Praise for *A Weekend wi...*

"*A Weekend with Mr. Darcy* is the leader of the pack! Brava Ms. Connelly!"

—*Austenprose*

"Connelly has created a magical world for Janeites… a must-read for Austen fans."

—*Diary of an Eccentric*

"A great romp in the English countryside with some gal pals and hot men that will make you giggle, squirm, and sit on the edge of your seat."

—*Savvy Verse & Wit*

"Jane Austen fans, rejoice! This one is a solid winner… clever, romantic, and intriguing."

—*Psychotic State Book Reviews*

"You don't have to be an Austen addict to enjoy this one. It's full of humor and wit."

—*Debbie's Book Bag*

"Victoria Connelly is an engaging and skilled storyteller… I felt I was able to see, feel, and hear all the wondrous things about Jane Austen's Hampshire firsthand."

—*Austenesque Reviews*

"Comprised of eventful love stories, unbelievable twists, and numerous bits of Jane Austen facts, *A Weekend with Mr. Darcy* is a breezy novel that you will simply devour. The characters are charming as well as relatable and the plot is fantastic."

—*Royal Reviews*

"Fantastically witty… it definitely put Connelly on my radar."

—*Read All Over Reviews*

"Sweet romance filled with fabulous Jane Austen references and history."

—*Book Addict*

"A delightful novel, and a fun, romantic read. I related to all of the Austen love in the novel, and I thought it had one of the best twists in a book that I've read for quite awhile."

—*Laura's Reviews*

'Do not be in a hurry: depend upon it, the right Man will come at last.'

Jane Austen, *Letters 1817*

To my wonderful friend Caroline.
You are such an inspiration.

Published by Sourcebooks Landmark, an imprint of Sourcebooks, Inc.
P.O. Box 4410, Naperville, Illinois 60567-4410
(630) 961-3900
FAX: (630) 961-2168
www.sourcebooks.com

Library of Congress Cataloging-in-Publication Data

Connelly, Victoria.
  Mr. Darcy forever / by Victoria Connelly.
    p. cm.
  1. Austen, Jane, 1775-1817—Influence—Fiction. 2. Sisters—Fiction. I. Title.
  PR6103.O547M7 2012
  823'.92—dc23

2011050595

Printed and bound in the United States of America
BG 10 9 8 7 6 5 4 3 2 1

Mr. Darcy Forever

VICTORIA CONNELLY

sourcebooks
landmark

Chapter 1

SARAH CASTLE WASN'T IN THE HABIT OF BLINDFOLDING PEOPLE, but her sister's twenty-first birthday was a delightful exception. As she drove through the winding lanes of Devon, she glanced quickly at Mia. She did look funny with the red polka-dotted scarf tied around her eyes and her curly dark hair flattened into submission.

Slowing down to take a bend in the road, Sarah tried to think how she'd spent her own twenty-first birthday. With a nine-year gap between them, Mia would have been just twelve and had probably been at school.

I would have just finished university, Sarah thought, remembering that summer. It had been the summer their mother had walked out on them and the summer Sarah's role had changed. There had been no note of explanation and no telephone call to check up on them. It was as if Monica Castle had decided she'd completed her role as a mother and moved on to other things somewhere else. Of course, neither of their fathers wanted to know, although the occasional check arrived to pay the rent and assuage some guilt.

From the wide-eyed graduate who was going to conquer the world, Sarah became a surrogate mother, tidying up after her little sister and making sure she always had clean clothes and was eating properly. Her own life had taken a back seat and, whilst working part-time at a restaurant, she'd studied to become an accountant.

No wonder she hadn't had time to celebrate her twenty-first birthday, but this weekend was going to make up for it.

She glanced quickly at Mia and smiled. Some sisters might not have survived the kind of relationship that was forced on them, but it brought Sarah and Mia closer together, and now that Mia had also graduated, she was about to leave home and start leading her own life. She'd already been talking about sharing a flat in Ealing with her friend Shelley, and Sarah was desperately trying not to act like a mother hen, fussing around Mia and making life impossible with endless questions. Mia was a grown woman, and Sarah had to remember that, although, looking at Mia now, she still seemed young and naive. She'd always reminded Sarah of Marianne from Jane Austen's *Sense and Sensibility*. She had the same drive and passion, teamed with inexperience. A lethal combination, Sarah thought.

Oh, stop worrying. Stop worrying, she told herself. This week was about pure unadulterated pleasure. She wasn't going to think about Mia living in an appalling flat, unable to pay her bills, and getting into all sorts of trouble because she wouldn't have her big sister to keep an eye on her. Oh, no. It was going to be a week of 'busy nothings.' They would walk. They would talk. They would eat and read and watch films. Sarah had a suitcase that was almost completely full of films, from the 2005 adaptation of *Pride and Prejudice* to the BBC version of *Persuasion*. She had been forced to take out some of her clothes, because they wouldn't all fit in. Of course she could have put the films in a separate case, but that would never have done. Sarah was very particular about such things. You took *one* suitcase away on holiday, and that was all. She only hoped that the warm weather would continue and that she wouldn't have need of the big woolly sweater she pulled out at the last minute.

Banishing thoughts of a freak May snowstorm, Sarah thought about the week that lay ahead. No doubt there would be the usual arguments about who was the best Elizabeth Bennet and who made the most dashing Mr Darcy. This disagreement was when their difference in age became most pronounced, as Sarah would be singing the praises of Colin Firth as Mr Darcy and Ciarán Hinds as Captain Wentworth, whereas Mia would be swooning over Matthew Macfadyen and Rupert Penry-Jones.

'But he's *far* too pale to be a convincing Captain Wentworth,' Sarah would say. 'He doesn't even look as if he knows where the sea is!'

'Well *your* Captain Wentworth looks like a grandfather,' Mia would retort.

Sarah grinned. There were some things about which they would never agree, but one thing they agreed on was that this week was going to be free from men. Sarah had just ended a relationship that had been a complete disaster from start to finish, and Mia was still nursing a broken heart after her latest boyfriend, Guido, had gone back to his mama in Italy. Sarah sincerely hoped there were no men in Devon or, at least, not in their little corner of it. She was fed up with living in a city where there was a rogue around every corner. The only men she wanted to think about were the fictional heroes in her Jane Austen novels. They were the only perfect men in the universe, weren't they? They never broke your heart. Living safely within the confines of a novel, they were the very best kind of lover.

'Are we nearly there yet?' Mia asked, breaking into Sarah's thoughts.

Sarah laughed at the childlike question. 'Nearly,' she said. 'You're not feeling dizzy, are you?'

'No, I'm fine,' Mia said.

'Because we can take the scarf off, if you'd like.'

'Oh, no! I like surprises,' Mia said.

'And you've no idea where we are?'

Mia shook her head. 'Somewhere complicated,' she said. 'All these twists and turns.'

It had certainly been a complicated journey, with Mia coming from London and Sarah from Winchester. They'd finally managed to meet up in Exeter and had driven through the rolling Devon countryside together, both glorying in being released from their city lives for a few days. Sarah couldn't wait to get out of the car and stretch her legs and stride across a few fields like Elizabeth Bennet or Marianne Dashwood.

It was then that she saw the track that she'd been looking out for and turned off the main road onto the private one. Mia swayed in the seat beside her.

'We're getting close, aren't we?'

'Not long now,' Sarah said, although she had never been there before herself, so had no real idea of where they were going. Still, she could feel a bubble of excitement inside her. It had been such a hard secret to keep from Mia. Sarah didn't like secrets. She liked openness and honesty, but, she told herself, this was different. This was a secret to beat all secrets, and she couldn't wait for it to be revealed.

The turnoff came quickly, and Sarah slowed the car, parked it, and turned off the engine.

'Can I take the scarf off?'

'No!' Sarah said. 'Stay right there.' She got out of the car and ran around to open Mia's door, releasing her seat belt and taking her arm.

'I feel like an invalid,' Mia said.

'Come on,' Sarah said.

'It's steep,' Mia said.

'It's all right. I've got you.' Sarah led the way down a path and then up a grassy bank until she reached a small wooden gate. She placed Mia's hands on top of the gate, and only then did she untie the scarf.

'Happy birthday,' she said, leaning forward and kissing her sister's pink cheek.

For a moment, Mia just stood blinking, as if getting used to seeing again, but then she gasped and her mouth dropped open.

'Oh, my goodness! It's Barton Cottage! You found Barton Cottage!' Mia jumped up and down on the spot like a little girl, which, Sarah knew, she would always seem to her. She would always be her little sister. She smiled as Mia's eyes widened in delight at the sight that greeted her. It was truly beautiful—the perfect Georgian country manor, its pale walls and large sash windows so open and friendly. But it was more than just a beautiful house—it was the house used in the 1995 film adaptation of *Sense and Sensibility*—the one to which the Dashwood sisters have to move after their father dies.

'It's so beautiful,' Mia said. 'This really is it, isn't it?'

'It really is.'

Mia turned to face Sarah, her dark eyes brimming with tears. 'I can't believe you found it, and I can't believe we're really staying here.' She opened her arms wide and then wrapped them around Sarah, squeezing her until she begged for mercy.

'Don't you want to see inside?' Sarah asked, extricating herself from Mia's embrace.

Mia nodded, her smile reaching gigantic proportions.

They opened the little wooden gate and walked up through the garden. Everything was lush and lovely. Frothy cow parsley grew in abundance, and bright red campion blazed in the hedgerows. To the left of the house lay a field of bright bluebells, and a beautiful lawn stretched out in front of the house in green splendor. It was as if spring had danced over everything, leaving no surface untouched.

As they reached the front door, Sarah turned around to admire the view down to the estuary. It was flanked with pale blond reed beds, and a little lane ran alongside it.

Mia gasped. 'That's the lane Willoughby rode along, isn't it?'

'And Colonel Brandon too,' Sarah said, wistfully glancing along it in the hopes that Alan Rickman might show up on horseback at any moment.

'We're going to have the best week ever here!' Mia said.

'Of course we are,' Sarah said. 'A perfect week.'

But perfection is hard to come by, even in Devon, and Sarah had been wishfully thinking when she'd hoped there were no men in their little corner of the English countryside.

Chapter 2

Three years later

S ARAH CASTLE WOKE UP AND COULDN'T BELIEVE WHAT SHE WAS seeing. What on earth had she been thinking? How had she let it happen? She felt absolutely mortified and tried to shut her eyes, banishing the image from her brain, but it was no good— it had to be faced head on.

Sitting upright, she flattened down her hair with her hands and then swung her legs out of bed. She placed her left foot into its slipper and then the right one, careful not to touch the carpet.

It wasn't the first time this had happened, and she swore silently to herself that it would never ever happen again. Taking a deep breath, she stood up and straightened the offending curtain, shaking her head at the kink that had somehow been left in it overnight, and then she sighed in relief. That was better. Now the morning could begin properly.

There followed a strict routine of bed making, washing, and tidying before Sarah allowed herself to have breakfast. Not for her was the slatternly slippered shuffle into the kitchen for that morning cup of coffee. Oh, no. Sarah had to be immaculately dressed before she graced the kitchen. There she would take breakfast whilst writing her first list of the day, which was actually a list of lists. She would need to make a list of jobs for the week ahead, a list of all the jobs that needed doing that day, and a list of things that needed doing around the house.

Today was different, however, because she was going away. Work could be forgotten for the next few days. Well, not completely forgotten—she wasn't the type of person who could wholly switch off from work—but being a self-employed accountant, she found it easy to take time off when she needed, and the Jane Austen Festival in Bath each September was an annual treat.

People would come from all over the world for the festival, taking part in the great costumed promenade through the beautiful Georgian streets and going to talks, dance lessons, and classes in etiquette and costume. It was an event that no true Janeite could miss.

Sarah had booked herself into a small bed and breakfast just off Great Pulteney Street, an area that would have been familiar to Jane Austen. Sarah had already made one trip ahead of her time in Bath, to see the bed and breakfast, because she couldn't risk staying somewhere that wasn't suitable. She'd only made that mistake once, booking a hotel room in Glasgow for an accountancy training day. It had been a disaster. The carpets looked as if they hadn't been vacuumed for at least two days, there had been a strip of wallpaper in her room that had unfurled itself in a most unbecoming manner, and nothing had been straight—the pictures on the walls, the curtains across the landing, and the dining-room place settings. Sarah had to spend a good half hour of her own time going around straightening things before she could settle. It really wasn't the sort of thing she wanted to worry about when she was on holiday, but it was impossible to switch off from such things.

Sarah had always known she was different. It had nothing to do with her looks, because she was very pretty, with rich brown hair and eyes to match. Neither did it have anything to do with her intelligence, which was way above average, but even from a young age, she felt removed from those around her, because she seemed to see the world differently.

The earliest recollection she could pinpoint was when she was ten years old. She'd been shopping in Oxford Street with her mother and paid a visit to the ladies' toilets in a big department store.

Sarah had been very careful not to touch anything she didn't need to touch and had washed her hands twice, and then her mother asked her something. It was a simple enough question, but it stopped Sarah in her path.

'Open the door, will you, darling?'

Sarah stared at the big, wide door handle, a handle people would have touched, people who might not have washed their hands twice, as she had, or even washed their hands at all.

Her mother sighed. 'Sarah, open the door for me.'

Sarah turned to her mother and saw that she was carrying four big bags and didn't have a hand free. She bit her lip and looked, once more, at the door in front of her.

'What is the matter with you, child?'

'I've just washed my hands,' she said, but her mother didn't seem to understand her and, if it hadn't been for the little old lady who had come into the ladies', Sarah and her mother might still be standing there today.

Her mother never understood Sarah's profound fear of dirt—not just the sort of dirt that clumps around a pair of Wellington boots or blows in the summer wind and sticks to your sun cream. There was other dirt too, the invisible sort that came from other people and could make you ill. Microbes, bacteria, and viruses—they were all out there, and one had to be constantly on one's guard against them.

Sarah tried to avoid public toilets as much as possible now. If it was at all possible, she'd much rather go in a nice clean field where one didn't have to worry about door handles or picking up a bar of soap that would probably do more harm than good.

It wasn't just her fear of dirt that marked her out as being different, though. Growing up, Sarah had earned herself the nickname 'The Neat Freak,' because she was forever tidying up and not just after herself, but after everybody around her, as well. Everything had to be in its right place. Didn't that make sense? Wasn't that the way things were meant to be? Why didn't everyone agree with her? Why did everybody else seem to like living in chaos where keys and purses and umbrellas were constantly lost? It baffled her, it really did.

This determination for everything to be just right was noted by her first boss—Mr Henderson—who couldn't understand why the teenage Sarah was taking so long to stack the supermarket shelves, but every tin had to be exactly right, with the label not just facing out but also facing out symmetrically. She then noticed some of the other products on the shelves that had been put out by others, and had to straighten those. It was all very time consuming, and Mr Henderson had thought she was a slow worker, so she was fired. How ridiculous was that, to be fired for being too good at her job?

It wasn't until Sarah was twenty-four that she heard the term OCD. Obsessive–compulsive disorder—that's what she had. It was a well-recognized condition, and she was by no means the only person to suffer from it. All over the world, people were straightening things and washing their hands until they cracked.

People with OCD were counting things and scrubbing things, making lists, and ordering their lives into a set of neat and regular routines. It was their way of controlling the world, and it made perfect sense to them. There was no other way to live, and even though it might drive them crazy and they knew it was illogical, they couldn't stop themselves.

Sarah often tried to imagine what life might be like without OCD. She tried to envisage a different version of herself—a Sarah who was more relaxed, who could get out of bed and not worry about straightening the pillow and covers. A Sarah who didn't need to brush her hair with one hundred strokes and start all over again if she was interrupted.

Or, perhaps, OCD could be something that you could choose to suffer from on certain days of the week; you could mark it in your diary for Mondays and Thursdays, leaving the other days of the week free, so you could behave like a normal human being. But that was never going to happen, and there was no use in wishing it so.

As she packed her suitcase for the festival, Sarah's eye caught a little framed silhouette of Jane Austen that hung on the wall beside her bed. It was a dear little thing, framed in oval brass and with a traditional acorn hanger, bought on a previous trip to Bath. The reason it caught her eye now was that, like the curtain before, it wasn't hanging quite straight. She must have knocked it whilst dusting. Neatly folding her pair of jeans and placing them in the bottom of the suitcase, she walked across the room to straighten the little frame. As she did so, she couldn't help remembering another frame she'd once straightened and how much trouble it had got her into.

She'd been about twelve and was visiting a very posh art gallery in London with her school. She still remembered walking into a large, airy room hung with beautiful landscapes in large gold frames and standing in the middle of the room to admire them. It had been perfect. Even at the tender age of twelve, Sarah had been drawn to Georgian architecture. There was something intrinsically pleasing about the straight lines and symmetry of the rooms that made her feel calm and gave her a feeling of being oh-so-right.

But it hadn't all been perfect that day, because one of the paintings hadn't been straight. It was a landscape—a simple river flowing through the mountains—but it was distinctly wonky. Sarah looked around her, because she felt sure that she wouldn't be the only one to notice it, but nobody seemed to be paying it any attention.

Sarah shook her head, bemused as to how it had gone unnoticed. In such a symmetrically pleasing room, the wonky painting was virtually screaming out loud to be straightened, and without even pausing to question her actions, she crossed the room and took the painting in both hands.

The alarm that went off had never been equalled in loudness before or since, and it still made Sarah shudder to think of it.

'What on earth were you doing?' Her teacher's face was scarlet with embarrassment as security staff sprang into action and she and her teacher were escorted into a book-lined office.

It was soon pretty obvious that a twelve-year-old girl had no intentions of stealing the priceless artwork, and she was allowed to go on her way without further questioning. Now, as she fixed the little silhouette on the wall, she couldn't help smiling. OCD had certainly made her life interesting.

Catching sight of her reflection in the mirror, Sarah smoothed down her hair with her hands. She kept it in a neat bob, its edges so sharp that it looked in danger of slicing her cheekbones. Her mother used to let Sarah's hair get completely out of control, and Sarah had hated her for it, because she knew that once it got to chin length, one side curled outwards and the other inwards, which was absolutely appalling and not to be endured.

Everything about her was controlled, from the way she styled her hair to the neat skirts and jackets she wore for work. Straight lines were featured heavily. Not for her were the ruffles and flounces that came in and out of fashion—they were far too messy and unpredictable. You knew where you were with a straight line; it didn't mess around.

Mia often made fun of her for dressing so neatly and precisely.

'You work from home! You could hang around in your pajamas all day, and nobody would notice.'

'But I don't want to hang around in my pajamas all day,' Sarah said. 'It just isn't right.'

One of the reasons Sarah had become an accountant was so that she could work from home. Home was an environment she could control. She didn't have to worry about co-workers and the mess they made, and there was a certain calmness that came from knowing exactly where everything was at a given time. Imagine trying to work in an open-plan office with other people—the thought was just preposterous. She would have to share her space with total strangers, who might pick up her things. No, working from home was a much safer option.

Post was an issue, of course. She found it irritating that anybody could pop a filthy envelope through her mailbox, so she employed a pair of fine cotton gloves that she donned before touching anything that landed on her doormat.

Her clients were harder to control. When she could, she met them in a local pub that she knew to be clean.

If people turned up at her home, she showed them through to the room that she kept specifically for that purpose and would later vacuum and polish any surfaces she had seen them touch during their visit.

It really was an exhausting business, and there was never an end in sight. Sarah just seemed to lurch from one anxiety to another.

The only thing that could make her forget her OCD was Jane Austen. When she immersed herself in Austen, her lists were forgotten, and she managed to stop thinking about the dust that might be accumulating behind her wardrobe and the fact that the vacuum marks in the carpet were no longer visible. Whenever she picked up one of the six perfect books or switched on the television to watch one of the wonderful adaptations, she could truly relax and become a person that she barely recognized. That was the power of Austen.

She first discovered Jane Austen when she was at school. Her English teacher was meant to be teaching them Charles Dickens's *Hard Times* but had rebelled and given each pupil a copy of *Pride and Prejudice* instead, and thus began a lifetime of romance for Sarah. Whenever she was feeling stressed, whenever life got too much for her and even she couldn't organize or control it to her liking, she could lose herself in the magical world of heroes and heroines, where love and laughter were guaranteed, and where a happy ending was absolutely essential.

Then, a few years ago, she discovered the Jane Austen Festival in Bath. It had been a complete revelation to her that, all over the world, there were fans who were as obsessed as she was with the Austen books and films. She made many new friends, and they were the loveliest people in the world. Well, you couldn't imagine a mean, nasty person adoring Jane Austen, could you?

And here she was packing her suitcase once again, except she was a little nervous this time; she hadn't been for the past two years. She and Mia usually attended together, dressing up in Regency costume and giggling their way around Bath together, eyeing up any young man who might be a contender for Mr Darcy, but that was before things had gone wrong, wasn't it?

She sighed and picked up a tiny silver photo frame that sat on a highly polished table by the side of her bed. It was a picture of her and Mia at Barton Cottage in Devon three years earlier. They were both squinting into the sun and laughing. How happy they both looked, and how long ago that all seemed now!

'Three long years,' Sarah said.

And not a single word spoken between them in all that time.

Chapter 3

MIA CASTLE GOT OUT OF BED, IDLY THINKING HOW CLEVER SHE was not to have needed her alarm clock, when a sudden cold fear iced her spine and she remembered that the alarm clock had indeed gone off and that she had silenced it with an angry hand and then promptly fallen asleep again.

'I'm late!' she yelped, throwing back her duvet and leaping out of bed, tripping over the slippers that had been left among a tumble of clothes on the floor. Bending down quickly, she grabbed the pair of jeans and gave them a quick shake before shoving them into the suitcase at the end of the bed. They were mostly clean, after all.

Flinging open her tiny single wardrobe with the wonky door, she grabbed an armful of sweaters and shirts, most of them unironed, and dumped them into the suitcase. Next came the shoes. How many to take? It was an impossible question to answer, so they all went in: flat ones, heeled ones, scuffed ones, and cute ones.

Then it was the entire contents of the bathroom, from shampoo bottles to hairbrushes to an overstuffed bag of old bits of makeup. She didn't have time to be selective—not that her packing would have been any different if she had more time. Her suitcases were usually a big jumble of everything.

She then took the quickest of showers. She didn't have time to wash her hair, but let it tumble its way down her back, the dark curls as wild as briars as she pulled on a pair of jeans and a black T-shirt with the name of a rock band she'd seen when she'd been at drama school. She hadn't heard of the band since, but it was a very nice T-shirt and one of the few that didn't have great gaping holes in it.

Because she wasn't a complete slob, she opened her fridge and took out a pint of milk, pouring the contents down the sink and binning the empty carton. If her days of being a student had taught her nothing else, she'd learned about the perils of out-of-date food.

Putting on a watch with a leather strap almost worn away to a whisper, she glanced around her flat. She was looking forward to getting away from the dark, depressing place. Nine wonderful nights in Bath, she thought, where she wouldn't have to wear earplugs to shut out the noise of the traffic and her neighbors or worry about inhaling the pernicious damp in her shower room.

Reaching for her handbag, she checked her train tickets. She was only just going to make it in time.

'Handbag,' she said, grabbing it from her bedside chair. 'Suitcase,' she said, sitting down on top of it to squash it into submission. What on earth was in there to make it bulge so? she wondered. She hadn't packed *that* much stuff. Still, it was a whole nine days away from home, and at that time of year, it was impossible to know what to wear, so everything had to be packed.

She was just about to wheel the suitcase out of her front door when she suddenly remembered something.

'Costume!' she shouted. It was the most important item of clothing, and she'd almost forgotten it. She'd left it draped over the threadbare armchair that sat by the window overlooking the dirty street below. How white and pure and beautiful it looked in the dark, dingy bedsit! *I don't belong here,* it seemed to say. *I belong in a beautiful Georgian sitting room with candles and mirrors and a huge sash window overlooking an immaculate lawn.*

'Poor dress,' Mia said, picking it up and holding it against her. 'But don't worry, we're going to Bath. You'll love it there.'

What was she actually going to do with her costume, though? There was no way it was going to fit into her suitcase, and even if it did, it would get horribly creased. She looked around the tiny bedsit as if inspiration might strike, and surely enough, it did as she spied the overflowing bin in the corner of the room.

A bin bag would do the trick. It wasn't very dignified for such a lovely dress, but it would have to do.

With her suitcase threatening to explode at any moment, her handbag stuffed with books for the train ride—*Persuasion* and *Northanger Abbey* to get herself in the mood for Bath—and her bin bag, she left her flat, locking her door behind her and looking forward to getting as far away from it as possible for the next few days.

It really was a terrible flat, but it was all she could afford. Well, she couldn't really afford it, if she were honest. Who would have thought it? Three years after leaving drama school, and she was still in debt. What had happened to her dreams of being discovered and becoming an overnight success? She'd been so sure it would happen. Mind you, so had the thousands of other drama school students who had graduated the same year she had, to say nothing of those who had graduated before her and those who followed her. All of them had the same dreams and aspirations, and ninety-nine percent of them were probably stuck in a dingy bedsit and waiting tables at some terrible restaurant.

Success, it now seemed to Mia, was as elusive as a Jane Austen hero, but, as with her deep-rooted knowledge that she would find a modern-day Mr Darcy, Mia wasn't going to give up on her dream of becoming a singer. It was all she'd ever wanted to do. Her mother used to joke that, when a baby, Mia hadn't ever cried but rather had sung whenever she wanted something. Growing up, she'd taken every opportunity she could to show off her talents, from grabbing the microphone at her auntie's wedding and treating everyone to a very gutsy version of 'White Wedding' to hogging the karaoke at the local club. Mia sang at every opportunity, which could be particularly annoying if you were her neighbor, and she frequently received angry bangs on the flimsy walls if her rendition of 'Nessun Dorma' really was making it impossible for people to fall asleep.

What was to become of her, she dreaded to think. She lost count of how much she owed in back rent, and there was no way she could ever hope to save enough for a deposit on a place of her own with the money she was making from her job as a waitress.

And then there had been that recent audition. Mia shivered whenever she thought about it and tried to put it at the back of her mind, but it refused to go away. Just a fortnight before, she had auditioned for a new show in the West End. It was everything she ever dreamed of, and she queued up with the rest of the hopefuls, her heart hammering and her nerves jangling.

She shook her head. She wasn't going to think about it. She *refused* to think about that now. She had a train to catch and plenty of other things to worry about, such as sneaking by her landlord's door without being heard.

As she began to descend the stairs with her suitcase, she counted, remembering that the fourth stair was creaky in the middle and the fifth was creaky on the right side, but Mia had perfected a strange sort of ballet movement to avoid setting them off. It was a bit more difficult with a huge suitcase and bin bag in tow, but she managed to do it, making it down onto the next landing and the next flight of stairs. That was where Mr Crownor had his lodgings, and she did *not* want to run into him right now. He was the sort of man one tried to avoid at all costs, not only because he was most unpleasant in manner, but also because his personal hygiene left a lot to be desired. But just as Mia's foot hit the first stair, his door flung open, and he walked out onto the landing.

Mia froze and tried not to inhale, but the landing was soon ripe with the stench of garlic. Slowly she turned around, knowing she'd been caught and there was no escape.

'I've been hoping to run into you,' Mr Crownor said. 'You've been doing a pretty good job of avoiding me, haven't you, young miss?' He jabbed her left shoulder with a stubby, nicotine-stained finger. His thinning hair was slicked across his head in a greasy wave, his bloodshot eyes bulging out of their sockets as his stomach bulged over the waistband of his jeans. It was a sight that should only ever come out once a year, at Halloween.

'I've not been avoiding you, Mr Crownor,' Mia said, inching backwards down the stairs.

'Oh, you haven't? You sure about that? Because you know you're behind with your rent—*again*.'

'I know,' Mia said, swallowing, 'and I'm so sorry.'

'So where's my money?'

'It's coming, Mr Crownor. I just need a little bit more time.'

'Time, eh?' he said, his eyes bulging toward her most unnervingly. 'Well—see—I ain't got any more time to give you. I've got people queuing round the block for your flat. It isn't easy to find luxury apartments in this part of town.'

Luxury? Was he talking about the same pokey little bedsit with the moldy ceiling and the permanent smell of damp?

'Mr Crownor, as much as I'd love to talk to you, I really must go. I have a train to catch and—'

'So you've got money for a train ticket, have you? Well, I might have liked some of that money.'

'I promise I'll have the money for you when I get back,' Mia said.

'A working trip is it, then?' Mr Crownor's eyes narrowed suspiciously.

'Yes,' Mia lied. 'That's right.' Well, all those years in drama school had to be good for something, didn't they? 'Now, I've really got to go, or my boss will be furious with me, and I won't earn a single penny!' Before he could stop her, she trotted down the stairs, her suitcase banging behind her.

'Well, don't be surprised if I've let your room whilst you're away,' Mr Crownor shouted after her.

Mia ignored him, slamming the front door behind her and shuddering. Horrible, horrible man! That such men existed was just too depressing. Mia was a romantic and wanted to exist in the world where all men were handsome and eloquent and—above all—polite. Was that too much to ask? Unfortunately, her experience with men had been far removed from the novels she read. Life at drama school had been full of show-offs and fools. It had all been very depressing, and then she met Guido. He stepped on her toes outside Covent Garden tube and hadn't stopped apologizing for the rest of the day. He was tall, dark, and handsome, and she'd really fallen for him, but he was in town for only a month and then went back to his mama in Italy. It was the story of Mia's life.

'There are no heroes in London,' she said under her breath as she hailed a taxi, knowing that she was about to use the last ten-pound note in her purse, but not able to face the bus or tube with all her luggage. No wonder her best friend Shelley had swapped London for Bath two years before. Not only was she living in a beautiful house, but she was also very handy for the Jane Austen Festival.

Hopping in the back of a taxi a moment later, Mia closed her eyes. She was so looking forward to her trip to Bath, but something was worrying her, something she hadn't allowed herself to dwell on too much.

Sarah.

She hadn't spoken to her sister for three years. Prior to that, Bath had been their special place where they went together, taking part in as many Jane Austen activities as they could. But since their trip to Barton Cottage, Mia hadn't been to Bath for fear of running into Sarah.

'As long as she isn't there this year,' Mia said to herself.

But what if she was?

Chapter 4

Barton Cottage

'EDWARD FERRARS IS SUCH A WIMP!' MIA SAID THROUGH A mouthful of crisps.

'Edward Ferrars is *not* a wimp.'

'How can you say that?' Mia asked, leaning forward in the squashy sofa and throwing a cushion at Sarah, who was sitting opposite her. 'He's bullied by his sister, he never speaks his mind, and he almost loses the woman he loves because of it.'

'But he's trying to do the right thing,' Sarah said. 'It almost breaks his heart to think that he might lose Elinor, but he's intensely honorable and stands by Lucy Steele, even though he knows they'll be miserable together.'

'Oh, that's ridiculous! What sort of a man would marry somebody like Lucy Steele, when he's in love with somebody else?'

'An honorable man,' Sarah said. 'But perhaps honor isn't something you admire in a man. Perhaps you would have preferred Edward if he'd been more like Willoughby.'

'What do you mean?'

'I mean you're easily pleased. All you look for is a handsome face and a little bit of charm—you're just like Marianne.'

'And you're just like Elinor.'

'I am not like Elinor,' Sarah said.

'You so are! I can't believe you can't see it.'

'I can't see it because it's not there to see.'

'Oh, let's not have this conversation again.' Mia groaned. 'Every time we watch *Sense and Sensibility*, we end up fighting.'

'That's only because you have no common sense. You'd have forgiven Willoughby, wouldn't you? You'd have taken him back and had him break your heart all over again.'

'No, I wouldn't have.'

'Yes, you would.'

Mia stretched to her right and picked up another cushion, throwing it across the room at her sister.

'Hey!' Sarah yelped when it hit her on the head. She grabbed a cushion of her own and hurled it back toward Mia. There then ensued a major cushion fight, with both sisters grabbing every piece of soft furnishing they could find.

Finally, Sarah stood up. 'Enough!' she bellowed. 'I can't breathe!'

Mia fell into a giggling heap on the floor. 'I haven't laughed like that in years,' she said.

'I think I've pulled something in my back,' Sarah said, but she was still laughing. 'God, I can't believe I'm thirty. I feel so old.'

'You've always been old,' Mia said from the carpet.

'Thanks very much. It'll come to you soon enough.'

'No, it won't,' Mia said. 'I'm only twenty-one. You've got almost a decade on me.'

Sarah's mouth dropped open. 'What a thing to say! And to think I could have invited anyone here.'

'No, you couldn't have. You haven't got any friends. Who would put up with you as I do? Nobody, that's who.'

'You are a cruel, cruel sister!'

'No, I'm not,' Mia said. 'I'm just unrelentingly honest—like Marianne.'

'Yes, you are like Marianne, and that's your problem.' Sarah was smiling, but Mia knew she wasn't joking.

'Well, at least I can relax,' Mia said.

'What do you mean?'

'I mean, look at you—we're on holiday, and you're still dressed as if you're about to be interviewed.'

Sarah frowned and looked down at the neat pair of cotton trousers she was wearing and the slightly baggy blouse. For her, that was slumming it.

'You've got to learn to relax more.'

'I am relaxed,' Sarah said.

Mia sighed. She gave up on her sister—she really did. Mia had taken an early shower and was in a pair of comfy pajamas. Her hair was tied back in a ponytail, and she was halfway through a family-sized bag of crisps. Sarah didn't wear night clothes until she was ten minutes from getting into bed.

'I can't believe we're watching *Sense and Sensibility* in the very cottage where it was filmed,' Mia said, deciding to change the subject. She didn't want to fight with Sarah, even if it was a good-natured sort of a fight with cushions and everything.

Sarah sat down on the floor next to Mia. 'I've been wanting to bring you here for ages. One of my clients came here with *Pride and Prejudice* Tours and showed me the photos. I couldn't believe you could actually hire it.'

'Well, it's the best birthday present ever,' Mia said, resting her head on her sister's shoulder.

There was a sudden knock on the door, and the sister's sprang apart.

'Oh, my goodness! It's Willoughby! We've conjured up the spirit of Willoughby,' Mia said excitedly, scrambling up from the carpet.

'What are you doing?'

'I'm trying to see who it is.'

'Well, can't you answer the door properly?' Sarah said.

'I can't answer looking like this,' Mia said, motioning to her pajamas.

'Well, I haven't got any makeup on.'

'Oh, I can't see who it is,' Mia said.

'Who on earth could be knocking? We're in the middle of Devon.'

'The owner?' Mia suggested. 'A mad axman?'

'Don't even joke about such things.'

Mia jiggled the curtains. 'It's no use. I can't see him.'

'How do you know it's a "him," then?'

'Just wishful thinking,' she said.

'I thought we made a pact to swear off men,' Sarah said. 'At least for a week.'

Mia shrugged. 'Those sorts of pacts never last.'

There was a second knock on the door.

'He's not giving up, whoever he is,' Mia said, and then she dived behind the curtain. 'Oh, my goodness! I think he saw me!'

'Is it a "he"?'

Mia nodded. 'A young he, too.'

Sarah got up from the floor and joined her sister by the curtain before daring to look out of the window herself. 'What do you think he wanted?'

'To meet two young beautiful women, of course.'

'Do you think we should call him back?'

'I'm still in my pajamas,' Mia said.

'You're right. We'll have to hope he calls again. Do you think he will?'

'I should think so,' Mia said, little knowing what problems it would cause them.

Chapter 5

SHELLEY QUANTOCK WAS EAGERLY LOOKING OUT OF THE window of her Georgian terrace. Mia was late, not that there was anything new in that. In all of their years together at drama school, she'd never known her friend to be punctual. Still, it didn't stop Shelley from hoping, and she continued to pace back and forth between the window and the bookcase until her friend arrived.

At least it was a nice room to pace in, she mused, thinking of the last phone call she had with Mia and how she hated the thought of her friend stuck in a grimy bedsit in London.

'Why don't you move in with me? There's plenty of room,' Shelley had pleaded.

'I can't leave London,' Mia said.

'Why not? I did, and it hasn't done me any harm.'

'Yes, but you don't want to set the world on fire, do you?'

It was true. Even at drama school, Shelley hadn't ever really burned with the same sort of ambition that most of the other students did. Was that a failing? she wondered. She'd never wanted to set the world alight—she'd only ever wanted to have fun. That's all drama school had been for her, an entertaining way of passing the time, but she knew that her friend was different. Her friend pined for the big time—of making a name for herself and seeing it up in lights, but if Shelley were absolutely honest, she herself rather preferred the quiet life. For all her loudness and easy confidence, she really couldn't imagine hankering after a life in the public eye, although she had once had a brief brush with fame doing the voice-over to one of her father's herbal tea commercials.

Hugh Quantock was huge in herbal teas and could quite easily have bought Shelley and Mia a deluxe flat in the very best part of London when they graduated, but he refused. A couple of years later, however, he purchased 6 Southville Terrace in Bath, a beautiful honey-colored house with a huge bay window. It had been an investment, he said, not wanting his daughter to think she was being mollycoddled. Besides, Bath was the gateway to the South West—an area he had his eye on, in terms of business development. Shelley felt as if she didn't deserve such a beautiful house, because she'd never really worked a day in her life, but her father bought it as an investment and expected her to pay him rent. As a result, she got a part-time job at Tumble Tots nursery and surprised herself by how much she loved to look after the little ones, which was funny, because she never imagined herself working with children.

As an only child, Shelley had no experience looking after anyone other than herself, but there was something very satisfying about picking up a child who had fallen over or buttoning up a coat before home time or wiping a nose that needed wiping. She'd always thought of herself as the least maternal of women, but perhaps things were changing.

She laughed at the thought. She'd have to get a love life before she had a child, and that prospect didn't look very likely at the moment. The only man in her life was a strange lodger called Pie. Shelley wasn't even sure if that was his first name or last name, because he didn't say much—he just sort of drifted in and out of 6 Southville Terrace on his way to and back from goodness only knew where. Even if he had been able to hold a half-decent conversation, he wasn't her type at all, spending most of his time filling the enormous armchair in the front room whilst watching dreadful sitcoms, his mop of brown hair hanging loose and hippie-like over his shoulders.

Here she was, living a contented life in Bath. It really was one of the most beautiful cities in the world, and she knew it was a privilege to live there. She still got a buzz from walking around the streets and discovering crescents and squares that Jane Austen and her family would have known. It was amazing to be living in the very city her idol once lived in.

Jane Austen was the reason that Shelley and Mia had bonded so quickly at drama school. Shelley would never forget walking into rehearsals one day and seeing Mia slumped against the wall, totally absorbed in a book that turned out to be *Sense and Sensibility*.

'Oh, my goodness!' Shelley had exclaimed. 'I just love that book.'

'You do?' Mia said, looking up from her book in surprise.

Shelley slumped down on to the floor next to her. 'I have to admit to being just a little bit in love with Willoughby.'

Mia giggled. 'Me too. Apart from his breaking Marianne's heart and almost being the cause of her death, that is.'

'Well, that goes without saying, but he's no different from most of the men I've dated. They were all handsome heartbreakers too.'

Mia nodded in sympathy. 'They're the best and the worst, aren't they?'

The two of them had been friends ever since.

It was whilst Shelley was remembering this that a taxi drew up to the curb and a crumpled-looking figure emerged.

'Mia!' Shelley cried, running to the front door and flinging it open. She watched as Mia struggled with her suitcase and a large bin bag.

'What on earth is all this?'

'Oh, you know me—I could never travel light.'

'Is it your costume?'

'Yes; don't crumple it.'

'I wouldn't,' Shelley said. 'Is it the old standby?'

Mia nodded. 'I couldn't afford a new one.'

'Well, we can retrim it and make it a bit special, can't we?' she said, daring to peer into the bin bag.

'Do you have any money for the taxi?' Mia interrupted just as the taxi driver honked his horn. 'I'm absolutely broke.'

Shelley nodded, running into the house and coming back out a moment later to pay the red-faced cabbie.

The two women then embraced.

'Gosh, I've missed you!' Shelley said.

'I've missed you more,' Mia said. 'London's not the same without you.'

'Well, of course it isn't, but you wouldn't expect the inhabitants of Bath to do without my scintillating wit and vibrant personality, would you?'

'I wish you'd come back.'

Shelley linked Mia's arm, and the two of them went inside with the bags. 'I can't come back. I've got this place now, and I've even got a job—a proper job, this time.'

'You mean you're not busking outside the abbey anymore?'

'I haven't done that for years!' Shelley said. 'I'm working at the nursery down the road.'

'A nursery? As in plants?'

'No, as in children.'

'Blimey,' Mia said. 'You're not getting broody, are you?'

'I might be,' Shelley said, the traces of a faint flush coloring her cheeks.

'What happens to our "No men, no children, just fame and fortune" plan?' Before Shelley could reply, Mia caught sight of somebody sitting in the front room.

'Who on earth is that?' Mia asked in a hushed tone.

'Oh, that's just Pie. He lives here.'

'He's not your—'

Shelley's mouth dropped open before Mia could even finish her offending question. 'No way! He's here so I can pay my father his blasted rent.'

A strange scraping sound came from the hallway at the back of the house.

'Oh, Pie! I thought I told you to close the kitchen door.'

An enormous chestnut beast hurled itself along the corridor and almost knocked Mia on her back.

'Oh, Bingley!' Shelley shouted, grabbing hold of the dog's red collar and trying to restore some sort of order. 'Are you okay, Mia? He didn't mean to scare you. He's friendly, really.'

'What breed is he?' Mia asked with a grin. 'I can't tell.'

Shelley shook her head. 'He's a cross.'

'What's he crossed with?'

'I don't know. Something fat and greedy.'

'He's lovely, though.'

'Don't you believe it,' Shelley said. 'Nobody wanted him, and I'm beginning to see why.'

'I had no idea you had a dog.'

'No, and neither does my father. He'd kill me if he knew I had an animal here.'

Mia bent down to pat the dog. 'He is rather beautiful,' she said. 'I can see why you fell for him.'

'You can take him home, if you want.'

'I think Mr Crownor would be even less sympathetic than your father to my having a dog.'

'You're not still in the awful bedsit, are you?'

Mia nodded. 'Just for the time being.'

'I know,' Shelley said, 'fame and fortune are just round the corner, aren't they?'

Mia smiled, but there was a sad look in her eyes, and the first time, Shelley saw doubt there.

'Come on,' she said, 'let's have a cup of tea.'

Mia looked anxious.

'A *proper* cup of tea,' Shelley added, 'although Dad sent his usual testers, if you fancy giving them a try.'

'And what have we this week?'

'Erm, Camomile Dreams, Nettle Surprise, and Fennel Twist.'

'I think I'll give those a miss, if you don't mind.'

'That's probably a good move. I mean, Camomile Dreams isn't too bad, but you really don't want to smell the Fennel Twist. I came home last night, there was the strangest fug imaginable, and I found Pie in the kitchen with a mug of the stuff. I swear the whole kitchen had turned green.'

'You'd better let your dad know.'

'Yes, I think I shall fine him this time, say six months' rent.'

The two of them ventured into the kitchen, but luckily there was no green fug to greet them.

'There's nothing like Quantock Teas to put you off herbal for life,' Shelley said as she reached for a canister filled with regular tea bag.

'Hey, that's a pretty good slogan, if you wanted your father's business to go bust overnight.'

Shelley laughed.

'What happened to your commercial?' Mia asked.

'Daddy withdrew it,' Shelley said.

'Why? I thought it was brilliant! How did it go again?'

Shelley took a deep breath and then recited the commercial for which she'd done the voice-over. 'Tick-tock. Quantock. It's time for tea.'

Mia roared with laughter at the husky voice Shelley used. 'Daddy said it was way too sexy and gave the completely wrong impression about the tea bags.'

'I bet sales would have soared if he'd let it run its course.'

'I guess we'll never know,' Shelley said, silently bemoaning a lost career as a voice-over artist.

Mia looked out the kitchen window onto a small patch of emerald lawn.

'Who's that?' she suddenly asked, seeing a man in the garden next door across the low fence that divided the terrace.

'That's Gabe Sanders,' Shelley said, her eyes lighting up. 'You'll like him. In fact, I must introduce you.'

'Why?'

'Because you're single.'

'Oh, don't start all that again,' Mia said.

'But you are, aren't you?'

'So are you,' Mia said. 'Anyway, he's an old man.'

'He is not an old man! He's not even forty. Just come and say a quick hello.'

'I'm not into older men,' Mia said.

Shelley's eyebrows rose. 'There's a lot to be said for an older man. Just remember Colonel Brandon wasn't exactly in the first flush of youth, and he's one of my favorite heroes.'

'Yes, but Colonel Brandon probably wasn't a redhead.'

'Neither's Gabe,' Shelley said. 'He's more of a strawberry blond, wouldn't you say?'

Mia took another look at the neighbor and noticed that his arm was in a sling. 'He's broken his arm.'

Shelley nodded. 'Skiing accident. You wouldn't want for expensive holidays if you hooked up with him. Come on, let me introduce you!'

'Can't we just have a cup of tea and a chat? I'm exhausted and really haven't got the energy to be introduced to anyone, even if he could give Colonel Brandon a run for his money.'

Shelley sighed. 'All right, then,' she said, taking pity on her friend. 'I'll introduce you to him *tomorrow*.' She couldn't help grinning as Mia rolled her eyes at her.

Chapter 6

TRAVELING BY PUBLIC TRANSPORT WAS ALWAYS A TERRIFYING experience when one suffered from OCD. Sarah tried to stack the odds in her favor by booking a first-class train ticket, but as she sat down in her reserved seat, she could see several problems already. She'd booked a facing seat, because it was simply unnatural to travel backwards, and she'd opted for a nontable seat, because the thought of sharing a space with three strangers who might get out a big smelly picnic was not to be borne. She'd also booked the quiet carriage, which apparently meant that she'd be with like-minded people who weren't addicted to their mobile phones, iPods, or loud conversation with their neighbors. Half an hour into her journey, however, three mobile phones had gone off. Luckily for Sarah, a large-bosomed woman with a booming voice and zero-tolerance approach took the law into her own hands and reprimanded the hapless callers.

There weren't many people in the carriage with her that morning, but there were enough to annoy her. One thing she hadn't considered when she booked her ticket was the proximity of her seat to the door, which meant that there was a constant noise and draft as people got up to use the toilet. It really was very distracting when one was trying to enjoy the tranquility of the countryside.

There was also a businesswoman with a very runny nose who insisted on sniffing every eight or ten seconds. Sarah had been forced to count, and after the woman's thirty-fourth sniff, Sarah had resorted to her earplugs. Kept in a little pink tin, Sarah's earplugs were a lifesaver when traveling in public, instantly blocking out any annoying noises. If only she could block out the smells too, she thought, as somebody unwrapped a particularly stinky sandwich.

'You really have to learn to be more tolerant,' Mia often chided when observing her sister's little quirks. But it was no good—you couldn't tell someone with OCD to snap out of it. If only it were that simple. If anything, it was getting worse as she was getting older, and being a member of the general public was getting harder. Sarah found that she was becoming more and more reclusive, spending more time on her own in the solitude of her home, which was why something like the Jane Austen Festival was so important to her. It meant that she had to leave the safety of her sanctuary and venture out into the world, if only for a few days.

But something awful happens every time I do, she thought, remembering the week she spent with Mia in Devon. If only she'd stayed at home that week or had booked them into a house somewhere else—*anywhere* else, then it wouldn't have happened, would it? Why had she been so insistent that they go to Devon? It had seemed like the perfect idea at the time, but it had ruined everything.

She closed her eyes, wishing that she could turn back time, but then got angry with herself, because that wish was irrational. Not that she wasn't an irrational person—she knew that many of the symptoms of her OCD were completely irrational, like the counting every time she went up and down stairs and steps or whenever she did up her buttons.

She looked at her watch and wished that she was safely in her hotel room in Bath with the distractions of the city before her instead of stuck on a train with only her thoughts for company. No, that wasn't quite right. She had Jane Austen for company, didn't she? Opening her handbag, she took out her copy of *Northanger Abbey*, a smile instantly lighting her face at the thought of whiling away the time with Catherine Morland and Henry Tilney.

It seemed very special that Jane Austen had chosen Bath as the setting for her first novel, *Northanger Abbey*. It was also the setting for her last completed work, *Persuasion*, and Sarah often thought of how the two heroines, Catherine Morland and Anne Elliot, had opposing views about Bath; the young Catherine reveled in its bustle, whereas Anne had no affection for it. Sarah's own feelings about Bath always swung somewhere between the two heroines'. She adored the beautiful architecture and the enormous fun of seeing everybody looking so resplendent in their Regency costumes, but she often felt panicky at just being in a city and having to cope with the scary situations she found herself in. But she was determined that her time in Bath was going to be fabulous, and without further ado, she opened her book, turning to chapter three and the wonderful scene in which Catherine meets Henry Tilney for the first time. Sarah loved that scene. It was warm and funny, and she loved Tilney's gentle teasing of the young heroine. It was also a wonderful celebration of Bath and how one can 'step out of doors and get a thing in five minutes,' which reminded Sarah that she could treat herself to a little bit of shopping whilst in town.

How the time slipped by wondrously fast when reading a

favorite book! After just a few chapters, Sarah realized that they were about to arrive at Bath. She put her book away for later, because she didn't want to miss the approach.

Whether one arrived by train or car, one of the first things that struck you about Bath was how steep the roads were. They were as steep as any child would draw them, set among gentle hills, green fields, and verdant woods. It really was one of the most beautiful cities in the world. Sarah loved the innumerable church spires that shot up into the air and the neat square lines of the buildings. Georgian architecture was very comforting, she thought.

As the train pulled into the station, Sarah planned the next few hours. She would go to her hotel and take a long, hot shower. Public transport always made her feel grubby. Then she would have a bit of late lunch—there was a little bistro she knew that was clean and quiet with chairs that didn't wobble and cutlery that wasn't bent. If there was one thing that turned Sarah's stomach, it was a bent prong on a fork. Next she'd explore Bath. It seemed so long since she'd last been there, and she couldn't wait to lose herself among its streets. But first she had to endure the horrors of the train station, where other people might bump into her at any moment. She took a deep breath, and like Catherine Morland at the Upper Rooms, did her best to negotiate the crowds.

❧

'This is your room,' Shelley said, opening the door into a tiny room at the back of the house. 'Dad's been banging on at me to rent it out, but I think I've got enough to cope with having Pie living here.'

Mia placed her suitcase by the bed and sat down. The room was at the back of the house, and there was a view out across allotments.

It certainly beat the view of the dusty, dirty road that Mia had from her bedsit in London.

'So, tell me what's been happening. I haven't heard from you for weeks. You never ring me, you naughty girl.'

'My mobile is always out of credit, and I hate using the pay phone in the flats. The landlord is always hovering around, eavesdropping.'

'So what have you been up to?'

'Just the usual,' Mia said, anxious that Shelley might unearth all her secrets within five minutes.

'That isn't anywhere *near* good enough,' Shelley said, flopping down on the bed beside her.

'But my life is so boring,' Mia said. 'I go to work, I go to auditions, I write the occasional song, and I never have enough money to do anything remotely interesting.'

Shelley puffed out her cheeks. 'Goodness,' she said. 'That does sound bleak.'

Mia nodded. 'I often wonder how I got here. This isn't the life I envisaged when we were at drama school. Remember how full of hope we were? How everything was going to be so brilliant?'

Shelley grinned. 'You were going to conquer the West End, and I was going to dazzle Hollywood or, at least, marry into Hollywood royalty.'

'So what happened?'

'Life, my dear. That's what usually happens. It's the great gulf between fantasy and reality. It'll get you every time.' She placed an arm around her friend's shoulder. 'But it can't all be doom and gloom, can it? You must have *something* juicy to tell me. What about men?'

'What about them?'

'Are you seeing any?'

'Not seriously,' Mia said in a little voice. 'I'm just not ready.'

'But sweetheart, it's been over three years now, hasn't it? Do you really mean to tell me you've not seen anyone else in all that time?'

'It's—it's not easy,' she said. 'Do you mind if we don't talk about it? Bath is my special place, and I don't want to spoil it by talking about the past.'

Shelley sighed, and Mia knew she'd upset her. 'But it's not the past, is it? It's still hurting you right now—in the *present*.'

Mia shook her head. 'Not this week,' she said. 'This is Jane Austen week, and I'm not going to think about anything else.'

Chapter 7

Barton Cottage

T HAT FIRST PERFECT MORNING OF A HOLIDAY WAS ALWAYS magical. It was a time when everything was new, and an adventure might be waiting around the very next corner.

Mia drew back the curtains and gazed out across the sloping lawn down toward the estuary. It really was the most perfect view, and a far more pleasing sight first thing on a morning than the noisy road that greeted her from behind the net curtain of her grotty London bedsit.

It was lovely to wake up without the aid of an alarm clock. She and Sarah hadn't gone to bed much before one o'clock in the morning, because they'd been up talking half the night and enjoying a few glasses of wine. Well, that's what holidays were all about, weren't they?

Taking a quick shower and getting dressed in her tracksuit bottoms and her I Love Mr Darcy T-shirt, she walked down the stairs, smiling as she saw the very spot where Emma Thompson had sat in the film version of *Sense and Sensibility*. She could just imagine her sitting there right then, her cup of tea balancing on her knees as she listened to the painful sobs of her two sisters and her mother.

She knew that Sarah was up already, because she was never one to have a lie in, even on holiday. Besides, she'd heard her polishing doorknobs at an obscenely early hour. But she didn't find her in the kitchen as she'd expected to; she was in one of the front rooms, and Mia instantly knew what she was doing.

'You're not going to spray Barton Cottage,' she said as she entered the room and saw her sister with a tiny glass bottle in her hand.

'Good morning,' Sarah said with a bright smile.

'Sarah! What are you doing?' Mia asked, watching as her sister continued to spray her way around the two reception rooms.

'Other people have been here before us, and you can't be too careful,' Sarah said as she squirted a blast of lavender into the air. 'Mrs Dashwood would have approved; I'm sure of it, and Betsy and Thomas too.'

'I suppose,' Mia said, trying to imagine the Dashwoods' servants administering Sarah's lavender spray. 'But don't go mad, or the whole house will smell like a big lavender bag.'

'Where are you going?' Sarah asked as Mia bent down to put on the pair of trainers she'd left by the front door.

'I thought I'd go for a jog.'

'Before breakfast?'

'Best time,' Mia said.

'Well, don't be long, will you? I'm going to make you a proper breakfast, and you look like you need it.'

Mia rolled her eyes, but she secretly liked being looked after by her big sister.

Leaving the house, she did a few warm-up stretches in the

front garden before jogging across the lawn to the little wooden gate, which was almost completely hidden in a froth of white cow parsley, and on down to the private lane that skirted the estuary. Mia felt that she had entered the world of *Sense and Sensibility*, for the lane had been used in the film. She remembered how both Colonel Brandon and Mr Willoughby had ridden their horses along the lane, and she could almost see Marianne Dashwood among the pale blond rushes by the water's edge.

Opening another gate, she began her run, following the path along the estuary. The morning May sunshine was bright and dazzled her eyes when she looked at the water. Bright pink campions lined the path, and the air was sweet and warm. It was a pleasure to run in such surroundings. Mia's usual route was through a scruffy park near her flat, full of litter, broken glass, and dangerous dogs, but there was nothing threatening about this place, and she couldn't help smiling as she ran.

The path skirted a perfect blue pond before climbing toward a wood. She knew that it would eventually lead to the sea but was eager to be back in time for Sarah's breakfast.

Mia's breathing deepened as she continued. She loved the steady rhythm she built up as she ran—the gentle thud-thud of her trainers hitting the earth and the light perspiration beading her skin, the wind in her hair, and the heat of her face as she warmed up. There was nothing like it for forgetting your troubles, because the only thing you thought about was putting one foot in front of the other. Also, that morning, she was thinking about Marianne Dashwood. She liked to try to imagine Jane Austen's characters if they were around today. What would their modern counterparts be like? It had long been a running joke between her and Sarah that they were the modern incarnations of Elinor and Marianne

Dashwood, because Sarah was so sensible and in control, and Mia was energetic and headstrong.

She could imagine Marianne would like jogging. She practically ran everywhere in *Sense and Sensibility*, didn't she? Whether she caught sight of her beloved Willoughby or a patch of blue sky, she had to run toward it. Yes, she could imagine Marianne Dashwood sporting the latest pair of trainers and racing through the countryside.

As she reached a fork in the path, she slowed down. She had a feeling that if she took the one to the left, she would soon reach the sea. How tempting it was, but Sarah would probably be banging the bottom of the pan with a wooden spoon by now, in an attempt to call her home, so reluctantly, Mia retraced her steps and made her way back to Barton Cottage, running once more through the cool of the beech woods and back past the pond and alongside the estuary.

As she was running around the final corner, she collided with something solid. Dazed, she fell to the ground, where she lay stunned for a moment.

'Are you okay?' a man's voice asked, and a face appeared.

Mia looked up and nodded, although she felt a little shaky.

'Here, let me help you,' he said, taking her arm and helping her up. 'Nothing broken, I hope,' he said.

'I… I don't think so,' she said, looking up and seeing him for the first time. He was tall with neat dark hair and bright gray eyes that winked at her in the sunlight. His face was lightly tanned, and he was wearing a navy T-shirt and dark tracksuit bottoms that skimmed over an athletic build.

'I'd be absolutely mortified if I'd hurt you.'

'But it wasn't your fault. I wasn't looking where I was going.'

'No, I wasn't looking where I was going.'

'I didn't expect anyone else to be around. I'm afraid I was in a world of my own,' Mia said.

'And you're sure you're all right?' he asked as they walked slowly along the path together, her arm linked in his.

'I think so,' she said. 'Just a little dazed.' She looked up into his face and noted how very handsome it was. Yes, she was feeling dazed, all right. Something dawned on her. 'You're the man who called at the house last night, aren't you?'

He nodded. 'I hope I didn't scare you,' he said. 'You didn't think I was some mad axman?'

Mia stifled a giggle. 'Oh, no. We just wondered who it was. I mean, one doesn't expect visitors in the middle of nowhere.'

'I was just jogging by, and I noticed your car window was open.'

'Really?' Mia said. 'Gosh! That's very unlike my sister—she's usually a stickler for that sort of thing.'

'Not that anything would be stolen around here.'

'Well, thanks for thinking of us. Ouch!'

'You okay?'

'Yes,' Mia said with a little hobble. 'I think I grazed my knee. It stings a bit.'

'Let's get you back. My name's Alec, by the way,' he said. 'Alec Burrows.'

'I'm Mia,' she said with a little smile, thinking that a grazed knee was definitely worth the introduction.

Chapter 8

S HELLEY WAS DOWNSTAIRS FLIPPING THROUGH A COPY OF *Regency World Magazine* when Mia entered the room.

'Oh, it's you,' she said, looking up. 'I'd forgotten you were here.'

Mia sat on the sofa next to her. 'Sorry,' she said.

'It's okay.'

'No, it's not. I didn't mean to be rude. It's just—'

'You can't help it?' Shelley interrupted.

Mia groaned. She'd forgotten how annoying it was to be teased by Shelley.

'I was going to say it just feels odd being back in Bath. It seems an age since I was here.'

'It seems an age since you were anywhere outside that grotty little flat of yours. What have you been doing there?'

'What do you mean?'

'You haven't told me anything. You don't keep in touch. You don't return my phone calls. I've been worried about you.'

'I've sent you postcards.'

'Oh, yes, the informative postcards,' Shelley said. 'They really keep me up to date with what's been happening.'

'I'm sorry,' Mia said. 'I've been a crap friend.'

'Yes, you have, but at least you're admitting it, and at least you're here now. That's the main thing. We can do some serious catching up now, can't we?'

Mia nodded. 'But shouldn't we get our costumes sorted out for tomorrow first?'

Shelley's eyes widened, and a huge grin filled her face as she nodded manically. 'Wait until you've seen the ribbon I bought. It's the most amazing yellow you've ever seen. It's like a little piece of sunshine.'

Shelley was up from the sofa and out of the room before you could say *Northanger Abbey*, and Mia followed her.

'I hope you've still got that sewing machine, because I think my dress needs letting out a little.'

'You haven't put on weight, have you?'

'Well, not much.'

'Better bring your dress in, and we'll see what the damage is.'

They met up a moment later in Shelley's bedroom. It was the largest room upstairs and was wondrously light and airy, with a double bed on one side and a little workshop on the other. Shelley adored fiddling around with little bits of fabric and had made Mia's dress and her own in perfect Regency style.

As Mia entered, she smiled at the scene before her. By the window was an old pine table on which sat an ancient sewing machine and little heaps of ribbon and swatches of fabric in every color imaginable. There was a rail against the wall from which dresses were hanging. Mia remembered Shelley's obsession with rooting around charity shops and jumble sales when they'd been students.

'You never know what you're going to discover,' she'd say with a jolly smile on her face.

Judging by how full the rail was, Shelley had discovered

everything. There were dresses, skirts, shirts, and scarves in all the colors of the rainbow. Stripes jostled with dots, and cottons snuggled up next to velvets. It was a feast for the eyes, and Mia couldn't help reaching out and stroking a gold brocade jacket.

'This is lovely,' she said.

Shelley turned around and nodded. 'I think I'll be able to make the most gorgeous Spencer jacket from that.'

'Gosh, you're so clever. I wish I had a skill like that. You could make a fortune.'

'Well, it's funny you should say that,' Shelley began, picking up a length of scarlet ribbon, 'because I have sold a few things recently.'

'You have?'

Shelley nodded. 'I made up a dress for someone I met at last year's festival, and she told a friend, and then... well, it's snowballed a bit.'

'That's brilliant!'

'Yes, but it's so time-consuming. I mean, I love sourcing the materials and picking out designs from all my old books and making the garments, but not all the other stuff, like fittings and posting them and chasing checks. It's a bit too businesslike, you know?'

Mia nodded, knowing that her friend had always loved the practical side of drama school but had floundered miserably when it came to writing coursework.

'You need an assistant,' Mia said.

'Are you offering?'

'I can't leave London.'

'No? Are you sure? I mean, I have this spare room here just begging for a lovely tenant, and Bath is so much fun. Honestly, you wouldn't miss London at all.'

'But what about auditions?' Mia said.

Shelley sighed. 'You're still hung up about that life, aren't you?'

'And you're not?'

'I guess I never was,' Shelley said. 'It was fun as a student, but I think I only went to drama school to annoy Dad. He wanted me to go into his business as some lowly paid tea bag tester or something.'

Mia giggled. 'But you're doing that now.'

'I know,' Shelley said, rolling her eyes to the ceiling. 'I think I missed my true calling. I should've done something in fashion.'

Mia nodded. At drama school, Shelley had always been far more interested in the costumes than in the acting and could often be found backstage with a mouthful of pins.

'Okay, then. Let's be having you,' Shelley said, and Mia began to disrobe. Shelley immediately leapt across the room to push the door closed.

'Don't want Pie copping an eyeful, do we?' she said. 'He doesn't seem to care if I see him naked. He's always walking around with no clothes on. I really must say something.'

'Aren't you a bit—well, anxious, living with a total stranger?' Mia asked.

Shelley looked thoughtful for a moment. 'No,' she said at last. 'I feel wonderfully safe around him. Isn't that funny?'

Standing in her underwear, Mia picked up the sweet muslin dress that hadn't been worn for more than three years and pulled it on over her head.

'Oh, my goodness!' Shelley said at once. 'You *have* put on weight! This dress will never do up. I'll have to get to work on it right away.'

Mia's face flushed scarlet. 'Sorry, Shelley. I guess I eat when I'm unhappy.'

'Oh, I'm lucky. I starve.'

Mia smiled. Her friend had always had a full figure, and Mia had never seen her off her food ever. She *always* had an appetite.

'Look at me, I'm skin and bone,' she said.

Mia admired her comely figure. 'Yes, like Marilyn Monroe,' she said.

'Well, not to worry. I can soon fix this,' Shelley said, taking a seat at her trusty sewing machine. 'And I've got the perfect piece of ribbon to finish it off. You'll look just perfect tomorrow. Why don't you go and make yourself a cup of tea? I've left the 1995 copy of *Persuasion* in the DVD player. You can watch that, if you want. I'll give you a call when I'm ready for you.'

Mia nodded. She knew Shelley preferred to work without an audience, and she couldn't resist the pull of *Persuasion*. Amanda Root and Ciarán Hinds would be just the thing to get her in the mood for the promenade the next day. It was one of Mia's favorite film adaptations, and she loved trying to recognize the locations used in Bath, imagining herself walking in those same locations in her own Regency costume. That was one of the privileges of the Jane Austen Festival—one could make believe that one was in the very heart of an Austen novel or, at the very least, a film adaptation. The streets of Bath were among the most beautiful in the world and were certainly the most romantic to walk around in costume.

There was something very special about wearing a costume. It made you feel as if you were somebody else entirely. It was like armor against reality, and you could make believe that you were quite another person, which was a very seductive feeling.

Going through to the kitchen at the back of the house, Mia made herself a cup of tea in one of the I Love Darcy mugs, smiling at her friend's collection of Austen paraphernalia. There was a Jane Austen tea towel hanging over the cooker door, a film-locations calendar on the wall, from which a handsome Henry Tilney was staring down, and a shopping bag with the words 'Obstinate, headstrong girl!' hanging on the back of the door.

Stirring a spoonful of sugar into her mug, Mia left the Austen-infested kitchen and walked through to the sitting room, stopping abruptly at the door. Shelley's lodger, Pie, was slouched in a chair in the corner of the sitting room, his head in the racing pages of a newspaper. He didn't look up as Mia took a seat but made some sort of a grunt, perhaps in recognition of her presence; she couldn't really be sure. For a moment, she looked at his shock of brown hair and his stubbly chin. He was rather striking, she thought, in a very rough sort of way.

Deciding not to grunt back in response, she placed her mug on a little table and sat on the sofa.

'You don't mind if I watch something, do you?' she asked, thinking it polite to check.

A grunt came from behind the racing pages, and Mia took it as a form of consent. She picked up the remote controls, switched on the TV, and then pressed play on the DVD player. The bright image of the Cobb at Lyme Regis filled the screen. Shelley had obviously started watching it yet again, and Mia decided not to rewind it. The Lyme Regis scenes were among her favorite.

She was just reaching the famous moment, when Louisa Musgrove flings herself from the Cobb steps, when Pie mumbled something incomprehensible and left the room.

'I guess he's not an Austen fan,' Mia said with a little smile. Either that or he'd already overdosed on Austen since sharing a house with Shelley. She did, after all, have just about every single Jane Austen adaptation that had ever been made. There were two *Persuasions* in her collection, and wasn't there a new version to look forward to? Mia had read on one of the Austen forums that Oli Wade Owen and Gemma Reilly had been filming in Bath in May and June. If only she could have seen that! She was a big Oli Wade Owen fan, but perhaps the sight of him dressed as Captain Wentworth would have been more then she could have borne. She would have been sure to have swooned in the streets, which would never do.

Mia forwarded the 1995 film to the Bath scenes and recognized the house in Sydney Place. She'd once taken a walk there and regretted wearing her little ballet pumps instead of a sensible pair of trainers, because it was a good walk from the center of Bath, but it had been worth it. She had felt like she entered one of the scenes from the film and could just imagine Anne Elliot emerging from the front door. That was part of the magic of Bath; it was like one big, glorious film set, and one could happily imagine that an Austen character would materialize from a shop or a side street at any moment.

~ා

It was getting dark by the time Shelley finished Mia's dress. Mia had watched to the end of *Persuasion* and then returned upstairs.

'There you go, sweetie,' Shelley said as Mia entered the room. 'Try that on for size.'

Mia did as she was told, and Shelley helped her do the dress up at the back.

'That certainly feels a lot better,' Mia said.

'It looks gorgeous,' Shelley said, peering at Mia's reflection in the mirror from behind her shoulder.

Mia nodded.

'What is it?' Shelley asked with a frown.

'Nothing,' Mia said.

'Don't you like it?'

'I love it. It looks great.'

'Then what is it? What's wrong, Mia?' Shelley asked. 'I wish you'd tell me. All the energy seems to have drained out of you.'

Mia moved away from her and tried to get out of the dress, which was, of course, impossible without Shelley's help.

'You used to tell me everything,' Shelley said, following her and unbuttoning the back of the dress.

'There's nothing to tell. Why do you think I have something to tell you?'

'Because I know you. Or at least I used to know you.'

'What could I possibly have to tell you?'

'Well, I don't know,' Shelley said, exasperation filling her voice. 'I was kind of hoping you'd fill me in on that one.'

Mia sighed. 'If I had something to tell you, I'd tell you; believe me.'

With that, Mia left the room, and it was Shelley's turn to sigh.

'I wish I believed you,' Shelley whispered to herself, 'but I don't. I really don't.'

Chapter 9

In her hotel just off Great Pulteney Street, Sarah had unpacked and hung up all her clothes, frowning at the barely noticeable wrinkles that her journey had produced.

Her promenade dress in cream muslin with burgundy trim was laid out across the bed, and she was trying to remember the last time she'd worn it. It would have been the September before they visited Barton Cottage.

'Because we certainly didn't come here the September after,' she said quietly to herself, sitting on the edge of the bed and stroking the dress. She remembered the day that she and Mia had their dresses made by Shelley. It had been a wonderful day, and Sarah smiled as she remembered it. Their love of Jane Austen had certainly led to some fabulous adventures over the years, but it had cost them their friendship, too.

Sarah stood and walked to the window, which looked out over Great Pulteney Street. Just a few years before, Bath had been their special place, and they'd looked forward to the Jane Austen Festival each year, taking time out from their busy lives to spend some high-quality Austen time together. The last few years had meant no trip to Bath, though, and Sarah had missed it so much that it hurt.

What had brought her here now? she wondered. It didn't seem right for her to be here without her sister. For a moment, she thought about the weeks that had led up to her making her decision. She'd been working hard—harder than usual, which was saying something, because she was a renowned workaholic—but even she had realized that she couldn't keep up the pace. When she realized the festival was fast approaching, she booked her tickets for the events, telling herself that it was a well-deserved treat.

There was just one fear that hovered in the back of her mind. Would Mia be there? She must have asked the question a hundred times, but there was no way of knowing the answer. Even if she was there, they might not even see each other. Bath was a large place, there were many events to attend, and it was quite possible that they might just keep missing each other. But what if they didn't? What if Mia was there and they ran right into each other at the very first opportunity? What would happen then?

'Don't think about it,' Sarah said to herself as she began to pleat the bottom of her sweater between her fingers; it was an action she took whenever she was anxious.

That evening she took a walk, making her way toward Pulteney Bridge, where she listened to the River Avon wending its way through the city from under the three fine stone arches. She then made her way to the abbey, which was lit up like a magical lantern, and although she felt more peace than she had in a long time, she couldn't help looking out for Mia, imagining she might emerge from behind one of the Bath stone colonnades at any moment.

The streets were still busy with people out in search of an evening meal, and Sarah smiled as she saw a couple of young women dressed in Regency costume. They obviously couldn't wait for the official beginning of the festival the next day.

For a moment, Sarah felt a little lonely. Everybody seemed to be in pairs, walking and laughing with a companion and sharing their delight in the evening, but Sarah had nobody to share her evening with. Not anymore.

It's your own fault, a little voice said. *You have only yourself to blame.*

She took a deep breath. There was nothing she could do about that now.

Ever practical, she looked at her watch and decided it was high time she had something to eat. On her own. It wasn't ideal, but it was the only option available to her, so she had to get on with it.

Eating out was fraught with worries when one suffered from OCD, and Sarah was always a bag of nerves. She managed to survive by returning over and over again to places she knew, and she did so now, wending her way through the streets to a little bistro with not so much as a napkin out of place.

Luckily for her, her favorite table in the corner was available. Sarah didn't like window tables, because people would stare in and look at you eating, which was most unnerving. Nor did she like tables in thoroughfares where waiters would brush by you or fellow eaters could bump into you, so that left very few choices available to her when she ate out. Tonight, though, she had her favorite table, and it made her happy, even though she was dining alone.

She was halfway through her main course, when somebody caught her eye. It was a man sitting in the opposite corner of the restaurant reading a book. He had short, dark hair that was cut exceptionally neatly and closely to his head, and he was wearing an immaculate navy jacket. He was handsome but didn't look aware of the fact, even though he obviously took pride in how he presented himself. It seemed to Sarah that he wasn't out to impress other people, and he was totally unaware of her staring at him. But it wasn't his face Sarah was trying to get a good look at, but rather the cover of his book. She was always fascinated by what people were reading and couldn't help wanting to know what appealed to the handsome stranger. Would it be a historical biography or the latest bestselling thriller? Sarah wondered.

She didn't get to find out until she finished her meal. It was then that the gentleman stood up, and Sarah's eyes widened in surprise when she saw that the book he'd been reading was the collected letters of Jane Austen. He didn't look like a Janeite, but one could never tell. Jane Austen's appeal went far beyond romantic females.

She watched as he paid for his meal and placed his book very carefully inside a neat leather briefcase that fastened with a satisfying snap. He then walked toward her, and before leaving the restaurant, he gave her a small smile. Sarah instantly felt her face flush. She'd been caught staring. She never stared—it was so rude. Still, if she hadn't been staring, she'd never have seen his smile, and it had been a very cute smile indeed.

Later that night, Mia lay awake in the guest bedroom at Southville Terrace, staring at the ceiling. She'd felt awful at having been so mean to Shelley. After all, she'd only wanted to help. But she couldn't. That was the truth of the matter, and Mia knew it was probably best that Shelley knew as little as possible about her life in London.

How she missed her dear friend! Not long before, they would have confided in each other about everything. No event in their daily lives was too small or insignificant to muse over and dissect, along with a bottle of cheap wine and a box of chocolates. Mia missed those conversations. She remembered how the two women would sit on the carpet in their scruffy rented flat in London, their backs up against the sofa as they made themselves a little picnic on the carpet, Jane Austen adaptation playing on the TV before them. How many evenings they passed that way, bemoaning failed relationships, stressing about the scripts they had to learn for drama school, and musing about the future, which would invariably feature a tall, dark hero striding into their lives and making everything perfect.

'Not that I don't want to be an independent woman,' Shelley would say, 'but I'd be quite happy for the man in my life to own an estate like Pemberley.'

Mia had agreed wholeheartedly. Fine country estates had to be owned by somebody, so why shouldn't they belong to the men they would one day date? But a Fitzwilliam Darcy or a Henry Tilney had yet to make an appearance on the horizon, and both Mia and Shelley had to get their fix from fiction rather than real life.

Mia wondered what had been going on in her friend's life. They'd talked so little over the last few years, and Mia realized that much had changed between them. Perhaps the next few days would make amends and they'd open up to one another.

Shelley had known that something was wrong straightaway, hadn't she? And Mia realized that her friend probably wouldn't let the matter drop until she got to the bottom of things. And here she was thinking she could leave all her problems behind her in London. She didn't want them following her to Bath, but you took your problems with you wherever you went. A beautiful place didn't have magical qualities that vanquished all your troubles. Even if Mia were to find herself whisked into the very heart of

Pemberley, she'd still have to deal with the problems she accumulated in her life. She couldn't just shut them out.

'I know I can't,' she whispered into the darkness of the room, 'but let me forget about them for a little while, at least.'

Tomorrow was the promenade and the official beginning of the Jane Austen Festival. It was always a day to look forward to, and Mia had no intentions of her past clouding over such a day, so she closed her eyes, quite determined to dream of frivolous things, like girls in bright bonnets and men in tight breeches.

Chapter 10

T HE DAY OF THE PROMENADE DAWNED, AND AS THE CLOUDS
cleared, the sun got brighter and brighter, making the honey-
colored stone of the houses of Bath glow with warmth.

As Sarah stood looking out of the window down onto the street
below, she couldn't help feeling excited about the morning ahead.
She hadn't slept very well, but that was normal when she was in a
strange place. At one point, she got out of bed and sat in a little
chair with a lamp on, reading a few chapters from *Northanger
Abbey*. Sarah loved the line 'Catherine felt herself in high luck'
from chapter three, and she hoped that some of that luck might
come her way. She felt ready for it. The past few years had been
rather luck*less*, but Bath was a magical place where anything could
happen. It was where Catherine Morland had met Henry Tilney,
and it was where Captain Wentworth had declared his love to
Anne Elliot.

Sarah had gone down to breakfast in a pair of jeans and a T-shirt
but was now in full Regency splendor; her white muslin dress
trimmed with burgundy looked serenely understated and elegant
and was very much Sarah. She loved the neatness and grace of
fashion in Jane Austen's time and often wished that fashion would

forgo the graceless jeans and trainers of the twenty-first century and return to a time when women flitted around in pretty dresses and weren't afraid to be feminine.

She had removed all vestiges of her modern self, from the gold digital watch to the contact lenses she wore. Even though the items would never be noticed, Sarah liked to do things properly, although her hair was sporting a color that probably hadn't been available in Regency England. She looked in the mirror, thinking that the color looked natural enough, tucked neatly under her bonnet.

Leaving her hotel, Sarah walked out onto the street and felt conspicuous in her costume, for she was the only one she could see who was wearing such an outfit. An awful horror struck her. What if she'd got the date wrong? What if she'd arrived in Bath a week early? But that could never happen to somebody like Sarah, who planned every day down to the last minute in it.

Sure enough, when she approached the bridge into town, she saw a young couple ahead of her, both in Regency costume. How happy they looked together, their arms intertwined. Once again, Sarah felt the full weight of being on her own. She liked to think of herself as an independent woman. She was happy being her own boss, and she didn't feel that she needed anybody to tell her what to do in life, but it was at times like this, when a companion made all the difference. She thought about Jane Austen's novels and how most of her heroines had confidantes. Elinor had Marianne; Elizabeth had Jane and Charlotte; and Catherine Morland had Isabella, who may not have been the most trustworthy of companions, but she'd been a companion nevertheless. Walking through the streets of Bath on her own, though, Sarah felt more like Anne Elliot, for she had never quite been a part of things, but always hovered on the outskirts of companionship. Even Anne's relationship with Lady Russell had been wanting, for she could never tell her mentor her true feelings.

'But Anne got her happy ending,' Sarah told herself, 'right here in Bath too. She had to wait for it, but it came.'

With a feeling of optimism, Sarah took a deep breath and headed into the heart of the city.

～⑤

'Mia! Have you seen my bonnet?' Shelley shouted from the hallway. As Mia walked out of her bedroom to look down the stairs, she couldn't help thinking that it wasn't often you'd hear such a question in twenty-first-century life.

'Wasn't it on your mannequin?'

'Lady Catherine? Yes, but it isn't there now,' Shelley said. 'My goodness—if Bingley has got hold of it, I swear he'll be sent to the dogs' home before the end of the day.'

Mia hunted the missing bonnet upstairs, but it wasn't in any of the rooms. 'It's not upstairs,' Mia called as she joined Shelley in the kitchen.

'I can't go without my bonnet,' Shelley said. 'I've been looking forward to wearing it all year.' She was buzzing around the kitchen looking under tables and chairs, when Pie entered the room.

'Oh, Pie—you've got my bonnet,' Shelley said.

He muttered something and handed it to her.

'What did he say?' Mia asked as he left the room.

'I have absolutely no idea.'

'Maybe he's a secret cross-dresser with a fetish for Austensian bonnets,' Mia said, and they both giggled.

At that precise moment, Bingley crashed into the room like a cannonball, careening into Shelley at full speed.

'*Bingley!*' she shouted. '*Must* you do that?'

Mia laughed.

'Lord Almighty! Why can't he simply walk into a room? He always has to be firing on all cylinders.'

'He's adorable,' Mia said, giving him a pat on his chestnut head. He looked up at her and must have decided that Mia wanted to get to know him better, because before she knew what was happening, his front paws had left the ground and had been placed on Mia's shoulders.

'*Noooooooooo!*' Shelley cried out on Mia's behalf. Mia took a step back, and Bingley collapsed to the ground. 'Oh, your dress!' Shelley said, stepping forward to examine it for damage.

'It's okay, I think,' Mia said.

'Yes, apart from one great dirty paw print on your left shoulder.' She maneuvered her friend toward the sink and started dabbing at her with a damp cloth. 'I'm so sorry! That dog is a thorough nuisance. I can't think why I got him. Only last week, he ate my entire lasagna, and the week before that, he completely destroyed my limited edition Captain Wentworth cushion.'

'I'm sure he didn't mean to,' Mia said, 'and don't worry about my dress. I think Elizabeth Bennet might very well have sported a paw print on her shoulder, don't you think?'

Shelley grimaced, not looking convinced. 'How about a shawl?'

Mia nodded. The shawl was the epitome of Austen heroine elegance and was very handy for accidentally dropping, if one saw a handsome hero to pick it up.

Shelley disappeared upstairs and returned with a pretty sky-blue shawl that matched the trim of Mia's dress perfectly. She draped it over her friend's shoulders, covering up the offending paw print.

'We'd better get going,' Mia said, and Shelley nodded.

'Bonnets at the ready?'

Mia smiled. 'Oh, yes.'

They left the house, their tiny purses hooked over their arms and hiding all manner of modern necessities, like lip glosses and mobile phones. Shelley was also holding a pretty white parasol, which she'd told Mia was for fighting off any potential rivals, if there was a real-life Mr Darcy at the promenade, rather than for shielding herself from the sun.

'Are you sure Pie's all right giving us a lift into town?' Mia asked.

'It's the least he can do, after all the tidying up I do after him,' Shelley said. 'But he'll have to get a move on, if we're going to be on time.' She turned back to look at the house, but there was no sign of Pie.

'Oh, look—there's Gabe!' Shelley said, waving her parasol in the air at him.

'Hello,' he said from his front door. 'I wish I had a hat to tip. You look splendid—both of you! Off to promenade the streets?'

'Of course,' Shelley said. 'Oh, won't you come too, Gabe? You'd look fabulous in costume. Wouldn't he, Mia?'

Mia glanced at him quickly. 'Any man looks good in costume,' she said, and then bit her lip. She had sounded very rude, and she hadn't meant to.

'And what about my arm?' Gabe said, tapping his sling.

'You could be Horatio Nelson,' Shelley said, suddenly inspired. 'Now there's a real hero for you.'

'But wouldn't I have to lose an eye as well?' Gabe said with a laugh.

Mia smiled at his comment and noticed that he was looking at her. What was his problem? Had he never seen a woman in Regency costume before?

'Bingley not accompanying you?' Gabe asked.

'You must be joking! He'd rampage and wreck the whole promenade. I've shut him in the kitchen,' Shelley said. 'He's been a bad boy this morning. Just look what he's done to Mia's dress.' She pulled Mia's shawl down to reveal the offending mark.

'Oh, dear,' Gabe said, but there was the beginnings of a smile playing around his lips, and Mia couldn't help smiling too. 'Shall I give him a walk?'

'Oh, would you?'

'It would be my pleasure.'

'He's always such a darling for you. I can never handle him properly.'

'That's because he knows he can get away with things with you. You've got to be firmer with him, Shelley.'

'I know, but it's so hard.'

'I'll get him now, shall I?'

Shelley smiled and nodded, watching as Gabe entered the house. 'Honestly, I don't know what I'd do without Gabe. He really is marvelous. You should get to know him.'

Before Mia could protest, Shelley was shouting again.

'*Pie!* Oh, where is he? How very provoking he can be! Honestly, he wouldn't get a job as a taxi driver.'

Mia grinned as Pie emerged from the house. His hair was in disarray as usual, and he wasn't smiling.

'If only Pie could be more like Gabe,' Shelley whispered.

They followed Pie out into the road, and Mia smiled when she saw the vehicle that was to take them into Bath. It was a small white van. Well, it had once been white, but it was now more of a dingy beige, owing to the layers of dirt that had accumulated over goodness only knew how long. It wasn't exactly the finest of vehicles on the road, but it looked functional enough, and it certainly beat the long walk into town in their fancy gowns and delicate shoes.

'What is it, exactly, that Pie does?' Mia whispered, looking around the van as they squashed into the back seat together.

'I'm not sure,' Shelley whispered back.

'Didn't you ask? I mean, when he came to rent your room?'

Shelley shook her head. 'He just handed me two references and a wad of fifty-pound notes, and I said thank you. I'm sure he did try to tell me, but I couldn't understand what he was saying.'

'Is he foreign, do you think?'

Shelley shrugged.

Mia thought it very mysterious, and she wasn't at all sure she'd want to be sharing a house with somebody she knew so little about, but there was also something a little romantic about it. It turned Pie into a sort of Heathcliff-type character, where one could imagine all sorts about his background. Maybe he was a prince from a faraway country—or maybe not. She couldn't imagine it, herself.

Putting all thoughts of Pie's romantic past out of her mind, Mia looked out of the window as the van descended the steep hill into town. It was this side of town around which Jane Austen and her sister used to walk, Lyncombe Hill, wasn't it? Mia tried to imagine the sisters making the ascent in the restricting fashions of the day. It wouldn't do for Mia. As much as she adored her muslin dress and dainty shoes, she still liked to be able to stride out in a pair of jeans and sturdy boots.

Pie stopped at the back of the abbey, and they got out of the van, straightening their dresses and adjusting their bonnets.

'I'm so excited,' Mia said. 'It feels like decades since I was last here.'

Shelley linked arms with her like a true heroine, and they rounded the abbey together and were soon lost in a sea of costumes.

'It's the busiest ever!' Shelley said. 'I've never seen so many people before. This *must* be a world record.'

The crowd seemed to hum with excitement, and Mia watched in delight as people posed in front of the great abbey doors and the Pump Room, all eager to have their photographs taken for posterity.

Mia had truly never seen quite so many people in costume in one place, but there was something rather surreal about it too, for these heroes and heroines were definitely from the twenty-first century, even though the clothes they wore begged to differ. Mia noticed that a number of them were pushing baby strollers and holding mobile phones, and there was even a Mrs Jenkins look-alike who was sneaking a quick cigarette. Then there were the giveaway shoes. Whilst a good majority did their best with replica shoes from the period, there were still a few kitten heels and trainers half hidden beneath the long dresses. What would Jane Austen have made of it all? Mia wondered.

There were so many magnificent costumes that it was hard to know where to look. Sky blue and white seemed to be favorites, and they made a fresh combination. Mia also loved the sweet apple green and white she spotted a young woman wearing. It was all such a wonderful feast for the eyes and was rather like looking at a cloud of beautiful butterflies.

Then they spotted a woman with bright purple hair.

'That's not very Austen appropriate,' Mia said in disgust. 'You'd think she could have toned it down a bit for the festival.'

'I wish there were more men,' Shelley said. 'Most of them are old enough to be my grandfather.'

Then she saw him—he was tall, with bright chestnut hair, and he was in full Regency costume.

'Oh, my goodness!' Shelley exclaimed, a gloved hand flying to her mouth. 'It's a real-life hero! Mr Darcy *does* exist!'

Mia looked in the direction Shelley was gazing, and there stood the most handsome man she had ever seen, although he actually had his back to them, so it was impossible to tell if he really was handsome, but if the long, slim-fitting coat and elegant black boots were anything to go by, then he was a real stunner.

'I'm going to propose to him right now,' Shelley said, 'and don't try to stop me. Men like that don't come along very often.'

Mia giggled. Shelley was right. The man really stood out from the crowd. Not only was there a sorry lack of men in general, but also the ones who did join in the promenade tended to be a little older than your average Jane Austen hero.

Before Shelley had time to go down on bended knee, the hero turned around.

'Oh!' Shelley gasped, not only because he was just as handsome as she'd hoped, but also because he was holding a tiny baby in a little papoose.

'Probably best that you not propose to him,' Mia said with a little smile. 'I think he's already taken.'

Sure enough, they then spotted a young woman with a tumble of fair curls tied loosely with a pale pink ribbon. She was wearing a simple white dress and a pretty rose-colored Spencer jacket. A topaz cross hung on a fine gold chain around her neck, and Mia immediately recognized it as a copy of Jane Austen's famous necklace.

Shelley, who adored babies, couldn't resist saying hello and had approached the couple before Mia could stop her.

'What an adorable baby!' Shelley said. 'What's her name?'

'Cassie,' the man said.

'Cassandra,' the woman corrected.

'Like Jane's sister?' Shelley said.

The young woman nodded. 'Cassandra Elizabeth Jane.'

'How perfect is that?' Shelley enthused.

'Cassie for short,' the man said.

'How old is she?' Mia asked, peering down at the baby.

'Five weeks,' the woman said.

Shelley's mouth dropped open in wonder. 'Oh!' she exclaimed. 'Then I'm guessing this is her first Jane Austen Festival.'

The woman laughed. 'And its youngest participant. It's Dan's first festival too,' the young mother said, nodding to the tall gentleman beside her. 'I've been before, but this is the first year I've dressed up, and it's so much fun.'

Shelley nodded enthusiastically. 'I come every year. I wouldn't miss it for the world.'

It was then that the announcement came: the promenade was about to begin. Mia felt a funny fluttering in her stomach, which she normally only ever felt when attending auditions.

'Come on, Robyn,' the gentleman with the baby said, and Mia and Shelley watched as she linked arms with him and they began to promenade.

'Isn't that the most perfect family you've ever seen?' Shelley asked with a romantic sigh.

Mia nodded. 'They looked so happy together, didn't they?'

'That might be us one day,' Shelley said. 'In fact, I'm not going to even consider getting married to a man unless he is willing to don Regency costume.'

'Me neither,' Mia said.

'I think he was the only real hero here today, and he's taken,' Shelley said.

'We can still look,' Mia said, her eyes still fixed firmly on the gentleman.

'My, you really have got a bit of a crush on him, haven't you?' Shelley teased.

'Don't be silly,' Mia said. 'I was only looking at the baby.'

Chapter 11

O NCE SARAH REACHED THE ABBEY, SHE WASN'T ON HER OWN for long. She was adopted by a group of Americans who had come over from New York especially for the festival. She also spoke to a couple from Hong Kong and two girls from Sweden. Jane Austen was truly a global phenomenon.

By the time the group reached Milsom Street, they'd all discussed their favorite heroines (Elizabeth Bennet and Anne Elliot, although Sarah put in a special word for Elinor Dashwood), their favorite heroes (Mr Darcy, Captain Wentworth, with a heartfelt mention of Henry Tilney, owing to their being in Bath), and the house that they'd all like to be mistress of (Pemberley was voted unanimously, although Sarah thought of Barton Cottage, but she kept her thoughts to herself).

It was always an honor to walk the length of Milsom Street, and Sarah thought of how it was this very street that General Tilney had lodged in with Henry and Eleanor in *Northanger Abbey*. Anne Elliot had also walked this very street and, of course, Jane Austen too. Sarah often thought it funny how she would think of the characters as if they were real people who had really lived, occupying this very world with the same strength of mind and passion as their creator. How many of the shoppers today knew of the Austen connection, though? Sarah wondered. Did they think about Tilney teasing Catherine, and Captain Wentworth brooding over Anne as they went from shop to shop? Or was it just the select few like her, who could never walk through the streets of Bath without imagining a whole host of fictional characters swarming around her? Whatever the answer, Sarah knew that Bath would always hold a very special place in her heart, and she thought of Catherine Morland's assertion, 'Oh! Who can ever be tired of Bath?'

Mia and Shelley were rather enjoying being photographed by the Saturday shoppers who all took a moment out of their time to stop and watch the promenaders.

'He should definitely be in costume,' Shelley said, nodding toward a handsome man who was taking a photo of them with his mobile phone. 'Wouldn't he look splendid?'

'Like Gabe?'

'So you noticed how splendid Gabe is?'

'No,' Mia said, 'I've just noticed how you want to dress up half of the male population of Bath.'

'It wouldn't do them any harm,' Shelley said. 'I hate modern men's clothes. All these ripped jeans and oversized trainers. Most unattractive.'

Mia nodded. Very few modern men dressed well, she had to admit.

'Good morning, ladies.' A voice suddenly accosted them, and they turned around to see a gentleman in naval uniform. Unfortunately, he was about sixty-five and had a bushy beard in which you could lose a whole battalion.

They nodded politely as he continued on his way.

'I'm afraid that's all that's left for us,' Mia said.

'I think you're right,' Shelley said. 'Why is life a constant disappointment?'

'Because we read fiction,' Mia said, and Shelley nodded, knowing it was true.

It wasn't long before they were walking along the elegant curved pavements of The Circus. From there, they walked into Brock Street and on toward the Royal Crescent. It was always a highlight to enter the famous crescent, and there was an opportunity to stop for photographs whilst a group of dancers entertained the crowds. The sunny weather had brought more people out than ever before, and everyone stopped to watch the promenade.

'How beautiful everyone looks,' Mia said as she surveyed the sea of bright costumes in the sunshine. There were many sumptuous colors and fabrics, and everyone looked at home in the Georgian surroundings. Mia's heart swelled with pride at being a part of it all.

After the dancing ended, the promenaders ambled along the famous Gravel Walk, which was beautifully shady after the brilliant light in the crescent, but parasols remained up. After all, one didn't get to use them very often.

The walk ended in a flight of shallow steps, and then the party turned to head back into town.

Shelley shook her head and sighed. 'It's all over,' she said. 'All over for another year.'

Mia turned to look at her friend. 'But there's the rest of the festival to look forward to. We've got all sorts booked, haven't we?'

'Yes, but this is my favorite bit, and it always goes much too quickly.'

Mia smiled, but then she grabbed Shelley's arm.

'What is it?'

Mia's mouth dropped open, and she could hardly speak. 'I think I saw someone.'

'Who? The ghost of Captain Wentworth? I'm told he haunts these parts.' Shelley grinned.

Mia didn't say anything, but her eyes were fixed on the crowd ahead. She could have sworn she'd seen Sarah, but she lost her almost as soon as her gaze had alighted on her, so no, she couldn't be sure. Had her eyes played tricks on her? Had she only *thought* she'd seen her, because she'd been thinking about her? Maybe it was just a blend of an overactive imagination and her anxiety that her sister would be there.

'She wouldn't be here, would she?'

'Sarah? Why not? She is as much a fan as you are, and you are here.'

Mia sighed. Why indeed should Sarah not be there? She had as much right to attend the festival as Mia did.

'But she wouldn't,' Mia reasoned with herself. 'She can barely make it to the supermarket on her own.'

Shelley placed a hand on Mia's shoulder. 'Well, maybe she's changed. Maybe she got help for her OCD. I mean, you don't know, do you?'

The question stung Mia. Shelley was right. She wouldn't know, would she? She had missed out on more than three years of her sister's life, just as her sister had missed out on three years of *her* life. So much could have happened—so much *had* happened—in that time.

'It probably wasn't her at all,' Shelley said. 'Everybody looks the same in costume. It could have been any number of people.'

Mia nodded. Shelley was probably right, but Mia kept wondering if the woman she'd seen really had been her sister.

When the promenade reached the Pump Room again, Sarah felt a little lost. A great crowd of people were gathering outside the entrance to the Pump Room, luxuriating in having lunch in the sumptuous surroundings whilst wearing the most appropriate of clothing. Others were sitting on chairs outside cafés, happy to mingle with the modern world and not the least bit embarrassed by the looks they were getting.

It was always a sad moment to see the crowd dispersing and knowing it would be a full year before everybody met again. Of course, the festival was far from over, and Austen stalwarts would continue to wear a costume until the last event closed and it was time for Bath to return to the modern world.

Sarah paused for a moment outside the Pump Room, wondering where she should go. She had lost her new friends in the crowd and wasn't at all sure what to do with herself.

'Don't be such a child,' she told herself. 'You're a grown woman and can fend for yourself. Just get a sandwich and sit on the bench.'

A few minutes later, she had bought herself some lunch and walked to the square by the abbey. There was a busker playing a guitar and singing, and the benches were full of tourists and workers on their lunch break. In fact, there was only one bench that was free, but a man had spotted it just before her and was making his way toward it. Sarah was just about to turn in search of somewhere else to sit, when she realized it was the man from the restaurant. She recognized his shock of dark hair and kind brown eyes.

She watched in fascination as he got out a large tissue and dusted the bench. It hadn't been raining and the bench didn't look dirty, but he wiped each slat of wood before walking across to a nearby bin and placing the tissue in it. Returning to the bench, he sat down, placing a large bag next to himself.

Sarah wasn't usually forward when it came to men, but she really didn't fancy going in search of another place to sit, and the dark-haired man looked slightly less threatening a proposition than most.

'Okay if I sit here?' she asked as she approached the bench.

He looked up, shielding his eyes from the sun. 'Please,' he said with a nod.

Sarah sat down. She was terribly hungry. In fact, she could feel her stomach rumbling, but she felt funny about eating in front of a stranger, so left her pack of sandwiches in her handbag.

'Weren't you at the restaurant last night?' he said.

Sarah gave a little smile—half thrilled, half shy. 'Yes.'

'Good restaurant,' he said.

'Yes.'

'Clean.'

'Yes,' Sarah said.

'I mean, all restaurants should be, of course, but they're not. At least, not to—' He stopped. 'Sorry,' he said.

'What for?'

'I'm boring you.'

'No, you're not.'

He shook his head, looking embarrassed. 'Really, I can go on sometimes.' He cleared his throat and turned toward her. 'I'm Lloyd,' he said.

'I'm Sarah.' She was relieved when he didn't offer his hand

to shake, another potential minefield for the OCD sufferer. Not everyone took as much care of their hands as someone with OCD, although Lloyd had been talking about clean restaurants and had wiped the bench before sitting on it, so his hands were probably cleaner than the average person's. Something struck Sarah. He hadn't shaken hands with her not because he knew she wouldn't want to, but because he probably thought that *her* hands weren't clean. Sarah bit her lip and she immediately wanted to say something, but she couldn't blurt out, 'My hands are clean,' could she? It wouldn't be very gracious.

'What brings you to Bath?' Lloyd said, and Sarah was glad to be diverted from the unpleasant subject of how clean her hands were perceived to be.

'The Jane Austen Festival,' she said, motioning to her costume.

'Oh, of course,' he said with a smile. 'That's why I'm here.'

Sarah frowned. He didn't look like a fan, but maybe he was a secret one. After all, not everybody went around sporting breaches and cravats, and hadn't she spotted him reading *Jane Austen's Collected Letters* the night before?

'I'm a photographer. I'm here to photograph the festival,' he went on.

'Oh!' Sarah said.

'For *Vive!*'

Sarah grimaced at the name of the tabloid newspaper.

'Not for the newspaper itself,' he said. 'They've got a new Sunday magazine called *The Difference*.' He gave a groan. '*Vive!—The Difference*, get it? The photographs are for that.'

'I don't like that newspaper,' Sarah said. 'It's full of appalling stories that just aren't true.'

'I know,' Lloyd said. 'My mother's horrified that I'm working for them, but you can't be too choosy when you're freelancing, and it's good exposure.'

'I suppose,' Sarah said. 'But I do hope they're not going to make fun of the festival. Jane Austen fans in costume are an easy target, I'm afraid.'

'You've got no worries there. It's a totally sincere piece to coincide with one of the Austen anniversaries.'

Sarah breathed a sigh of relief.

'Perhaps I could take a photo of you?' he said.

'Oh, I don't know,' Sarah said, feeling a blush creep over her cheeks. 'I'm not very photogenic.'

Lloyd frowned and peered at her. 'I wouldn't say that. You look very photogenic from where I'm sitting.'

'No, no,' Sarah said, in fear that he was about to get his camera out. 'I much prefer to be on the other side of the camera.' She opened her handbag and got out her tiny silver camera. 'See?' She showed him the screen and scrolled through some of the photographs she'd taken of the promenade.

'Very nice,' he said.

'Well, they won't be as good as yours.' She watched as he opened up his bag and got out a very impressive camera.

'I think there are one or two I can use,' he said and scrolled through the photos taken that morning.

Sarah gasped. They were stunning. He had caught the buoyant mood of the morning, and the light was exquisite, capturing the smiling faces, swirls of fabulous fabric, and the beautiful surroundings perfectly.

And then her heart stopped. As picture followed picture, Sarah's eyes picked out the image of a young woman she thought she recognized. Could it have been Mia?

'Go back!' she suddenly blurted. 'Back!'

Lloyd looked surprised but scrolled back through the photos.

'Stop!' Sarah grabbed the camera from him and zoomed into the figure, but it was impossible to tell whether it was her sister or not. It could be, but it could just as easily be half a dozen other young women.

She handed the camera back to him. 'Sorry,' she said, suddenly realizing how odd her behavior must have seemed to him.

'Did you recognize someone?'

'No,' she said, shaking her head. 'I thought I did for a moment, but I was wrong.'

He gave a little smile.

'Your pictures are wonderful,' she said.

'Thanks,' he said, putting the camera back in the bag. As he did so, a piece of paper fluttered to the ground and, at once, Sarah noticed what it was.

'Oh, you have a list!' she said.

Lloyd cleared his throat as he retrieved it, obviously embarrassed. 'I—er—yes,' he said.

'I make lists too… all the time. I can't leave the house without them.'

'Really?'

Sarah nodded. 'You don't think that's weird, do you?'

'No,' he said quickly. 'That's absolutely normal. I think people who leave home *without* lists are the strange ones.'

'Yes,' Sarah said. 'I've always thought so too. I mean, how do people remember everything without a list? How do they make the best use of their time?'

Lloyd nodded. 'People might think they'll remember everything, but something usually gets forgotten.'

Their eyes met, and they both smiled as if they'd found a kindred spirit.

'I'm afraid I've got to go now,' he said, standing up. 'There's an event on at the Guildhall.'

'Yes, the Country Fayre. I'm going to it later,' Sarah said.

'Here's my card,' he said, fumbling for one in a jacket pocket.

Sarah took it from him and read the name in bold script across the top: Lloyd Anderson.

'Maybe I'll see you there,' he said, a definite invitation in his voice.

'Yes,' she said, shielding her eyes from the sun as she looked up and smiled at him. 'Maybe.'

She watched as he walked away and became immersed in the crowds, thinking that her 'maybe' was a definite *probably*.

Chapter 12

Barton Cottage

THE WALK BACK UP TO BARTON COTTAGE WAS TAKING MIA longer than it should have, not because her knee was sore, but because she was rather enjoying linking arms with Alec Burrows.

'Okay?' he asked as they squeezed through the gate together. 'We're nearly there.'

'Where are you staying?' Mia asked.

'The little place just through the wood. It's right down by the water and has the most amazing views.'

'This one does too.'

'Yes,' he said, looking back down toward the estuary. 'My aunt used to live in Devon, and we'd stay here on family holidays. I guess I never outgrew them.'

'Where do you live?'

'London,' he said.

'Oh, I live in London too!' Mia said, a bit too enthusiastically. She could almost hear Sarah admonishing her. 'I'm in Ealing at the moment with a friend. I've just finished drama school.'

'Really? You're an actress?'

'Yes. Well, more of a singer. I'm auditioning in the West End.'

'Wow!' he said. 'I've never met an actress or singer before. I'll have to come and see you when you're on stage.'

'Would you?'

'Of course. I'll give you my card. Just let me know when and where.'

'I will,' she said, imagining him sending red roses to her dressing room and taking her out for a champagne supper after her first stunning performance. But she was getting too ahead of herself; she hadn't known him for even five minutes.

'Now, let's get you to the nearest sofa,' he said, and the two of them walked across the lawn and into Barton Cottage.

'Sarah?' Mia called through the house. 'Sarah?'

'What is it?' a voice called from the back of the house where the kitchen was. 'Oh, my goodness! What's happened to you?' Sarah asked as soon as she saw her sister.

'Nothing. I just fell.'

'I'm afraid we had a sort of collision,' Alec said.

'And I tumbled right over, just like Marianne.'

'Marianne?' Alec said.

'Marianne Dashwood from *Sense and Sensibility*.'

He didn't look any the wiser.

'It's a book by Jane Austen,' Sarah explained.

'Oh, she's a heroine,' he said.

'Yes,' Mia said. 'And she gets swept up by a dashing hero.'

Sarah looked aghast at her sister's forwardness.

'Well, I hope I didn't disappoint you.'

Mia smiled at him. 'This is Alec,' she said to Sarah, by way of an afterthought.

Alec stretched out a hand and shook Sarah's.

'I'm Sarah.'

'This is about as strange as introductions get, isn't it?'

'I guess so,' Sarah said.

'I feel just awful about what has happened. If there's anything I can do—'

'Oh, I'm fine,' Mia said, flopping into the nearest chair and rolling up the left leg of her tracksuit bottoms.

Sarah gasped. 'You're bleeding!' She rushed out of the room.

'My sister loves a crisis,' Mia said. 'Oh, sit down, please!'

Alec sat on a chair beside her and shook his head. 'I'll never forgive myself for this.'

'But it's nothing. Really. It doesn't hurt at all. You're probably bleeding too. Have you checked?'

Alec cleared his throat and then dared to roll up the legs of his own tracksuit bottoms. Sure enough, a small graze greeted him.

Mia's mouth dropped open. 'See! You're hurt too. Let me see.' Without thinking, Mia was on the floor and kneeling beside him in a moment. 'It's not too bad, but it's still bleeding.'

Sarah walked into the room with a bowl of warm water, cotton wool, and a box of plasters. Her eyes widened at the sight of her sister on the floor in front of a pair of bare legs.

'See to him first, Sarah,' Mia said, scrambling up from the floor.

'I wouldn't hear of it,' Alec said, rolling his tracksuit legs down again. 'I'll take care of it at home.'

'You're not going, are you?'

'I think I've probably done quite enough damage for one morning,' he said, getting up from the chair.

'Why not stay for breakfast? I'm sure Sarah's made plenty,' Mia said with what she hoped was a winning smile.

'No, thank you,' he said. 'That's very kind of you, but I should be getting back. But perhaps I can call again? Maybe tomorrow—to see how you are.'

Mia nodded and couldn't help smiling once again.

The two women watched as he walked down the path toward the little wooden gate, from where he turned around and waved.

'Isn't he wonderful?' Mia said. 'Wasn't it kind of him to see me home?'

'I think it's the very least he could do if he caused you to fall in the first place.'

'But it was all my fault. You know what I'm like. I was running along not paying any attention to the world around me, and I ran right into him.'

'Mia, you really should be more careful. You could have been seriously hurt.'

'Oh, I'm fine.'

Sarah pushed her sister back into the house. 'I want to get a proper look at that graze.'

Mia sighed, turning around to catch a last glimpse of Alec, who'd broken into a jog and was heading out of view.

'It was he who called last night,' Mia said. 'He wanted to let us know that the car window was open.'

Sarah's mouth dropped open. 'I left it open—all night?' She looked absolutely horrified. 'I'd better check on it after I've seen to you.'

'And then breakfast.'

Sarah nodded and then shook her head. 'What a start to the morning!'

Mia thought it was a brilliant start to the morning. In fact, it was better than she could ever have imagined.

Chapter 13

THE COUNTRY FAYRE ALWAYS ATTRACTED A GOOD CROWD, AND the Guildhall was full of costumed customers eager to sample what was on offer. There were bookstalls and fabric stalls, stalls selling bonnets, ribbons, and dress patterns. A woman was reading palms, and a man was cutting out silhouettes.

Grand portraits looked down on the proceedings from the pale green walls, and golden columns soared up to an ornate ceiling from which hung the most splendid chandeliers.

Tables and chairs were set out in the middle of the room, and it was the perfect place for people to meet and chat and catch up on all the festival gossip. On a small stage, musicians played.

Shelley was loving it all, feeling as if she had stepped back in time and that Mrs Bennet and her daughters were bound to enter the room at any moment.

'Isn't this wonderful?' she said, grabbing Mia's arm. 'Mia?'

'What?'

'What's the matter? You're all twitchy!'

'No, I'm not.'

'Yes, you are. You've been miles away, and you're twitching like an anxious rabbit.'

Mia pulled away and went over to a stall and idly picked out an old hardback copy of *Northanger Abbey* with a torn dust jacket and mottled pages.

'Mia?'

'What?'

'I wish you'd talk to me.'

'I am talking to you.'

'No, you're not. You're only half there.'

Mia returned the book to its shelf and turned to face Shelley. 'I'm sorry,' she said. 'I just feel strange being here.'

'Without Sarah?'

Mia nodded. 'It doesn't feel right, you know?'

'I know,' Shelley said. 'I miss her too. I always thought of her as an honorary sister.'

Mia sighed. 'I still can't get my head around it all. I'm sorry.'

'There's no need to apologize, silly.'

'I promised myself that I wouldn't spoil this trip to Bath, but I can't help thinking of her. Every corner we walk around, I see her standing there or I remember one of our funny holiday moments together, like when she got a fit of sneezes in the middle of that really boring lecture about card games.'

'There *must* be a way of you two making up.'

Mia shook her head. 'I can't see how.'

'But you were so close. I always admired that. My mum has two sisters, and she can't stand either of them, but you two were different. You were more like twins, and it pains me to see you like this now.'

For one awful moment, Shelley felt quite sure that Mia was about to cry, so she looked around the room in desperation until she found the perfect distraction. 'Come on,' she said. 'Let's get our silhouettes cut. I've always wanted mine done.'

A little smile lit up Mia's face, and the two of them headed over toward the stall to be immortalized in card.

If it hadn't been for Sarah's enormous bonnet half hiding her face, Mia might have spotted her as she entered the Guildhall, but she didn't, and Sarah was no longer on the lookout for Mia either. She was far too busy trying to spot Lloyd, which wasn't hard, because she practically bumped into him at the palm-reading stall.

'Hello,' he said, putting his camera down and smiling at her.

'Hello,' she replied.

'Come to have your palm read?' he asked.

'Oh, I don't believe in such things,' she said. 'Anyway, I know about my past and present, and I'm not at all sure I want to know about my future.'

'It would make a great photo, though,' Lloyd said, taking some money out of his wallet and handing it over to the palm reader. 'Go on,' he said, 'my treat.'

Before she could object, the palm reader grabbed hold of Sarah's hand, and she was forced to take a seat.

'What a beautiful hand you have,' she began, her piercing blue eyes taking in the shape of Sarah's hand. She nodded. 'But it tells a sad story. You have been hurt—recently too. It's a hurt that you're still carrying with you, but you must learn to let it go. It's time to move on.'

Sarah tutted at the words. She could have taken them personally if she'd wanted to, but they seemed vague and could have applied to any number of people in the room.

'You're a romantic, and life is often a disappointment to you.'

Sarah shook her head. Well, she'd got that wrong, hadn't she? She wasn't a romantic. It was Mia who was the romantic, not her—*she* was practical beyond belief.

'You are,' the palm reader said, as if reading her thoughts, 'but you hide it well. I can see that you believe in happy endings, even though you haven't found your own yet, but you're going to meet somebody—somebody who won't let you down this time. In fact, you might have already met him.'

Sarah blinked in surprise. 'Really?' She bit her tongue. It was the standard procedure of palm readers, she believed. They took your money and gave you a little bit of hope for the future.

'Oh, yes,' the palm reader went on. 'He's tall and dark and very handsome.'

Sarah rolled her eyes at the declaration. It was a horrible cliché, even though Lloyd happened to be all three of those things.

'And the two of you will be very happy together. You are alike; I can sense that. You've never met anyone like him before, but he is right for you.'

Sarah's time was over, and she stood up.

'What did she say?' Lloyd asked as she joined him.

'You mean you didn't hear?'

'I was taking photos.'

Sarah was glad that he'd been concentrating on something else. 'It was just the usual rubbish.'

'I thought you'd never had your palm read before.'

'I haven't, but I still know that it was all rubbish.'

'My sister once had her palm read, and she was told she would be married and pregnant within a year.'

'And what happened?'

'By the following summer, I had a brother-in-law and nephew.'

Sarah shook her head. 'Coincidence,' she said.

Lloyd laughed and Sarah smiled. She liked the way his eyes twinkled when he laughed.

'I just want to get a few shots of that person cutting the silhouettes. Have you seen them? They're amazing.'

Sarah nodded. 'They're wonderful, aren't they?'

'Do you want to have yours done?'

'Oh, no,' Sarah said. 'I think I'll just browse the books on this stall.'

'Okay,' he said. 'And then maybe we could get a cup of tea or something.'

Sarah paused for a moment, thinking back to what the palm reader had told her about her future partner. *You might have already met him.* Could it be Lloyd?

'A cup of tea would be lovely,' she told him with a smile, wondering if she was tempting fate, even though she didn't really believe in it.

~

Mia and Shelley would have loved to have been photographed for *Vive!* magazine, but they'd already left the Guildhall by the time Lloyd walked across the room with his camera. They'd both been delighted with their silhouettes and placed them carefully in their purses.

'What next?' Mia asked.

'I didn't book anything else for today, but I thought we could do a bit of shopping whilst we're in costume. Oh, and Lorna Warwick is doing a book signing. I thought we could go to that. I'm desperate to read her latest.'

'*His* latest, don't you mean? Lorna's a man—didn't you hear?'

Shelley frowned. 'A man? You're kidding.'

'No,' Mia said. 'And a rather gorgeous man too. Wait until you see!'

'Well, I'm always in the mood to meet gorgeous men,' Shelley said with a grin. 'Oh, my God!' she suddenly cried. 'Hide!'

'Hide? From what?'

'Him—him in the costume over there!' Shelley nodded toward a short, stocky man who was wearing a Regency naval uniform.

'But I thought you said you liked a man in costume.'

'I do—I mean, I usually do.'

'Who is he?'

'Arthur something or other. I forget. I met him at last year's festival. He just sort of latched on to me and wouldn't let go. It was awful. I'd forgotten about him until just now. Oh, blimey! He's seen us! Let's just go—quickly!'

It was too late.

'Shelley!' the man called, his hand flapping madly in recognition. 'How are you?' He pushed his way through the crowd and grabbed hold of Shelley's shoulders before leaning forwards and planting a sloppy kiss on her cheek. 'You're looking as gorgeous as ever,' he enthused.

'I'm fine,' Shelley said in a small voice as she tried to extricate herself from his grasp.

'You didn't call me. I did give you my card, didn't I?'

Shelley nodded. 'One or two of them.'

'That's right, but it's been a *whole year*. I thought we would have seen each other again. I was waiting for you to call me, you naughty girl!'

'Oh, you know how it goes. Busy, busy!'

He nodded, but he couldn't hide his disappointment. 'Well, here we are again, and don't you look a picture?' He tweaked her bonnet. 'Aren't you going to introduce me to your friend?'

Mia, who'd been watching in amusement, suddenly wished she could shrink away.

'This is Mia,' Shelley said.

Arthur moved forward and leaned in for a second sloppy kiss in as many minutes. He reached into a pocket before thrusting a business card into Mia's hand.

'Now at least your friend can call me if she wants.'

Mia's eyes widened at the suggestion.

'Anyway,' Shelley said, spying an opportunity to get away, 'we really must go. We've booked an event.'

'Oh, I didn't think there was an event until three. Are you going to the Tea with Jane Austen? Maybe I'll see you there—'

Shelley didn't stop to answer him. She grabbed Mia's hand and ran.

'That was awfully rude, wasn't it?' Mia said a moment later, when they stopped.

'You have to be rude with Arthur, believe me,' Shelley said.

Mia giggled. 'You do attract them, Shelley.'

'Yes,' she said, wiping her cheek with a tissue. 'I don't know what it is, but I seem to have the knack.'

'You don't think he'll follow us, do you? I don't think I could stand another of those wet kisses. The Navy really should know better.'

'Yes, he's no Captain Wentworth, is he? But I don't think he'll follow us. He's probably attached himself onto some other unsuspecting girl by now,' Shelley said. 'Come on; let's go shopping.'

Chapter 14

Barton Cottage

AFTER THE SURPRISE MEETING WITH ALEC BURROWS, SARAH and Mia had enjoyed a full English breakfast before taking a walk to the private beach on the estate. The May sunshine was gloriously warm, and Mia wore a white dress covered in scarlet poppies and a sunhat Sarah had forced onto her head before leaving. Ever-practical, Sarah was wearing a pair of light beige trousers and a sky-blue shirt with pockets full of tissues.

Mia led the way through the wood she'd jogged through earlier, pointing out the place where she had collided with Alec.

They soon found the track to the beach and ambled along together, taking in deep lungfuls of pure air.

'I won't want to go back to London,' Mia said.

'Yes, you will. You've got all those auditions lined up, haven't you?'

'I suppose,' Mia said, and then she thought of another reason to look forward to going back to London—Alec. 'What do you suppose he does?' she asked.

'Who?'

'Alec!'

'I thought we came here to escape men. I seem to remember that was the bargain.'

'Really? I don't remember that at all,' Mia said, thinking of his bright gray eyes and the cute smile she'd drawn from him.

The rest of the day passed peacefully and with very little happening, which was just how Sarah had envisaged it when she booked Barton Cottage. If only Mia hadn't run into that man. Trust her sister to be knocked over by the only man in Devon, and now she wouldn't stop talking about him. There was only one thing for it in such situations, and that was Jane Austen, so that evening, after Mia cooked a light student-inspired supper of spaghetti, they settled down to watch the Emma Thompson version of *Sense and Sensibility*, screaming in delight every time they saw Barton Cottage.

Mia should have been out like a light that evening, but she wasn't. Instead, she walked across to her window and drew back the curtains. The night was inky black, but as her eyes adjusted, they were soon dazzled by stars.

Being the kind of person who always wanted to share her thoughts and feelings with the entire world, Mia knew that she'd have to wake up Sarah immediately, so leaving her bedroom, she crept across the landing to her sister's bedroom and opened the door.

'Sarah? Are you awake?'

A muffled noise came from the bed in the corner of the room.

'Come on—wake up! You've got to see this!'

'See what? It's the middle of the night.'

'Wow!' Mia said. She was at the window and had drawn back the curtains. 'Look out of the window. You can't see anything. Come and see! Sarah—come and *see*.'

'Why would I want to look out of a window if I can't see anything?'

'It's so dark,' Mia said. 'I can't see a single house. We're the only people in the world,' Mia said.

'I'm afraid not.'

'But you could believe it in a place like this. It's just us and the stars. Look how bright they are! Come on, Sarah—look!'

Sarah obviously realized that she was going to get no peace until she joined her sister at the window. She pushed the duvet away from her, carefully placed her feet in her slippers so that they didn't touch the floor, and bleary-eyed with sleep, shuffled in the direction she hoped was the window.

'Can you see them?' Mia asked.

'Not yet,' Sarah said.

'Let your eyes adjust.'

Sarah kept looking. It was an odd experience and almost impossible to tell whether her eyes were really open, for she could see nothing.

But then…

'Oh!' she exclaimed.

'Yes,' Mia said. 'So many stars. I wonder if Alec is looking at them too.'

Sarah sighed. 'You mustn't keep going on about him.'

'Why not?'

'Because we don't know that much about him.'

'We know enough to know that he's wonderful.'

'We don't know that at all,' Sarah said. 'And I thought we agreed, Mia—no men this week.'

'Yes, but that was before we met any men,' Mia said with her usual warped logic.

'You really are incorrigible. Goodness knows what he thinks of you. You were so forward!'

'He probably thinks I'm a very approachable young woman, which is just what I am, and I really don't mind his knowing that. How else are we to meet men? We don't get introduced to them by our families or a master of ceremonies anymore. You have to do it yourself when you can. You don't bump into them every day of the week,' she said, giggling at the aptness of her wording. 'I just got lucky today.'

'I'm going back to bed, and you should too.'

Mia groaned. 'All right then, grumpy!' She returned to her own room, eager to snuggle back under her duvet, her bare limbs chilly.

Honestly, she thought, Sarah really could be a spoilsport. Mia knew she was just being protective; it was a role she'd been playing as long as Mia could remember. After all, she hadn't had a mother to guide her through the perils of love, but what possible harm could there be in a little holiday romance? she thought. It was probably just what she needed.

Chapter 15

SARAH AND LLOYD FOUND A TEAROOM AWAY FROM THE CENTER of Bath. It was small and pretty with pale pink tablecloths and white china cups.

Lloyd pulled out a chair for Sarah and placed his heavy camera bag underneath the table.

'It must be cumbersome carrying that around with you everywhere,' Sarah said.

'I don't really notice it now,' he said. 'It's like a part of me, I guess. I'd feel naked without it.'

They ordered a pot of tea and couldn't resist a slice of cake each. Sarah opted for lemon sponge, and Lloyd ordered a slice of ginger cake.

'I always worry about eating out,' Lloyd said, picking up his cup and examining it. 'But it looks clean enough in here, doesn't it?'

'I think so,' Sarah said, giving a slight smile. 'You have it too, don't you?'

'What's that?'

'OCD.'

Lloyd laughed loudly. 'Is it that obvious?'

'Only to another sufferer,' Sarah said.

They smiled at one another.

'How long have you had it?' he asked.

'All my life, I think. There's always been something vaguely odd about me,' she said with a laugh and then realized that it was probably not the best thing to say to promote herself.

'I know what you mean,' he said.

'You mean, you think I'm odd?'

'No!' he said with a laugh. 'I mean, *I've* always felt odd too.'

'Oh!' Sarah said with relief.

The tea and cake arrived, and Lloyd took a mouthful of ginger cake as Sarah poured the tea.

'I used to get endlessly teased at school,' Lloyd said. 'Everything had to be neat and tidy. Science apparatus for experiments, the books in the library, the sports equipment in the cupboard. Everyone thought I was teacher's pet, but it was the OCD. I had no interest in pleasing anyone other than myself. Things had to be in order.'

Sarah nodded in recognition.

'But not many people knew about OCD back then,' he continued. 'You were just branded as strange or effeminate.'

'That must have been difficult. At least girls can disguise it some of the time. We're meant to be neat and tidy, so it can often go unnoticed. I must say, I didn't have much trouble at school. It was home that was the problem for me. My mother had real trouble understanding what was happening. She thought I did things just to annoy her, like the time I took down all the washing from the line and hung it up again properly.' She took a sip of tea.

'There are certainly more people around who understand now. There isn't such a stigma attached to it, is there?'

'I suppose not,' Sarah said, 'but it still takes some understanding.

I've never really met anyone who's understood it properly. Well, apart from one person.'

'Who's that?'

'My sister. She's the only one in the world who doesn't judge me for it. Except that—'

'What?' Lloyd asked.

'We're not really speaking at the moment.' Sarah bit her lip. She hadn't meant to divulge so much to the man. After all, he was a relative stranger.

'Why aren't you speaking?' he asked in a gentle voice. 'What happened?'

What happened? Sarah closed her eyes for a moment, knowing that she couldn't tell him. 'We... we had an argument. Over a man.'

'That will usually do it,' Lloyd said.

'Yes,' Sarah said, finishing her tea before pouring a second cup. 'I'm afraid it will.'

Chapter 16

Barton Cottage

THE WEATHER WAS MORE LIKE THE MIDDLE OF SUMMER THAN the middle of May, and when Alec called for them in the late morning, they were ready to hit the beach.

The tide was out and there were miles of perfect sandy beach to greet them.

'Isn't this the most perfect place in the world?' Mia asked. 'We have to come back here *every* year.'

'I don't think we'll be able to afford it,' Sarah said.

'But you're a rich accountant.'

'And you're going to be a rich actress and singer,' Sarah said. 'You can pay for the next trip.'

'You think I can't, don't you?'

'I didn't say that.'

Mia tutted. 'Oh, let's not argue.'

'I'm not arguing.'

Mia caught Alec's gaze and giggled. 'Sisters!' she said. 'Always fighting.'

'We're not always fighting,' Sarah protested.

'Do you have any brothers or sisters?' Mia asked Alec.

'A younger brother. I call him my younger *bother* because he's always getting into trouble.'

'Oh, dear,' Sarah said.

'What sort of trouble?'

'The sort that involves money,' Alec said. 'He has these madcap ideas that he's convinced will make him rich, but they usually fall apart, and I'm left picking up the pieces.'

'So you're rich?' Mia asked.

'Mia!' Sarah scolded.

Alec laughed. 'I get by,' he said.

'What do you do?' Mia crossed her legs in a yoga-type position, making her long, denim-clad legs look even longer.

'I'm a business consultant specializing in small-company management.'

'Oh,' Mia said, sounding none the wiser.

He grinned. 'Basically, I help small companies maximize their profits.'

'It sounds very rewarding,' Sarah said.

'Yes, it is,' he said. 'I've seen many businesses flourish, which is a wonderful thing.'

Mia was trying to mask how disappointed she was by his choice of professions. It wasn't very romantic. It was a shame that he wasn't a musician or a poet or something. There wasn't anything remotely romantic about being a business consultant, was there? But it was hard to find a perfect man, wasn't it? And he was exceptionally handsome, so perhaps you couldn't have a handsome man who also had an interesting job, she reasoned.

'I haven't had a picnic for years,' Alec said, changing the subject. 'This is just like when I visited my aunt. She'd make up the best hampers in the world. She used to get up at the crack of dawn, when the rest of us were still asleep, and make mountains of sandwiches and cake and flapjacks and all sorts of other goodies.'

'You must miss her,' Sarah said.

Alec nodded. 'Every day.'

Mia looked across at him. 'We never had an aunt. We barely had a mother.'

Alec looked puzzled.

'Don't bore him, Mia.'

'I'm not boring him. Am I boring you?'

'Of course not. You couldn't possibly bore me.'

Mia smiled. 'See, Sarah? I couldn't possibly bore him.'

'Tell me about her,' he said. 'I'd like to know more about you both.'

'Well, there's not much to tell, really,' Mia said. 'Our mother left us. I was only eleven, and I came home from school one day and she'd gone.'

'Just like that?'

Mia nodded.

'It had been coming on for some time,' Sarah added. 'I don't think she was a natural mother, to be honest. We'd often go whole days without seeing her at all.'

'But that's terrible. Wasn't there anyone else to look after you? A father? Or a grandparent?'

'Not really,' Sarah said. 'Neither of our fathers were around much.'

'I never got to know mine,' Mia said with a dramatic wave of her hand. 'I am a complete enigma, but I bet he was a prince.'

'Or a criminal,' Sarah said with a little smile.

'Oh, you always like to burst my bubble!'

'Just keeping your feet on the ground.'

'But they don't want to be on the ground. They want to be tiptoeing up in the clouds.'

Sarah sighed. 'What can you do with such a flibbertigibbet?'

Alec laughed. 'I'm not sure there is much you can do, except sit back and enjoy the show.'

'You see?' Mia said. 'Alec knows how to appreciate me.' Mia was suddenly on her feet, brushing the sand from her legs. 'I'm going for a walk,' she announced. 'Do you want to come, Alec?' She waited for a moment, a big smile fixed on her face, her eyes wide.

'Sure,' he said, getting up from the sand. 'You coming, Sarah?'

'Oh, she'd rather sit with a book, wouldn't you, Sarah?'

Sarah nodded, understanding her sister perfectly.

Mia and Alec walked along the beach before finding a path into the wood where the dappled shade cooled their sun-warmed limbs.

'Are you sure Sarah won't be lonely?' Alec asked.

'There's no need to worry about her. She prefers her own company,' Mia said. 'Come on.' She led the way along the path as it climbed steeply among a carpet of bluebells. She inhaled deeply. 'Smell that! Isn't it wonderful?'

Alec took a deep lungful of the heady perfume. 'It's my favorite time of year.'

'Mine too,' Mia said. 'I mean, not only because it's my birthday, but also because the flowers are so beautiful right now. There are bluebells, campion, primroses, and that lovely frothy elderflower—'

Alec interrupted. 'It's your birthday?'

'Well, it was last week, really, but neither of us could get away then, so we're celebrating it now. I'm the ripe old age of twenty-one.'

'I'm so sorry,' he said. 'I had no idea it was your birthday, and such a special one too.'

'That's okay,' Mia said.

'I would have got you something if I'd known,' he said. They stopped under the shade of a beech tree, its new leaves the brightest green.

'Would you?'

'Of course,' he said with a smile.

Mia smiled back, noticing the way his eyes crinkled at the edges. 'What would you have given me?' she asked, moving a step closer toward him.

'What would you have liked?'

She was inches away from him and could feel his warm breath on her face. 'How about a birthday kiss?' she said, knowing that Sarah would be appalled at such forwardness, but if a girl couldn't take liberties on her birthday, when could she? Besides, he looked as though he wanted to kiss her.

She waited for what seemed like forever, the world suddenly concentrated on the tiny space that separated them. A warm breeze blew her hair back from her face and the scent of bluebells seemed to permeate her skin.

'I think I can manage a kiss,' Alec whispered. 'If that's what you really want.'

Mia nodded and closed her eyes as his lips sought hers. It was a sweet, tender kiss that made her skin tingle with pleasure, and it took a moment to realize that he had stopped kissing her.

'Well,' he said, 'I wasn't expecting this today.'

Mia opened her eyes. 'No?' she said. 'Why ever not?'

He frowned at her, half puzzled, half amused. 'You are the most surprising girl I've ever met.'

'But I'm not a girl anymore,' she said. 'I'm twenty-one now.'

'Yes, you are.'

She looked up at him, her eyes wide and bright. 'That kiss,' she began, 'was very nice, but it was over much too quickly, didn't you think?'

'Well, I—'

She leaned up toward him and pressed her mouth against his, closing her eyes and experiencing the wondrously warm sensation again.

'Is that better?' he asked her a moment later.

'That was very nice too, but it was only our second kiss. What do you say we make it twenty-one?'

Down on the beach, Sarah had long forgotten her novel, placing it back in her rucksack so that it wouldn't discolor in the sun. Where had Mia and Alec got to? She worried. Mia might be twenty-one, but she was as impetuous and impulsive as when she was an eight-year-old. She never liked to admit it, but she needed somebody to keep an eye on her, and Sarah saw it as being her job. For a moment she wondered about going in search of her sister, but she knew that Mia wouldn't thank her for it. She'd give her another ten minutes before she really started to worry.

She got out her copy of *Sense and Sensibility* again, but when she tried to read it, it wasn't the faces of Marianne and Willoughby she was seeing but those of Mia and Alec. She returned the book to the bag and stretched out on the tartan.

She was *always* worrying about Mia, she thought as she closed her eyes against the sun. Why couldn't they have a less stressful relationship, like Jane and Elizabeth Bennet? For a moment, Sarah thought about sisters in the novels of Jane Austen. There was Jane and Elizabeth in *Pride and Prejudice*, who shared every confidence—well, *almost* every confidence. At the other end of the sisterly spectrum were the Elliot sisters from *Persuasion* and the poor put-upon Anne who was left to do all the unpleasant chores.

Then, of course, there was Elinor and Marianne from *Sense and Sensibility*—the sisters who adored each other but were worlds apart. That's who Sarah was reminded of, whenever she thought of her own relationship with Mia.

Please don't let her fall in love, she said to herself. *He isn't right for her. I just know it.* But Mia wouldn't stop to think about such things. She'd see a handsome face and be flattered by a few smiles and fall headlong into love. Sarah had seen it before, and it never ended well. Take that time with—what was his name? Robbie Merton. Even Sarah had to admit that he was handsome. Mia met him whilst at sixth form. He was one of those boys who drove a beaten-up old car way too fast whilst playing terrible music way too loudly. And Mia had adored him. She scribbled his name a hundred times across pieces of paper that were meant to be filled with thought-provoking essays. Of course, he'd broken her heart by being caught with another girl in his car. He hadn't even bothered to drive off anywhere first. Mia walked right past him on the way to her drama class.

'Poor Mia,' Sarah said as she silently cursed handsome men.

$\sim$

'Won't Sarah be wondering where we are?' Alec asked as they followed the footpath out of the woods.

'Oh, stop worrying about her. She'll have her head stuck so far in that book that the rest of the world will have ceased to exist a long time ago.'

Alec laughed. 'So where are we going?'

Mia shrugged. 'Questions, questions.' She turned back and smiled at him. 'Don't you trust me?'

'I'm not sure.'

Mia's mouth dropped open. 'What a thing to say!'

'But we've only just met.'

'Yes, but—' Her eyes widened, and then she sighed. 'I feel as if I know you. Does that make sense? I know it sounds crazy, and I've heard that line in a thousand movies and read it in a million books, but it's exactly how I feel about you.'

She held his gaze for a moment, anxious about what he would say. Had she gone too far? He was right; they had only just met. Maybe she was being too forward. She knew Sarah would be having fits if she knew what was going on here, yet Mia couldn't help saying those words. She'd always had to express her feelings and worry about the consequences later, so here she was again, wondering if her feelings were about to get her into trouble. 'Is that crazy?' she asked.

'No, it's not crazy,' he said. 'I feel it too. I feel like I've known you both forever.'

'You do?'

He nodded, and Mia smiled. 'Good,' she said, leading the way down some steps and onto a perfect little beach. For a moment she just stood there, shielding her eyes against the sun.

'What are you looking at?' Alec asked her.

'That's the field, isn't it?'

'What field?'

'The field where Marianne twists her ankle and Willoughby carries her home.'

'Friends of yours?'

Mia laughed. 'No, they're from a film. *Sense and Sensibility.* The Emma Thompson adaptation of the novel.'

'So you're saying that a pair of fictional characters had some sort of mishap in that field?'

Mia nodded enthusiastically. 'I think that's definitely the one.' She pointed to the spot where she was sure it had happened.

'You are funny,' he said.

'Why?'

'Because you care about things that didn't really happen.'

'But it did. It was filmed right there.'

'By actors playing fictional characters,' Alec said.

'You don't read fiction?'

'Only the occasional thriller.'

Mia sighed. 'Men just don't get Jane Austen, do they?'

'I guess not.'

Mia looked into his dark eyes, which were twinkling delight-fully in the sunshine, and decided to forgive him. He was just too handsome not to forgive.

Chapter 17

THE QUEUE FOR THE LORNA WARWICK TALK WAS LENGTHY.

'I didn't realize she—I mean *he*—was so popular,' Mia said.

'Look at all the women here!' Shelley said. 'I don't think I'll stand a chance.'

'Nonsense,' Mia said. 'You're gorgeous. He'd be absolutely mad not to notice you. Have you got your book?'

'No. I didn't have room in my little purse. Anyway, I was going to buy a brand-new one. My others are all creased or covered in dog slobber.'

Mia frowned.

'Don't ask!' Shelley prompted.

The queue surged forward and there was a mad scrambling for the few chairs that had been put out in the shop. Mia and Shelley were pushed and elbowed to within an inch of their lives.

'I didn't think people in muslin could shove so hard,' Mia said.

'Just shove right back,' Shelley advised.

Even with a few tactfully placed elbows, they didn't make it to a seat, but they got a very good position at the front of the room, close to the table where Lorna Warwick would be talking and signing.

'I don't think Jane Austen herself could command such a crowd,' Mia said, looking at the bookshop that housed more people than books.

There were stacks of Lorna Warwick's latest book—*Christina and the Count*—everywhere, and its wildly romantic cover featuring a beautiful young heroine and a Gothic castle was drawing lots of attention from the fans. Two enormous posters advertised the event, but neither alluded to the fact that Lorna Warwick was a man.

Mia had to admit to being a bit of a fan, and Lorna Warwick's books had certainly been there to distract her when the real world got too much for her. She'd lost count of the number of evenings she had spent in the company of fictional characters. Once she opened a book and nose-dived into its pages, she could almost forget about the roar of the traffic outside and the bass from her neighbor's stereo coming through the walls. Fiction was always her medicine, and Jane Austen never failed to cure a heart that had been bruised by life, but her favorite writer had left only six novels behind. They were wonderful, of course, and could weather any number of reads, but what did a fan do when she wanted something new?

Luckily, Mia had recently found the Austen Authors website and discovered there was a whole world of Austen sequels, prequels, and spin-offs with irresistible titles such as *Mr Darcy's Secret*, *Murder at Mansfield Park*, and *Wickham's Diary*. She'd already seen a fine collection of such titles at Shelley's.

Then there were the Lorna Warwicks, with their jewel-bright covers, handsome heroes, and beautiful, spirited heroines. Shelley had a full set of paperbacks and, judging by their cracked spines and creased covers, they were well loved.

'Where *is* he?' Shelley asked, bringing Mia back to the present.

A member of staff appeared, and next to him walked a tall man with broad shoulders and a shock of dark hair. He was wearing a dark suit and a crisp white shirt that was open at the throat.

An enormous cheer sounded and even a couple of wolf whistles.

'Wow!' Shelley said. 'He's gorgeous! I do hope they start to put his photograph in his books now. It would be worth buying them for that alone.'

Mia smiled and nodded in agreement. Lorna Warwick was the best-looking man she'd seen in a long time.

They watched as he walked to the center of the shop and waited for some sort of order to return before he spoke.

'Thank you!' he said at last. 'It's a very great pleasure to be in Bath today as part of the amazing Jane Austen Festival. I'm Lorna Warwick, although I'm sure you all realize that isn't my real name.'

The audience laughed and clapped as if he'd said the funniest thing in the world.

'I'm actually Warwick Lawton, but please don't hold that against me.'

There was more laughter, and then he went on to talk about how he wrote and how much Jane Austen's books had influenced him. He then read an extract from *Christina and the Count*, leaving the narrative at the sort of cliffhanger that would have readers running to the till in record time so that they could buy their own copy and find out what happened next.

There was then the most almighty scrum to queue up and meet Warwick.

'I'm going to get him to put lots of kisses in my book,' Shelley said once they both queued to buy their copies. 'And can you take a photo of me and him with my phone?'

Mia nodded and grinned. It was all quite exciting. She'd never met an author before. Her favorite authors were usually people who'd been dead for at least a century. She wondered what kind of author Jane Austen would be if she were alive today. Would she give talks and appear at book signings? Would she chat live on websites?

Before she knew it, Mia and Shelley reached the front of the queue and Warwick Lawton was signing their books.

'Put "To Shelley with my undying love,"' Shelley said, batting her eyelashes.

Warwick looked up, his pen hovering over the title page of the book. 'Well,' he began, 'as much as I'd like to, I think my fiancée would have something to say about it.'

'Oh!' Shelley said. 'Is that Katherine? The woman you dedicated your book to?'

Mia nudged Shelley in the ribs, and Warwick cleared his throat.

'It is, indeed,' Warwick said, signing the book with a big flourish.

Shelley scampered around to his side of the table, and Mia took a quick photo with her phone.

'Thank you,' she said. 'Have you ever thought of using the name Shelley for a heroine?'

Warwick smiled.

'Because you can use it, if you want. I don't mind.'

Mia grabbed her arm and marched her away.

'I think he liked me,' Shelley said. 'Don't you think?' Before reaching the door, she paused for a moment and opened her book to see what Warwick Lawton had written. 'To Shelley with my very best wishes,' she read with a down-turned mouth. 'And there's only one kiss.'

'But it's a very big kiss,' Mia said.

'Yes,' Shelley said. 'It's probably a kiss with tongues.'

They both burst out laughing and left the shop together, arm in arm.

⚬

Lloyd looked at his watch, and Sarah bit her lip. He was bored with her already, wasn't he? He was trying to think of an excuse to get up and leave. She knew she shouldn't have told him about her OCD. Even though he had it himself, it didn't mean that he'd want to spend time with a woman who had it.

She twisted her hands under the table and counted silently to ten. It was one of the ways she used to calm herself and take control of a situation.

Eight. Nine. Ten.

'Well, I think it's about time I got on,' she said.

Lloyd looked at her, surprise in his eyes.

'And you must be busy too,' she added. It was better to be in charge of these things, she told herself.

'Well, I've got an appointment at the Jane Austen Centre,' he said. 'Just to take a few photographs for the article.'

'Oh, right,' Sarah said. So this was it, was it? A short but sweet meeting that didn't come to anything.

'Would you like to come with me?' he asked.

At first, Sarah thought she must have imagined his invitation, but he repeated it, and she smiled in relief that she wasn't being dumped in a Bath tearoom. 'Well, I've never turned down an excuse to visit the Jane Austen Centre.'

'Good,' he said.

They paid for their tea and left the shop together, wending their way through the beautiful back streets until they came out at Gay Street.

'She lived here, you know,' Sarah said.

'What—in the Jane Austen Centre?'

'No—Gay Street—just a few houses up. It was one of her many addresses in Bath.'

'Seems that you can't move around Bath without stumbling across a blue plaque or some sort of literary reference to the great lady.'

'That's what I love about being here. She's in the very air.'

Lloyd smiled. 'So what is it about Jane Austen?'

'What do you mean?'

'I mean, what's this great hold she has over the female imagination?'

'It's not just a female thing,' Sarah said. 'Have you not seen all the men in costume too?'

'Yes, but they're far outnumbered by the women, and I have yet to see a man sporting an I Love Darcy T-shirt.'

Sarah grinned. 'I suppose.'

'So what's her secret? Why are people still so fascinated by her after two hundred years?'

Sarah paused for a moment. 'Well, it's the stories. To begin with, they're just wonderfully warm, optimistic stories about love and forgiveness. Her characters have such life, and they're still recognizable today, from the vivacity of Elizabeth Bennet to the appallingly snobbish Mr Collins.'

'But Jane Austen wrote only six books, and so many other books have been written since them.'

'I know,' Sarah said. 'You've only to go into a bookshop to be stunned by the number of stories out there. It's truly baffling some-times to know what to choose, but the magic of Jane Austen is that you can return to her six books any number of times and always find something new to enjoy. If you read them when you're young, it's the love stories you're interested in—the "will they, won't they?" But later you become fascinated by other things too. There's the humor, for a start, and the intricacies of the relationships. It's a whole world, and I can't tell you what a joy it is to escape into that world.' She stopped. 'I'm gushing now.'

'No,' Lloyd said. 'Well, yes, but it's wonderful. I've never heard anyone talk so passionately about books before.'

'You're not a reader?'

'Only a bit of nonfiction, I'm afraid.'

'But you're missing out on so much,' Sarah said. 'Novels can tell us so much about life. They have the power to enrich our own lives in so many different ways. They're not just for entertaining us, although that would be enough.'

'And how have they enriched your life?'

Sarah smiled. 'I can't imagine my life without novels—especially Jane Austen's. They're like the very best of friends. They're always there for you. At the end of a hard day, you can reach out and know that they'll give you the sort of comfort that's rare to find in life.'

'You speak like somebody who—' he stopped.

'What?'

'Like somebody who's needed that comfort,' he said, looking down at the pavement. 'I'm sorry—I shouldn't have said that. I didn't mean to pry.'

'You're not prying,' Sarah said. 'And you're right. Jane Austen's always been there for me. Even in the very worst of times.'

Chapter 18

Barton Cottage

It was evening at Barton Cottage. The sun had dipped low in the sky, and a cold breeze sent the sisters inside. As Sarah was tidying in the kitchen, there was a knock at the door.

'I'll get it,' Mia sang. Not that Sarah had any choice. Ever since she was a small girl, Mia had been convinced that every phone call and every knock at the door was meant for her. This time, she was right, because as she opened the door, she saw Alec standing there holding a large birthday cake aflame with candles.

'Alec!' she screamed. 'It's wonderful!'

'Couldn't celebrate a birthday without a cake, could we?'

'That's so sweet of you. Come in! Come in!' Mia ushered him through to the kitchen where Sarah was making a cup of tea. 'Sarah—look what Alec brought!'

Sarah turned around and gasped at the sight of the cake.

'Can I put it down somewhere? I'm terrified I'll drop it at any moment.'

Sarah motioned, and Alec placed the cake on the worktop, where the twenty-one beautiful candles winked at them all.

'I can't believe you found such a brilliant cake. Wherever did you find it?'

'Ah, that would be telling,' he said with a grin.

'Well, we must all have a slice immediately.'

'Not before blowing the candles out and making a wish.'

'Okay,' Mia said, her cheeks flushed with excitement as she closed her eyes and blew. Every single last candle was extinguished.

'Did you make a wish?' Sarah asked.

'Oh, yes,' Mia said, blushing as she looked up at Alec. 'I did.'

That night, Sarah lay awake in her bed, listening to the distant hoot of an owl. She didn't mean to think about Alec. She'd been trying to shut him out of her mind all evening, but he wouldn't go away. His voice had echoed in her mind throughout dinner and, as she washed up, his face had hovered before her.

He's not interested in you, a little voice said. *It's Mia he likes, and why not? She's young and beautiful and full of vitality. Why would he look at you? You didn't have one interesting thing to say to him all day. Besides, you're meant to be having a break from men.*

For a moment she thought about her last relationship. It had been doomed from the beginning. Well, what could she expect, being the way she was? People just didn't understand her. Mia had often joked that she'd need to find a carbon copy of herself, in a male version, of course, who would put up with her little quirks, but where was she going to find such a man?

People with OCD didn't want to go around divulging their affliction, for fear of putting others off. It was bound to rear its ugly head at some point, and Sarah always hoped that whomever she was seeing would have fallen for her by then, and nothing would put him off. But that hadn't happened with Martin.

She'd been seeing him for six months and things had been going well, but only because he hadn't visited her home. They'd been out to restaurants, where Sarah behaved herself impeccably, even when faced with a dirty tablecloth and a rickety table leg that had driven her mad. She had bitten her tongue and not said a word.

But then she'd made the mistake of asking him to take his shoes off when she invited him in for coffee. He looked at her as if she were quite mad.

'I haven't been asked to do that since I was a kid,' he told her.

'I have new carpets,' she explained. Well, they weren't officially new, but they looked as though they were, because she took such good care of them. He'd taken his shoes off and followed her into the kitchen whilst she made the coffee, and that was mistake number two. She should never have let him into the kitchen.

'You file your herbs?' he asked, looking at the herb rack, a large grin bisecting his face.

'Of course,' she said. 'It makes perfect sense. How else would you find them?'

'Er... by looking?'

'But this saves time.'

After that, he'd given himself a private tour of her home, noting the way she folded her towels in the bathroom and laughing when he discovered her list of lists. He even opened her wardrobe and shook his head when he saw the way she color-coded her clothes.

'You've got that OCD thing, haven't you? I saw a program about that the other week and thought you had it. You're always straightening things that don't need to be straightened.'

Sarah hadn't known what to say, so she said nothing.

'You are one *crazy* lady,' Martin had said, shaking his head. 'Now I'm going to put my shoes back on and get the hell out of here.'

Those were his last words to her. Six months of friendship and kindness evaporated as he slammed her front door and drove away.

She certainly wasn't looking to leap into another relationship yet. That would be madness.

She beat her pillow with an angry fist and flopped back down again. Oh, why did Alec have to be there to spoil things? This week was meant to be about her and Mia. It was their special time together, and the only stressful thing was meant to be their fighting over which version of *Persuasion* to watch. Alec's appearance had given the weekend another dimension, one Sarah was sure was going to end in trouble.

There were several wooden sun loungers in front of the house, and the next morning, after a late breakfast, Sarah had made herself comfortable on one. She'd brought her copy of *Sense and Sensibility* out for company, but it had long since fallen out of favor as she closed her eyes, enjoying the warmth of the May sunshine.

This really was the life, she thought, wondering if she could afford to buy Barton Cottage if it ever came on the market, but even her decent earnings probably wouldn't stretch to purchasing a piece of heaven.

She took a few deep breaths, inhaling the sweet air as she listened to the rich song of a blackbird in a nearby hedge. It would be so very easy to shut oneself off completely from the rest of the world in such a place as this, she thought, and she could imagine doing it too. She had a sort of personality that didn't rely on others, and she'd be quite content to be alone with her books and her films and only herself for company. Mia wouldn't, though. She was enjoying her time at Barton Cottage and was definitely benefiting from being out of the city for a while, but she would go mad if she were expected to live in such a place. She'd already made friends with that stranger, Alec, hadn't she? No, her sister couldn't be happy unless there were others around her.

Sarah was just pondering what to have for lunch when a dark shadow fell across her, blocking out the sun. She opened her eyes and started as she saw the outline of a man before her.

'Hello,' he said.

'Alec?' She sat upright and adjusted the straps on her summer dress, which were doing their best to escape down her shoulders. 'You startled me.'

'Sorry,' he said, taking a seat next to her without invitation. 'You looked so peaceful there.'

'Yes,' she said, removing her sunglasses and smiling at him. 'It's that kind of a place, isn't it?'

He nodded and smiled back at her. He really did have a very lovely smile, she noticed.

'Mia's out,' she volunteered before he asked her.

'Jogging?'

'Yes.'

'I thought she might be. I expected to pass her as I walked through the wood.'

'I think she went the other way.'

'Ah,' he said.

'But you're welcome to wait for her. I'm sure she won't be long.'

'What makes you think I wanted to see her?' he asked.

Sarah frowned at him, not understanding.

'I might have wanted to talk to you,' he said, clearly seeing her confusion.

'Me? Whatever for?'

He laughed, and Sarah found that she was soon laughing with him.

'You are funny,' he said at last. 'Don't you know how fascinating you are?'

Sarah's eyes crinkled in merriment. 'You're joking, aren't you?'

'Why would I be joking?'

'Because—well, just because.'

He leaned forward and fixed her with a penetrating stare. 'Tell me about yourself.'

'What do you mean?'

'Your life story. I want to know everything.'

Sarah's eyes narrowed in suspicion behind her sunglasses. 'Why?'

'Why not?' he said.

'Well, there really isn't much to tell.'

'All the really interesting people say that,' he said.

'But it's true. You should be talking to Mia. She's far more interesting than I am.'

'But she's already told me everything. I want to know about *you*.'

Sarah felt uncomfortable. She was never happy when the attention was fully on her, but she was doubly uncomfortable with Alec's attention, because it seemed so clear to her that he'd been flirting with her sister. Why did he now seem so interested in her? Maybe it was to get around her, so that she wouldn't object to his being with Mia. Perhaps he saw her as a parent figure, a person who might stand in the way of him and Mia.

'You don't need to worry about that,' she said. 'I don't mind your seeing Mia.'

'What?' Alec asked, looking baffled.

Sarah didn't get a chance to explain, because Mia came running up the garden.

'Hey!' she shouted, waving at the two of them. 'Don't you both look lazy sitting there in the sunshine? What have you been talking about? Me?'

'Yes,' Sarah said. 'What else?'

Chapter 19

I T WAS THE SECOND DAY OF THE JANE AUSTEN FESTIVAL, AND MIA and Shelley were in the kitchen, looking out onto a bright Sunday morning sky.

'Are we wearing our dresses again today?' Shelley asked.

'Of course,' Mia said. 'I've been looking forward to wearing mine all year. I can't very well wear it in London, can I?'

'Imagine the looks you'd get on the tube!' Shelley said.

Mia collected the breakfast dishes and piled them into a bowl of hot soapy water.

'Your neighbor's out,' Mia said casually.

Shelley got up from her chair to look. 'Oh, just look at the poor lamb.'

Mia looked up from her soapy water and saw the rather pathetic sight of a man with a sling trying to hang a basket of washing out on the line.

'Do go and help him, Mia,'

'Why don't you go?'

'Because I'm doing the dishes,' she said, suddenly pushing Mia out of the way.

Mia rolled her eyes. 'You are the most unsubtle of matchmakers,' she said. 'I've told you, I'm not interested in men at the moment.'

'Yeah, yeah. What is it Mrs Smith said in *Persuasion*? "Every man is refused… till he offers."'

'But how am I even meant to help him? There's a great big fence between us.'

'Yes, but a bit's broken toward the back, courtesy of Bingley. Just nip through there.'

Mia rolled her eyes. She wasn't going to get any peace until she acquiesced, was she? Walking the length of the garden until she came to the gap in the fence, she looked back at the window. Shelley nodded her forward, her eyes wide and eager, and Mia slipped through the fence, careful not to snag her clothes on the Bingley-sized gap.

'Hello,' she said as Gabe looked up from his washing basket. 'Don't worry. I'm not a burglar. Shelley thought you looked like you needed a hand.'

Gabe turned around and gave her a smile that really was quite cute—for an older man, that is, Mia thought.

'I certainly could use another hand,' he said. 'It isn't easy with just one.'

'I hope you're not left-handed.'

He shook his head. 'Luckily, no.'

Mia bent down and picked up a checked shirt from the laundry basket and pegged it on the line. She couldn't remember the last time she'd hung washing outside. In her little flat in London, one had to do one's best with an airer above the bathtub and a rotating system on two small radiators, which fogged up the windows and caused the wallpaper to curl. It was rather nice to have a washing line and to see the clothes fluttering about in the warm autumn breeze.

'You don't have to do this,' Gabe said.

'It's no trouble,' Mia said.

'I mean, it's very good of you, but I can manage. Sort of.'

Mia smiled. 'I'm actually quite enjoying it. I don't have a washing line.'

Gabe stared at her as if she were an alien.

'I live in a bedsit in London,' she explained.

'As I did too. A long time ago.'

'Oh, did you?'

'Whilst I was training to become an architect. Had to slum it for a few years in dreadful accommodations, but got out as soon as I could.'

'Yes, it's lovely here. Shelley's lucky to have such a great place.' Mia bent down and retrieved a white shirt, clean and crisp, and pegged it on the line. It was followed by a pair of black boxer shorts, and Mia felt a blush creep over her cheeks.

Gabe cleared his throat. 'Sorry,' he said, taking them from her.

'It's okay.' Mia said it, but she still felt embarrassed. It wasn't the sort of situation to befall the heroine from a Jane Austen novel, was it? She delved back into the basket and chose a safe T-shirt, allowing her blush to ebb away.

'Thanks so much,' he said, a smile tickling his mouth as the last shirt was pegged onto the line.

'That's okay,' Mia said before hopping back through the broken fence.

'I was just going to make a cup of coffee,' Gabe called after her. 'Would you like one?'

Mia hesitated and looked back at the kitchen window, where Shelley was flapping her hands, as if to shoo Mia back whence she came.

'Okay,' Mia said, entering Gabe's garden again. She followed him into his house, taking one last look at Shelley, who was giving her the thumbs up.

The kitchen was a lovely bright room with pale blond cabinets and a fabulous gray slate floor, and there wasn't so much as a tea bag out of place. Having only dated young men or those who had recently graduated whilst she was at drama school, Mia was used to a totally different kind of kitchen. She grimaced as she remembered the filthy, sticky floors and sinks overflowing with crusty dishes. She'd never have accepted a cup of coffee from one of those kitchens. Perhaps there was something to be said about the older man, after all. Perhaps a modern-day Willoughby would have a kitchen that looked like a student's, whereas a modern-day Colonel Brandon's kitchen would be more akin to Gabe's.

She watched as Gabe rolled up his sleeves, displaying strong, toned arms, and went to put the kettle on. She gave his clothes the once-over. His shirt was checked and looked a little old-fashioned and made him look as if he'd stepped out of the magazine, *Country Life*. He was wearing fawn-colored corduroy trousers that also gave him the look of a landowner. All he needed was a Labrador and a couple of rifles slung over his shoulder.

'How do you like your coffee?' he asked, startling her out of her rural daydream.

'Milk, one sugar, please.'

A moment later, he handed her a terra-cotta mug and invited her into the living room next door.

Gabe's house was a mirror image of Shelley's, but unlike Shelley's, it seemed far less chaotic, even though it was crammed full. Mia whistled when she saw the book-lined front room. The far wall was packed from floor to ceiling with books, and there were neat bookcases along the other two walls as well. The rest of the wall space was taken up by framed prints of buildings that Mia didn't recognize. Perhaps they were buildings Gabe had designed.

'So you're here for the festival?' Gabe asked, sitting down on a dark red sofa and motioning for Mia to do the same, but she was too much of a fidget to sit. Besides, she was still looking around.

'Yes, I came through from London,' she said. 'I used to come every year, but… well, things get complicated, don't they?'

Gabe's eyebrows rose a fraction, as if he wanted her to explain. 'And you're obviously a Jane Austen fan?'

'Of course. I don't think anybody should live in Bath unless they adore Jane Austen.'

'Really?'

'Yes,' Mia said. 'Why—don't you?'

'Well, *adore* is a pretty strong word. I'm not sure I adore her, but I've read a bit.'

'A bit?' Mia stared in wide-eyed horror. 'What—bits from each book?'

Gabe laughed. 'I read *Pride and Prejudice* once. It was a long time ago, and I don't remember much about it. Is that awful?'

'Yes!' Mia said. 'That's *really* awful!'

'Then I shall try and remedy the situation. Which books would you recommend?'

'You have to *want* to read them,' Mia said. 'They shouldn't be forced upon you.'

'But I *do* want to read them. Perhaps then I'll understand what all the fuss is about.'

Mia sighed. 'You'll have to read *all* of them. There are only six, and you really shouldn't take any shortcuts. But I suppose you should start with *Northanger Abbey* and *Persuasion*, as they are both set in Bath. They were also her first and last completed novels, so they're a bit special.'

'Thank you,' he said. 'I shall buy myself some copies straightaway.'

'Good,' Mia said, nodding her approval.

Gabe smiled.

'What?'

'You don't mince your words, do you?'

'No,' Mia said. 'You have to say what you think in this life. There's no point hiding your feelings. That would just be a waste of time.'

Gabe nodded.

'You agree, then?'

'Although I'm not sure I'm able to follow your lead.'

'Why not?'

'Because if I told all my clients what I was really thinking, I'd never have any employment at all.'

Mia frowned. 'But how can you keep your thoughts back?'

'I hide behind a very thin veil of politeness. I listen to what my clients have to say, and if I disagree with them, I bite my tongue and then try to coerce them around to my way of thinking.'

'But doesn't that drive you crazy?'

Gabe shrugged. 'It's all part of the job. I just have to get on with it.'

'Oh, I always have to speak my mind,' Mia said.

'And doesn't that get you into trouble?'

'All the time,' she said and then gave a little laugh. 'But I can't be any other way, I'm afraid.'

Gabe stared at her.

'What?'

'I admire that,' he said. 'There aren't enough people who are honest and open in this world.'

'Shelley is,' Mia said.

'Oh, yes. Shelley's brilliant. Have you been friends long?'

'Since drama school.'

'She's been a really good friend to me,' Gabe said.

Mia smiled. 'Well, she certainly seems to like you.'

Gabe frowned and his eyes narrowed. 'What's she been saying?'

'Nothing. Only that you are very nice,' Mia said with a little blush.

'Shelley means well, but she's a meddler, I'm afraid—in the nicest possible way.'

'You mean she's tried to match you before?'

'Every other week,' he said.

'Oh, dear.'

'I mean, I don't mind. I've actually met some very interesting young ladies, like Mary the Goth, with the purple lipstick and eyes like a giant panda.'

Mia smiled.

'And Janice, who didn't stop talking the whole two hours she was here.'

'I suppose friends always think they know best,' Mia said.

'I think Shelley expects the world to be like one of those romantic novels she's always reading.'

'That's the only problem with novels,' Mia said. 'They give readers such high hopes that the real world can often be a bit of a letdown.'

Gabe looked as if he was about to say something, but a sudden mass of chestnut fur tore into the room.

'Bingley!' Mia said in shock.

'I must have left the back door open again,' Gabe said. 'He's always finding his way here.'

Mia watched as Bingley made himself at home by Gabe's feet.

'We're old buddies, aren't we?' Gabe said, bending down to pat Bingley's head.

'He certainly looks at home here. You really should adopt him. I don't think Shelley can handle him.'

'Oh, you'd be surprised. I've seen her with him, and she's brilliant. I think she just puts on an act about his being too much for her. We all like something to moan about, don't we?'

'I suppose so. What's yours, then?'

'I don't know,' he said. 'Aches and pains here and there.' He nodded to his arm. 'Exercise seems to do me more harm than good now.'

'But you're quite old now,' Mia said. 'I suppose that's to be expected.'

Gabe laughed. 'Don't sugar coat it for me, will you?'

Mia bit her lip. 'I didn't mean to sound rude, and I'm sorry if I did but...'

'What?'

Mia looked at him. 'Well, you said Shelley has been trying to matchmake, you but... well... do you think you will find someone? I mean if you haven't found the right person by now.'

'But I did find the right person.'

Mia frowned. 'Then what happened? Didn't she love you? Was it unrequited love?' she asked, imagining him writing reams of poetry to a callous woman who didn't return his affection.

'No, it wasn't unrequited love. In fact, we married.'

'Oh, so you're divorced? I'm so sorry.'

Gabe shook his head. 'It wasn't divorce that took her. It was meningitis.'

'She died?' Mia's eyes were wide with horror. 'I'm sorry—I didn't know.'

'Nobody does. It happened before I came here, and I try to

keep that part of my life private. I'd hate to think of the pity that would be laid at my doorstep if someone like Shelley knew the truth.'

'Was your wife very young?'

'Twenty-nine.'

Tears brimmed in Mia's eyes. 'That's awful. That's only a few years older than me.'

Gabe nodded. 'We'd been married only three years.' He paused for a moment, bending down again to pat Bingley's comforting head. Mia looked around the room.

'Is this her?' she asked, gazing down at a small silver photo frame on the bookcase. The photograph was of a young woman with long red hair and a smiling face.

'Yes,' Gabe said, looking at the photo.

'She's beautiful.'

Gabe got up from the chair and picked up the photo, and for one terrible moment, Mia thought he was going to cry. Her and her big mouth. Why was she so nosy, and why did she always have to ask too many questions?

'What was her name?' she said, knowing it was probably wrong to ask yet more questions but quite unable to help herself.

'Andrea,' he said.

'How did you meet her?'

Gabe smiled. 'It was a mutual friend.'

'Like Shelley trying to matchmake you?'

'Yes,' he said. 'Only she managed to get it right the first time.'

'Then it was love at first sight?'

'Not exactly. Well, not for Andrea, but it was for me.'

Mia smiled and noticed that his eyes were bright and wide, as if remembering the first time he'd seen Andrea.

'We'd both been invited to one of those awful dinners where you just know it's going to be awkward and that the host is setting you up. Anyway, I was sitting opposite Andrea. She'd been introduced to me but had immediately struck up a conversation with the host's husband that seemed to go on for hours, and I couldn't get a word in edgeways.'

'That's very rude of her.'

Gabe smiled. 'She told me later that she'd done it deliberately because she was too shy to talk to me.'

'Was she really shy?'

'Until the coffee was served, and then she looked up and smiled at me, and I was lost.'

Mia gasped. It was the most romantic thing she'd ever heard. He was *lost*. Had she ever had that effect on a man? She doubted it.

'I couldn't take my eyes off her after that. I must have looked like a fool, but I didn't care. Then, when we were about to leave, she held out her hand to shake mine and placed a little piece of paper in it with her phone number on it.'

'And you called her?'

'The very next day.'

'And then what happened?'

Gabe's forehead creased. 'You don't really want to know all this, do you?'

'Yes,' Mia said. 'I'm an Austen fan. There's nothing I like more than a love story.'

Gabe smiled. 'Okay,' he said, 'I'll tell you, but you have to let me top up that coffee first.'

Mia looked down at her empty cup. She couldn't actually remember drinking it, because she'd been enthralled by his story.

'Okay,' she said. 'But then I want *all* the details.'

Chapter 20

Shelley had a dilemma. She and Mia were due to head down into town to attend a walking tour of Jane Austen's Bath, but Mia hadn't yet come back from Gabe's.

'Do you think I should go and get her?' she asked as Pie walked into the living room, his mass of dark hair obscuring half his face. 'She's been in there for ages.'

Pie grunted his response, which wasn't very helpful at all.

'I mean, I did send her round there, but I thought she'd be gone only five minutes. Don't get me wrong, I'm delighted that things seem to be going well, but I'm just a bit worried. What on earth can they be doing?'

Pie grunted again.

'You don't think they're—?' Shelley's mouth dropped open, but then she shook her head. 'Gabe is a gentleman. They must just be talking.' She paced up and down the room. 'I've already lost my dog to Gabe, and now it seems I've lost my best friend too.' She looked up at Pie as if he might have something consoling to say to her, but he just stared at her. 'Haven't you got to get to work or somewhere?'

He shrugged his broad shoulders and left the room.

Shelley sighed, knowing there was nobody to blame but herself. She was the one who practically shoved Mia toward Gabe, and she couldn't very well complain if they really were getting on.

She walked through to the kitchen and gazed up into the face of Henry Tilney, who was smiling down at her from the calendar.

'What would you do, Henry? Do you think I should go and find out what's happening or leave them to it? What would Emma Woodhouse do? She was always matchmaking people, wasn't she?' Shelley puffed out her cheeks. She had no idea what a fraught business matchmaking was.

Next door, Gabe was making more coffee. Mia had followed him through to the kitchen and was watching him. He really was rather handsome, she thought, with his warm hazel eyes, thick fair hair, and a gentle smile. And he looked as if he kept himself in shape when he wasn't recovering from a broken arm. It seemed a shame that he was on his own. She was quite sure there were thousands of women out there who would beat a path to his door, if they knew he was available. He was too old for her, of course; she'd always dated men her own age and had never been tempted by the older man, but she was enjoying talking to Gabe. He was easy to listen to, and she felt like she'd known him for ages.

'So, come on—tell me what happened next,' she said, desperate to get back to the story he had been telling her about how he'd met his wife.

'Well, I gave Andrea a call, and we agreed to meet later that week. I chose a little Italian restaurant I knew. It was one of those amazing hot summer nights, and we ate outside in the courtyard. We hadn't talked to each other at all at the dinner party, and I was worried we had nothing to say to each other, but the problem was shutting us up,' he said, laughing at the memory. 'We were the last to leave the restaurant that night, and then we walked along the river, not wanting to leave each other's company.'

'What did you talk about?'

'Everything, really. Our jobs, our families, our hopes for the future, and the wonderful thing about it all was that it was so natural. Nothing was forced. You know when you're with somebody and you have no idea what to talk to them about and you have those painful silences? Well, there were none of those with Andrea.'

He handed Mia her coffee, and they returned to the living room. This time, Mia sat down on the sofa opposite him.

'You know, it feels funny to be talking about her like this. That's one of the things I haven't been able to do. When she died, there was so much sorting out to do—things to arrange and people to see and, well, there wasn't much time to just sit and talk about her. Even if there had been, I don't think people would have let me.'

'You mean your family?'

'My family, Andrea's family—nobody really wants to talk much. I think loss isolates a person. Everybody is far too nervous to ask you how you feel, in case you have a breakdown in front of them. It's much easier not to say anything and hope the pain goes away quickly and quietly.'

'Was there nobody you could talk to at all?' Mia asked.

Gabe shook his head. 'My family didn't know what to say to me, and I didn't want to burden them. Nothing like this had ever happened in my family.'

Mia looked at him, her eyes full of sympathy.

'And I don't mean to burden you now,' he said.

'But you aren't. I was the one who brought up the subject, and I want to talk about it. It's important.'

Gabe smiled at her. 'You're an extraordinary young lady,' he said.

She smiled back. 'No, I'm not. I'm just very nosy.' She got up from the sofa and walked across the room to one of the many bookshelves that lined the walls. 'Oh, you have a collection of poems,' she said, pulling out an old hardback book and admiring its green and gold cover. 'It's beautiful. I've never seen such fine pages. They're like tissue paper.'

Gabe cleared his throat. 'As much as I'd like to take credit for owning it, that was Andrea's.'

'But you've read it?'

'Alas, no.'

'No?' Mia said. 'Not ever?'

Gabe gave a little smile as if embarrassed. 'Not ever. Andrea would occasionally read some out loud to me.'

'Which ones?'

Gabe frowned. 'I... er... some of the shorter ones.'

'You mean you don't know?' Mia said.

'I have a bad memory,' he said with a little smile.

'How can anyone get through life without reading the Romantic poets? I mean, they *are* life!'

'So, along with Jane Austen, I should read all the Romantic poets?'

'Yes!'

'Anything else?' he said, his eyebrows rising.

Mia looked thoughtful for a moment. 'Well, you shouldn't miss out on Thomas Hardy, although you rarely get a happy ending. And then there are the Brontë sisters. You really shouldn't go through life without reading *Jane Eyre* or *Wuthering Heights*.'

'Okay,' he said. 'Well, that should keep me busy for a little while. Anything else I should add to the list?'

She looked at him. 'You're teasing me,' she said.

'No, no,' he said. 'Well, just a little.'

'I didn't mean to sound bossy. I know I usually do. It's a terrible fault of mine.' She bit her lip. 'I hope you didn't think I was—'

'Please, don't worry! It's just so nice to talk about these things. I usually don't get out much. Shelley says I'm a workaholic, and I guess she's right. I really don't socialize much.' He smiled. 'I sound like a sad old sod, don't I?'

Mia laughed. 'No! Well, yes. A little, perhaps.'

They looked at each other for a moment, and Bingley thumped his tail on the carpet as if in approval of the conversation.

'Was Andrea bossy?' Mia asked.

Gabe shook his head. 'No. Not at all. She was one of those laid-back people. She never minded if I left my clothes strewn all over the floor or left half-empty coffee cups all around the house.'

'That sort of thing would drive my sister crazy,' Mia said, and then she bit her lip.

'What is it?'

'Nothing. I just—I haven't talked about my sister for a while.' Mia felt as if she were holding her breath. She hadn't meant to mention her sister. She hadn't even meant to be thinking about her. Maybe it was being in Bath. Maybe Bath was bringing all the memories bubbling back to the surface.

'Did you want to talk about it now?'

Mia looked at Gabe's face. It was kind and open, the sort of face that one instantly trusted.

'You wouldn't want to hear about all that,' she said in a small voice.

'Sure, I would. You've been listening to me prattling on for ages.'

'Yes, but that was different. I kept asking all the questions.'

'Perhaps I could ask you some questions, then, if it would make you feel better.'

Mia smiled. Perhaps it would. Perhaps she should talk to

somebody about everything. It might be what she needed, and wasn't it better to talk to a stranger? Shelley had been trying to get her to talk to her, but Mia hadn't been able to, but Gabe—this felt right.

'You really want to hear all this?' she said.

'I really do,' he said, leaning forward.

'Well, okay,' Mia said. 'If you're absolutely sure.'

'Hello?' a voice called through from the kitchen, startling Mia. It was Shelley. 'Anyone there?'

'We're in here,' Gabe said.

Shelley appeared in the living room. 'There you all are! I'd lost both my dog and my friend.'

Bingley got up from his home by Gabe's feet and went to greet his mistress with a friendly sniff.

'I was getting worried about you,' she said, turning an accusatory look toward Mia.

'I thought you knew where I was,' Mia shot back.

'Yes, but I thought you'd have been back by now. I'm afraid we've missed the walking tour of Bath today.'

'I'm so sorry, Shelley. It's my fault,' Gabe said.

'No, it isn't,' Mia said. 'I kept asking you questions and—well—I didn't realize how late it was. So don't blame Gabe, Shelley. Blame me.'

Shelley looked confused. 'We can probably still make that talk this afternoon.'

'Okay, then,' Mia said, getting up from where she'd been sitting.

Gabe got up too. 'It's been a real pleasure talking to you, Mia,' he said.

'You too.'

'Perhaps we can... er... finish our conversation another time?' he said.

'Oh, did I interrupt something?' Shelley asked.

'No,' Mia assured her.

'No,' Gabe said.

Shelley frowned at them both. 'Come on, then,' she said. 'Come on, Bingley.' Mia and Bingley followed Shelley back through the kitchen to the garden and then through the gap in the fence.

'What were you two talking about for so long? You were gone for ages,' Shelley said as soon as they were out of earshot.

'But you sent me round there to make friends,' Mia said.

'I thought you must have both run off to Gretna Green.'

'Oh, don't be silly. We were just talking.'

'But what about? What did I interrupt?'

'Nothing. It was nothing.'

'Why don't I believe you?'

'I don't understand you, Shelley. I thought you wanted me to get on with him, and that's precisely what I've been doing.'

'But for so long?'

'You're beginning to sound jealous.'

'Ha! Why would I be jealous? If I liked Gabe myself, I wouldn't be pushing *you* toward him, would I?'

'Well, I don't know,' Mia said.

They reached the house, and Shelley opened the door, ushering Bingley inside before he could escape again.

'Why are we arguing? We shouldn't be arguing. This is crazy,' Mia said.

Shelley stopped. 'I'm sorry. Let's have a cup of tea.'

'No, thanks. I've just had a coffee.'

'Well, I'm making one for me.'

Mia sat down at the kitchen table, knowing that Shelley wasn't going to let the subject drop easily.

'So what did you talk about all that time?' she asked again, reaching for her favorite I Love Darcy mug and spooning an extra sugar into it.

Mia shrugged, not wanting to betray Gabe's trust. It was funny, but although she'd known him for only a brief while, she felt very loyal toward him.

'Oh, you know,' she said noncommittally.

'No, I don't, so hurry up and tell me.'

'Just stuff,' Mia said vaguely.

Shelley huffed. 'You come all this way to see me, and I can't get a word out of you, and then you spend the entire morning talking to my neighbor.'

'Sorry,' Mia said.

'So you do like him, then?' Shelley pressed.

'Of course I like him. He's a very nice man.'

Shelley's eyebrows rose suggestively.

'Shelley, I've only just met him. Stop trying to matchmake me for half a minute.'

'But he *is* very nice, isn't he?'

'I've already said he is. But he's much too old for me.'

'Isn't that what Marianne Dashwood said about Colonel Brandon?' Shelley asked.

'I'm *not* Marianne Dashwood,' Mia said. 'And Gabe certainly isn't Colonel Brandon.'

'I didn't say he was,' Shelley said with a little grin.

Mia decided to ignore it. She knew she didn't stand a chance of winning this particular battle.

Chapter 21

SARAH WAS EATING LUNCH IN A PIZZERIA BUT WASN'T HAPPY with the cutlery. The knife looked mottled, and there was a bent prong on the fork, which turned her stomach, so she asked for it to be replaced. She should never have come into the place. It was an unknown quantity, and she had broken her rule of eating somewhere she didn't know.

When her pasta dish arrived, she poked it around with her new replacement fork, making sure there weren't any hidden horrors before she placed the food in her mouth.

As she ate, she wondered where Lloyd was. She thought of the time they'd spent together the day before and how much she enjoyed it. It was comforting to talk to somebody who knew what it was like to cope with OCD. It was as if she were being herself for the very first time in her life. They had known each other for only a day, yet she felt as if she could give her OCD free rein in his company. If she needed to examine the prongs of a fork, she could. If she needed to calm herself by counting to ten, she could. He didn't judge her. There wouldn't even be any light teasing, which often happened in the company of her sister.

And he's going to stay in Bath!

Sarah tried not to get excited at the thought that he was staying in Bath because of her. He was a freelance photographer and was at liberty to make his own timetable, and it just happened that the city of Bath had thoroughly captivated him and he'd decided to stay on for a few more days after his Jane Austen Festival assignment.

He's probably only interested in the architecture, she told herself as she paused to examine a piece of pasta that didn't look quite as symmetrical as the other pieces. You mustn't assume that he is staying on because of you.

Sarah thought back to the time they spent together at the Jane Austen Centre. She'd watched him as he worked and liked the polite way he dealt with people and the joyous ease with which he went about his job. Each new angle he found had been a mini adventure, like discovering a new territory. It had been so much fun and, of course, a visit to the Jane Austen Centre was always a treat for an Austen fan. Sarah had promised herself that she would travel light on this trip; it was something she always prided herself on; however, the temptation in the shop was just too much, and she bought an armful of books and goodies, including a beautiful framed silhouette of Jane Austen, a Longbourn lip balm, and a marvelous Jane Austen Festival mug.

After she was quite sure she couldn't fit anything else in her suitcase, they left the shop, and Sarah posed for Lloyd for a quick photograph on the steps outside the center with the delightful 'meeter and greeter' who was dressed in full Regency costume.

'This is one extraordinary city,' Lloyd said as they walked up Gay Street toward The Circus.

Sarah nodded. 'It's my favorite,' she said. 'I never tire of it, no matter how many years I keep returning.'

'I wish I had longer here,' Lloyd said.

'You're leaving?' Sarah said all too quickly. She bit her lip. She had sounded far too much like Mia.

'Well, my assignment is more or less complete.'

'Oh,' Sarah said, trying desperately not to look at him, for fear that he would see the disappointment in her eyes.

'But I've been thinking,' he said as they entered The Circus. 'I don't really have to get back. It's easy enough to download and submit my chosen photographs from my laptop in my hotel room.'

'Is it?' Sarah said.

'And my next official assignment isn't until next week.'

'Right,' Sarah said, trying not to get her hopes up.

'So I've been thinking of staying on in Bath.'

'You have?'

He nodded, a little smile playing around his mouth. 'I'd really like to get to know this city better,' he said.

Sarah nodded, trying hard not to feel hurt that he hadn't said he wanted to get to know *her* better. After all, she knew that her own modest beauty couldn't possibly compare to that of Bath's.

'Well, I think that's as good a reason as any,' she told him. 'And I'm sure you'll find plenty to photograph.'

He stopped walking for a minute, and Sarah felt sure that he was about to reach into his bag for his camera, but he didn't. Instead, he turned to face her. 'That's not the only reason I'm staying,' he said.

'No?'

'No,' he said. 'I've just met somebody, and I'd really like to get to know her better.'

Sarah said nothing. She wanted to count to ten, because it always calmed her, but he'd be sure to see her lips moving if she did that, so she kept perfectly still and waited for him to say more.

'And I'm wondering if she'd like to get to know me better too.'

'Oh,' she said at last.

'Does she?'

'Well, I couldn't really say.'

'Couldn't you? That's a funny sort of response. Don't you like me at all?'

Sarah allowed herself a smile. 'You mean me?'

'Well, of course I mean you. Who else did you think?'

'One never likes to assume,' she said.

He laughed. 'You are funny,' he said, 'and I really do want to get to know you better. I want to know all about you. I want to know where you come from and what's made you the person that you are today. In short, *everything*. I want to know everything!'

'Are you sure?'

He nodded. 'I might even tell you a little bit about myself in return.'

'Okay,' Sarah said, 'I think I can cope with that.'

'So where do you want to begin?'

They stopped walking again, and Sarah looked up at the grand columns and fine sash windows of The Circus. What was she going to tell him? She liked him, she really did, and she didn't want to start this relationship by hiding the truth from him, but nor did she want to scare him off, and the truth might very well do that.

'Let's just take it nice and slow,' she said quietly and felt mightily relieved when he nodded in agreement.

Chapter 22

Barton Cottage

MIA HOVERED BY THE WINDOW IN THE FRONT ROOM OF Barton Cottage.

'Where is he? He should be here by now.'

'Calm down. You're going to wear holes in your sandals with all your pacing.'

'But it shouldn't take him long to get here. Maybe I should go and meet him halfway.'

'Mia! That'll look awful!'

'Why?'

'You'll look too keen. Just be patient and wait.'

Sarah watched as Mia flung herself into an armchair and pouted.

'You could make yourself useful and check on the food,' Sarah said, but Mia didn't get a chance to do her bit in the kitchen, because there was a smart knock on the door, and she was out of her chair like a jack-in-the-box.

'Don't rush!' Sarah cried. 'Let him wait a moment. It won't do him any harm.'

'You really are perverse, Sarah. Why should he wait, when I'm here to greet him right away?'

Sarah sighed. Mia had a lot to learn about propriety. Still, she got up from where she'd been sitting on the carpet, where she'd tried to get the DVD player working for their evening's entertainment, and walked through to the hallway just as Mia was opening the door.

'Hello, lovely ladies,' Alec said as he entered the house. He was carrying a bottle, and Mia immediately snatched it from him.

'Ooooh! It's champagne!' she cried with glee.

'Only the best for my girls,' Alec said, winking at Sarah.

Sarah smiled back, but she felt that he was being far too familiar with them both.

'Come into the kitchen, Alec. Sarah's been preparing all sorts of treats for us both.'

'Well, something certainly smells good,' he said.

They walked through to the kitchen at the back of the house, and Sarah opened the oven. There on a baking tray sat dozens of tiny party treats, from mini sausage rolls to onion bhajis.

'I thought it would be nicer to have lots of little bits to pick at whilst we're watching the film.'

'It looks great,' he said.

'I'll get some glasses,' Mia said. 'I want to get this champagne open.'

Ten minutes later, they were carrying their plates of food through to the living room. Alec sat down on the sofa opposite the television, and Sarah watched in horror as Mia sat herself down on the carpet by his feet.

'Wouldn't you be more comfortable on the sofa?' Sarah asked.

'Nonsense,' Mia said. 'I prefer sitting on the floor.'

Sarah frowned, not liking the proximity of her sister to Alec, nor the angle either.

'Did you manage to get the machine working again?' Mia asked.

Sarah nodded, brandishing the remote control and hitting Play. 'I don't think I've ever watched a Jane Austen adaptation with a man before,' she said.

'Why should it just be a girl thing?' Mia asked. 'I mean, they're great movies; nobody can dispute that. I think you're going to really love it,' she said, turning around to Alec and smiling at him.

'Good,' Alec said, taking a sip of champagne. 'Then we can watch *Killer Zombies Take Manhattan* afterwards, and you can tell me what you think of that.'

Mia laughed. 'You've got to be joking!'

'But I'm watching one of *your* favorite movies,' he said, a teasing lilt to his voice.

'Yes, but that's because it's good,' Mia said, 'and not filled with mindless violence.'

'There's a lot of great wit and lyricism in *Killer Zombies Take Manhattan*. It's a very underrated film,' Alec said.

'Yeah, right!' Mia said and then play-punched him.

The titles came up on the screen and a magical hush filled the room as if they were in a cinema. Sarah always loved the moment when a favorite film began. There was something immensely calming about it, even if one had seen it many times before, which, with all the Austen adaptations, she had. In fact, the pleasure seemed to increase with each viewing. A wonderful anticipation came from knowing exactly what was going to happen next—of being aware that the next scene would bring Colonel Brandon or the moment Marianne twisted her ankle was fast approaching. It was intensely pleasurable.

For a long time, Sarah had refused to go to the cinema. Not only were there issues of hygiene, but there were also issues of other people. She couldn't believe that people went to the cinema not to see a film but to eat endless amounts of popcorn and other noisy food and to sit sending text messages. That's what had happened the last time she went to the cinema. There had been a special showing of the 1940 version of *Pride and Prejudice* starring Laurence Olivier and Greer Garson. Sarah had seen it a dozen times, of course, but had never seen it on the big screen, so doing her best to overcome her fears of being a member of the general public, she got herself ready to go out and took great care to choose a seat that was central to the screen and equidistant from the screen and the exit. She also quickly clocked the man with the very large packet of crisps and the elderly woman with the enormous handkerchief and was careful to sit nowhere near either of them.

For a while she had been only one of a dozen or so people who bought tickets for the screening, and she was just congratulating herself on having chosen such a good seat when two young girls walked into the cinema.

'Where shall we sit?' one of them squealed.

'At the back?' the other one replied.

Yes, Sarah thought. *Sit at the back—miles away from me.*

'I don't like the back. It's creepy. I want to sit nearer the front.'

The lights dimmed and the trailers began, causing the two girls to trip over themselves on their hunt for a seat.

Hurry up! Sarah willed them, but they didn't seem in any hurry at all, nor were they conscious of disturbing anybody.

Sarah sighed in exasperation when they chose seats three rows directly in front of her. She knew she wouldn't be able to concentrate on the film with them sitting there, but she also knew that sitting in any seat that wasn't perfectly central would irritate her. She decided to choose the lesser of two evils and moved her seat.

The film started, and for a few blissful moments, Sarah was swept away, enraptured by the beauty and grace of Greer Garson and the handsome snobbery of Laurence Olivier, and then the chatter began.

'It's all black and white,' one of the girls shrieked. 'Why's it all black and white?'

'I thought this was the Keira Knightley version.'

'Well, it isn't, is it?'

'You mean we've wasted money seeing this rubbish?'

'I don't believe it!'

A phone suddenly beeped.

'Who's that?' her friend asked.

'It's Jo. I'll text her back and say we're stuck watching this boring film.'

Sarah could stand it no longer. '*Shush!*'

The two girls turned around in shock.

'What's your problem?'

'You're my problem! I'm trying to watch this film,' Sarah said, surprised by the authority in her voice.

The girls went quiet for a moment, but Sarah could see the little squares of blue light from their mobile phones and could no longer concentrate on the film. From somewhere behind her, a nose blew very loudly and the rattle and munch of crisps was heard.

Sarah counted slowly to ten, but she didn't feel any calmer once she reached the magic number.

'Will everyone just be quiet, *please!*' The loudness of her voice startled her. Had she really said that out loud? She soon got her answer, when a woman approached her from the aisle.

'I'm afraid I'm going to have to ask you to leave,' the woman said. 'You're disturbing everybody.'

'*I'm* disturbing everybody? Are you mad? I'm not the one with the noisy crisps or the mobile phone or the trumpeting nose. I'm the only one who came here to watch this film *properly!*'

'Madam, please lower your voice and leave the cinema.'

Sarah got up. In all truth, she was glad to leave. She hadn't been enjoying the whole cinema experience, and she had not been back to a cinema since. Instead, she waited for films to come out on DVD and then watched them in the peace and quiet of her own home.

Now, watching *Sense and Sensibility* with Mia and Alec, she didn't mind the polite nibble of sausage rolls, but she had to admit that she didn't like the way Mia's legs were stretched out in front of her or the number of buttons that were unfastened on her blouse, exposing an awful lot of bosom. She couldn't remember that many buttons being undone before Alec had arrived.

She looked at Alec's profile in the surreal light from the television screen and admired him. He was certainly handsome, with his high forehead and dark hair. She could see why Mia was so attracted to him.

But she mustn't make it so obvious to him. She's in danger of making a fool of herself. Sarah knew that Mia wouldn't see it like that. If she felt an emotion, she had to express it. It was as simple as that. Life was too short for subterfuge, she would say, in a way that was horribly reminiscent of Marianne Dashwood. In fact, this whole situation with Alec was reminding her of the *Sense and Sensibility* story they were watching together. Alec—like Willoughby—had appeared out of nowhere, helping a limping Mia back to Barton Cottage. He was tall, dark, handsome, and mysterious enough to be beguiling to an impressionable young romantic like Mia. And just like Willoughby, very little of substance was known about him. They didn't know much about his job, other than he helped small businesses. They didn't know anything at all about his family, other than an aunt who used to live in Devon. It was all very unsettling. At the least, it was unsettling to somebody like Sarah. Mia didn't seem to mind at all, but for the space of the evening, Sarah tried to shut off her worries.

It was wonderful to watch the film and to recognize the very cottage they were staying in.

'That's this room!' Mia shouted. 'And those are the stairs!'

'And the reed beds,' Sarah said.

It really was rather exciting to spot and know the locations in the film.

'Isn't it wonderful, Alec?' Mia said at one point. 'We've walked down that path—look!'

A strange noise occurred. Mia turned around from her place on the carpet and saw what it was. It was Alec, and he was snoring.

'I don't believe it! He's asleep!' Mia said, horrified at the discovery. 'We're not even halfway through. He's going to miss all the best bits unless we wake him up.'

'No, don't disturb him. He looks peaceful,' Sarah said.

'It's quite a cute snore, I suppose,' Mia said. 'Although you'd probably get fed up of it after a while. I mean, if he was in the same bed as you and you were trying to get to sleep.'

'Shush!' Sarah said. 'What a thing to say! What if he heard you?'

'He can't hear me—he's fast asleep.'

'He might be pretending.'

'Why?'

'So he can listen to us talking about him,' Sarah said.

'Well, then, he might hear something he doesn't want to hear, like he's got very peculiar socks on and a funny bit of hair that sticks out over his right ear.' Mia tugged the leg of one of his trousers, and Alec jolted awake.

'What?' he said, looking startled.

'You fell asleep,' Mia said, a wounded expression on her face. 'You fell asleep in the middle of our favorite Jane Austen adaptation.'

Alec straightened up on the sofa and rubbed his eyes. 'Goodness,' he said. 'That's so rude of me. It must be the champagne and the ten-mile jog this morning.'

'Ten miles?'

He nodded. 'I try to get my average up whenever I stay here, because it's not always easy when I'm working in town. I go to the gym, but it's not the same as being somewhere beautiful like this, is it?'

'No,' Mia said. 'It isn't.'

Sarah's eyes narrowed in suspicion, because she didn't completely believe what Alec was saying.

'It's important to keep yourself in shape, isn't it?' he said.

Mia nodded, and Sarah noticed the way her sister was looking up at his body, which had probably been his intention, she thought cynically.

'Shall we have a break from the film?' Sarah said.

'Yes,' Mia said. 'My bottom's getting a bit numb on the floor.' She got up and stretched, and Sarah watched Alec eyeing up her sister's bottom, which had probably been Mia's intention. The two of them reminded her of the scene in *Pride and Prejudice* when Mr Darcy makes the comment about Elizabeth Bennet and Miss Bingley walking around the room with the knowledge that their figures looked at their best that way.

'Anyone for coffee?' Sarah asked.

'I'm still on the champagne,' Mia said.

'Well, I need a coffee,' Sarah said leaving the room.

It was a relief to be alone in the kitchen for a moment. She hadn't felt comfortable in the living room with Alec and Mia flirting with each other. Oh, why did he have to be there that week and spoil things? This was meant to be *her* time with her sister. She'd been looking forward to it for so long, and now this man was coming between them and ruining everything.

'Hello,' Alec said, suddenly appearing in the door of the kitchen. 'You ran off.'

'I was getting a coffee,' Sarah said, suddenly remembering and busying herself with the kettle.

'What's wrong?'

'Nothing's wrong. Why should something be wrong?' Sarah said, a little too defensively even to her own ears.

'Just the way you're acting,' he said.

'I'm not acting. I'm just being me.' She took a mug from the draining board and checked that it was perfectly clean before popping a spoonful of coffee into it.

'Why are you behaving like this?' Alec asked, moving a step closer to her.

Sarah glared at him. 'What do you want, Alec?'

'What do you mean?'

'What are you doing here?'

'I don't understand. I thought I was invited here tonight.'

Sarah suddenly felt bad at having asked the question of him, but her heart was still thudding inside her chest, and she knew she had to speak her mind. 'I don't like the way you act around my sister.'

Alec frowned. 'I wasn't aware that I was acting in any particular kind of a way.'

'I've seen the way you look at her.'

Alec cleared his throat in the guilty kind of way someone might when he knew he'd been caught. 'Well, she's a very pretty girl. I can't help that, can I?'

'But you *can* help by not encouraging her.'

There was a pause, and a strange look passed between them.

'I see,' he said at last. 'Look, you seem to have got the wrong impression of me.'

'Have I?'

'Yes,' he said. 'I'm not interested in your sister. At least not beyond being a friend. She's bright and warm and attractive, but— well, she's just not my type.'

'But you've been flirting with her ever since she met you.'

'Have I? I thought she'd been flirting with me.'

'It takes two, you know.'

'Does it?'

He took a step toward her, and Sarah took one back. He was in her personal space, and she didn't like it.

'What do I have to do to convince you that I'm not interested in your sister?'

Sarah felt panicky and could feel her breaths were shortening. 'I don't know,' she said. 'Just—just—'

'Because this is very interesting to me. You think I'm interested in her. You think I've been flirting with her, when I haven't. You've got it completely wrong.'

'Have I?'

'Yes!' he said, the word flying from his mouth like a bullet. 'It's you I'm interested in, Sarah! *You!*'

Their eyes locked for a silent, suspense-laden moment as the kettle boiled behind them.

Alec was the first one to speak. 'Sarah,' he said, whispering the name desperately.

Sarah shook her head. 'No,' she said. 'Don't do this. I won't allow it. Mia—'

'Someone call my name?'

Sarah looked up and saw her sister standing in the doorway.

'What's going on?' Mia asked. 'Is everything all right?'

'Yes,' Sarah said, moving away from Alec. 'Everything's fine.'

Chapter 23

After leaving Gabe's, Mia and Shelley made it into Bath in time for a talk about food in Regency times. It wasn't the most riveting of talks, and Mia was soon wishing that they'd just gone shopping instead, especially when it was time for questions from the audience and a very rude lady with a massive bosom hogged all the time available, causing the rest of the audience to tut and sigh in annoyance.

'Oh, my goodness,' Shelley said. 'It's that dreadful Mrs Soames.'

'Who?' Mia asked, leaning forward in her seat.

'She comes to the festival every year and makes an absolute nuisance of herself.'

'Come on—let's sneak out,' Mia said, and the two of them got up and left the room as quietly as possible.

They hadn't quite made it out of the building when Mia stopped.

'What is it?' Shelley asked.

'Can you smell that?'

'Smell what?'

'Lavender!'

Shelley sniffed the air like Bingley might. 'I'm not sure.'

'Sarah's been here.'

'Your sister Sarah?'

Mia nodded. 'I'm sure of it. I'd recognize that smell anywhere.'

'The lavender? But it could be anyone. Any number of old ladies might be wearing lavender.'

Mia shook her head. 'It's Sarah and her spray. She never leaves home without it.'

Shelley sniffed the air again. 'Are you sure you're not imagining it?'

Mia wasn't listening. Her gaze roamed the foyer, anxious that she might see Sarah at any moment, and what would she do then?

'Do you think she was in that talk?' Shelley asked. 'Surely you would have seen her.'

'Not if she was wearing a bonnet.'

'Would she be likely to? I mean, after the promenade?'

'I'm not sure. She used to be far too self-conscious about her costume, but who knows?'

Walking out into Queen Square, Mia wondered if she'd really just spent an hour in the same room as Sarah and not seen her. How peculiar that felt, and yet despite the long years apart, she still wasn't sure she was ready to see her.

⁓

Sarah had, indeed, been in the talk about food in Regency times. She'd been sitting toward the back of the room and suddenly felt very hot and in need of some fresh air and had got up to leave before the questions began. She'd not seen Mia or Shelley and hadn't thought to look for them, either. Besides, she was too busy thinking about something else.

Lloyd.

She was due to meet him outside the abbey and was anxious

not to be late. He'd told her he was going to photograph the River Avon in the morning, and Sarah was pleased that he was staying in Bath. It took her mind off how lonely it was, being on her own there, despite the many festival events that were keeping her busy.

Now, walking through the city, she couldn't stop thinking how nice it was to have a man's company again. It felt as if she hadn't had such company in some time, and life was always a little bit duller without a companion.

As she approached the abbey, she began looking out for him and soon spotted him among the crowds in front of the great door. He was bent down at ground level, his broad shoulders taut as he found some new angle from which to photograph. Sarah sneaked up on him, wondering how close she could get before he saw her.

'Hello,' he said, without raising his eye from the viewfinder.

'How did you know it was me?' Sarah said, perplexed.

'I saw you as soon as you came into the square.'

'Did you?'

He got up and showed her a photograph he'd taken of her a few seconds before. Sure enough, there she was, wearing a soft, otherworldly expression on her face.

'What were you thinking of?' Lloyd asked her.

Sarah looked up at him. 'I was thinking of you.'

He smiled and she smiled back. It was the right answer.

'Did you get the photos you wanted of the river?'

'I got a few,' he said.

Sarah liked his modesty. They were sure to be brilliant photographs, but she knew he wouldn't boast about them.

'So,' he said, 'are you going to tell me the secret history of Sarah now?' His voice was full of warmth, but it made Sarah feel quite cold, and she sat down on a nearby bench feeling depleted.

When Lloyd had told Sarah that he wanted to know everything about her, she hadn't quite taken him at his word but he seemed intent on finding out about her.

This is your comeuppance, a little voice said. *You're going to be found out. You can't escape.*

'Sarah—what is it?' he asked. 'You've turned white! Are you okay?'

She nodded but then shook her head.

'I'm a bad person,' she whispered.

'What?'

'I'm a bad person. You don't want to know about me. You really don't want to get involved with me.'

'What are you talking about? How could you *possibly* be a bad person?'

'You don't know what I've done.'

Lloyd's forehead furrowed. 'I admit I don't know much about you,' he said, sitting down next to her, 'but I know enough to say that you're one of the sweetest people I've ever met.'

'I'm not,' Sarah said, shaking her head. 'I'm the very worst kind of person you could ever imagine.'

Lloyd laughed but then apologized when he saw the hurt expression on Sarah's face.

'Sarah,' he said, 'it seems to me like you're carrying some terrible weight around and—say no if you want; I won't be offended if you do, but—I might be able to help you.'

'How?' she asked. 'How can you help me?'

'I can listen to you,' he said. 'If you want to talk about it.'

Sarah sighed. It was the very thing she'd been dreading, because she hadn't ever talked about it to anyone.

'You probably won't want to have anything to do with me if I tell you,' she said.

Lloyd looked startled. 'I can promise you right now that you don't have to fear on that score.'

'But how can you say that?'

He smiled at her. 'Because I like you, and nothing you can say is going to change that.'

Sarah looked into his eyes, which were filled with kindness, and then she took a deep breath, hoping he wouldn't go back on his word once she told him the truth.

Chapter 24

Barton Cottage

'I WAS THINKING OF DRIVING INTO TAVISTOCK. ARE YOU SURE YOU
don't want to come?' Sarah asked Mia. They were sitting at the
breakfast table, and Mia was working her way steadily through
three slices of toast and marmalade.

'I don't understand why you want to go anywhere,' Mia said,
taking a slurp of tea.

'I just want a change of scene, that's all.'

'A change of scene? But I thought you said this was the most
beautiful place on earth.'

'But I want to explore,' Sarah said.

Mia frowned. This didn't sound like the Sarah she knew.
'What's the matter? Is something wrong?'

'Why should there be something wrong?'

'Because you sound strange. You don't sound like you.'

'What an odd thing to say,' Sarah said.

'No, it isn't,' Mia said. 'Not when you're acting all weird.'

'I'm not acting all weird.'

'Yes, you are—you're all distanced.'

'What, just because I fancy a trip to Tavistock?'

'No. You've been… I don't know—pensive.'

Sarah bit her lip. The trouble with having a sister was that she would always know when something was wrong, even if you didn't say anything and even when you were doing your very best to hide it.

'You're imagining things,' Sarah said, deciding to deny the whole thing. 'Now, are you coming with me or not?'

'I want to stay here.'

Sarah sighed, getting up to clear away the breakfast things. She knew what Mia meant, of course. She wanted to hang around in case Alec dropped by, and Sarah was in a terrible quandary about that. Should she stay too and try to make sure Mia didn't make a fool of herself? But it would run the risk of seeing Alec herself, and she really didn't want that to happen.

Yes you do, a little voice said as she entered the kitchen. *You want to see him more than anything else in the world.*

Which is why you mustn't, she told herself sternly, crashing the crockery into the sink. He's dangerous. He's flirting with both you and Mia, and there's only one way that will end, unless you do something about it right now.

Before either she or Mia could change her mind, Sarah finished washing up, brushed her hair with one hundred strokes, and grabbed her handbag and car keys.

'I'm off,' she called through the house.

Mia appeared in the doorway of the living room. She was wearing a light summer dress that clung to her figure in the sort of way that left nothing to the imagination.

'I hope you're going to put a cardigan on,' Sarah couldn't help saying.

Mia laughed. 'You're joking, aren't you?'

'There's a cool breeze around,' Sarah said, but she wasn't really thinking about breezes.

'When will you be back?'

'I'm not sure,' Sarah said, but she knew she didn't want to be back until it was dark. She wanted to stay away from Barton Cottage as long as possible.

'Okay,' Mia said. 'Well, drive safely. These country lanes can be dangerous.'

Sarah nodded. 'And you be careful too.'

'What do you mean? I don't think there's anything dangerous here at Barton Cottage.'

'Just… be careful, all the same.' Sarah swallowed hard, hoping she was doing the right thing in leaving.

As she left the private estate and drove along the deep green lanes of Devon, she breathed a sigh of relief. It felt good to get away, if only for a short time. At least she knew Alec couldn't find her.

Mia was quite relieved to see Sarah driving away. She was in a funny mood, and it was probably best if she was on her own now. Honestly, she could be worse than a mother, sometimes. Fancy suggesting that she wear a cardigan! The whole point of her choosing the yellow dress was because it showed off her figure, so why would she want to hide it under a saggy, baggy cardigan?

Once she was quite sure that Sarah had gone and wasn't likely to return because she'd forgotten anything—not that Sarah ever forgot anything—Mia left the house and walked along the track beside the estuary before following it through the wood. Sarah would not approve of what Mia was going to do, but the thought only spurred Mia on. She was old enough to make her own decisions. Twenty-one was a very special age. She was a grown woman now and didn't need her older sister constantly telling her what to do.

When she reached the driveway that led to the cottage where Alec was staying, she paused, as if having second thoughts. But what was there to have second thoughts about? She felt that they had made a real connection. It was as if she were meant to meet him—that he'd been waiting for her, and it was fate that Sarah had booked Barton Cottage.

It's meant to be, she told herself. *It's right.*

She walked down the driveway toward the cottage by the estuary.

Sarah wasn't in the mood for shopping. She poked around a few of the shops, and to acknowledge how close she was to Cornwall, bought copies of Daphne du Maurier's *Frenchman's Creek* and *Jamaica Inn* at the local book shop. She had to admit that Tavistock was one of the prettiest places she'd ever visited, with its grand town hall and Georgian buildings, but she needed to stride out. She needed to be somewhere vast and lonely, where there were no handsome men to disturb her equilibrium.

Being ever practical, she bought a few provisions to take back to Barton Cottage before she left Tavistock and then drove the short distance to Dartmoor. It was a landscape she'd never seen before, but the acres of boulder-strewn moorland pleased her eye. Pulling over to park, Sarah swapped her neat flat shoes for a pair of walking boots and then followed a footpath lined with deep green bracken.

The path led to a distant tor, which looked like a sleeping dragon in the afternoon light. She hadn't realized how high up she'd driven, but looking around, she saw tiny villages dotting the wide valleys and saw steeples of churches far below. In the distance, she spotted a group of dark ponies, free to wander wherever they wanted. Sarah envied them that freedom, knowing that at some point, she would have to return to face her problems. For now, though, with the wind in her hair and the sun on her face, she could pretend that everything was all right. She could refuse to think about Alec and the way he looked at her.

But you can't stop thinking about the way you look at him, a little voice told her.

As she reached the tor, she tried to distract herself by admiring the sculptural shapes of the stones around her. You could see for miles from up here, and as she tipped her head back and gazed into the never-ending sky, she knew that she had failed to run away from her problems, even for the brief space of a day, because no matter how far you ran, you couldn't run away from yourself.

She leaned back against the rough rock and closed her eyes, feeling the fall and rise of her chest as she breathed in the moorland air. It was quiet here, and that was just what she needed right now; it was just her and her thoughts. Finally she allowed herself to speak the words that had been hovering in her mind for days.

'I'm falling in love. I'm falling in love—'

∼◯

'I have never eaten so well in my life,' Mia said, finishing a lunch that Alec had thrown together with the ease of a professional chef.

'That's what holidays are all about, aren't they?'

'But I feel so guilty. I'll have to run around the whole estate at least ten times before we leave.'

'Don't talk about leaving,' Alec said.

'I don't want to,' Mia said. 'It's too awful to even think about.'

'Then let's not,' he said. 'Let's fill the day with happy things.'

Mia laughed. 'Yes! Let's do that!'

That afternoon, they walked along the coastal path for miles, the sun warm on their limbs and the salty tang of the sea in the air. Their conversation drifted easily and seamlessly from subject to subject, and the hours passed by.

The sun was beginning to fade as they retraced their steps, and reaching Alec's cottage, he turned to Mia.

'Well, I guess Sarah will be back now,' he said.

'Oh, she'll be out for hours yet.'

'Really? Where's she gone?'

'I don't know, some town where they sell lavender spray.'

Alec looked perplexed.

'Come on. I don't want the evening to end yet. It's so beautiful.'

'Where do you want to go?'

'I don't know. Let's make it up as we go along,' Mia said, taking his hand and leading the way.

They followed the path through the wood, the sweet scent of bluebells heavy in the evening air. Dusk had started to swirl around the trees as they left the main path, and their footsteps were soft and silent.

Mia had never felt more alive in her life. Although her limbs had cooled as she and Alec entered the wood, she still felt wonderfully warm.

It's because you're in love, a little voice said, and she knew it was true. She'd fallen head over heels in love with this man, and the knowledge made her feel giddy.

'Where *are* we going?' Alec asked after they'd been walking for a good ten minutes.

'You know where we're going,' Mia said. 'Into the woods.'

He laughed. 'But we're in the woods.'

Mia turned to look at him, and they stopped walking. She suddenly felt shy, as if she were with a stranger.

He is a stranger.

Mia shook her head. She did not need to hear Sarah's voice now. Anyway, she was wrong. Alec wasn't a stranger at all. They'd spent all day together, talking like old friends. She couldn't know him any better if they spent the next fifty years locked in deep conversation.

Doing her utmost to block out any feelings of doubt, Mia leaned toward him, gently pressing her lips against his until she felt him return her kiss. She couldn't remember the last time she'd wanted to be kissed by somebody so much, but she didn't want to stop at a kiss, and she could feel that Alec wanted more too.

She watched as he took off his coat and laid it down among the thick bluebells.

'You're sure about this?' he whispered. 'I mean—'

'Stop talking and just kiss me.'

His mouth descended, and she was instantly consumed by the moment, closing her eyes and surrendering herself to his touch, desperately trying to shut out the voice of her sister who was screaming at her.

What are you doing? Mia! Stop now!

But she didn't stop, and neither did Alec.

Chapter 25

When Sarah finished telling Lloyd about her drive up to Dartmoor and the terrible realization that she'd allowed herself to acknowledge there, he looked at her as if she were quite mad.

'You fell in love,' Lloyd said. 'Is that it? Is that what you think makes you a bad person?'

'You don't understand. That was just the beginning.'

He looked pensive. 'But it's not your fault,' he said. 'We can't always choose who we fall in love with.'

'Can't we?'

'No.'

'You sound like you're talking from experience,' she said. 'Are you?'

'Are you trying to change the subject?'

'Maybe,' she said with a tiny smile. 'And maybe it's time you told me a bit more about yourself.'

He looked surprised, but then nodded. 'I suppose it is,' he said, 'although there's not a lot to tell.'

'Tell me anyway,' Sarah said, really not wanting to say anything more about her past to Lloyd today.

'Okay,' he said with a sigh. 'There have been two relationships in my life. Two major ones, anyway. One was with Chrissie, a girl I met in my first job. We dated for a couple of years and then drifted apart. No hard feelings and all that.'

'And the second?' Sarah asked after he paused for what she deemed long enough.

'The second was more complicated. The second one moved in with me.'

'Did she have a name?'

'Oh, yes,' Lloyd said with a bitter laugh. 'April.'

'That's a pretty name.'

'And most unsuitable too,' Lloyd said. 'Not that she wasn't pretty, you understand. She was. Pretty as a spring day. That's when her birthday was, too. She was named after the month she was born in, but... what can I say?'

Sarah cocked her head to one side. 'I don't know, but I hope you're going to say something.'

Lloyd grinned. 'She was more like winter, I'm afraid. To me, at least, although not at first. It kind of crept up in our relationship like an ice age.'

'Oh, dear,' Sarah said.

'It was just little things at first, like a comment here or a frown there, but it all turned into some appalling relationship war in the end.'

'I'm sorry,' Sarah said.

'Don't be,' he said. 'It's all in the past, and that's where it should stay.'

Sarah frowned. 'How did it end, exactly?'

Lloyd let out a huge sigh. 'Exactly?'

Sarah nodded encouragingly.

'I came home from work one day, and I found the house—well—I'm not sure how you'd describe it.'

'She'd trashed it?'

'Not really,' Lloyd said. 'Not by a normal person's standards, but by yours and mine, I guess you'd consider it trashed.'

'How do you mean?'

'She'd gone right round the house unstraightening curtains, leaving dirty cups out and drawers half-open—that sort of thing. She'd unmade the bed and had even left the toilet seat up, but the really terrible thing was she was laughing—*hysterically*! She thought it was all hilarious, and she kept pointing at me and shouting, "Your face! You should see your face!" It was dreadful.'

'That's horrible!' Sarah said.

'Yes, she really knew how to push my buttons. She'd even re-arranged all the kitchen cupboards—every single one of them—so that everything was in the wrong place. Well, you'll know how disturbing it is to open a cupboard and come face to face with something that shouldn't be there.'

'That's so cruel. I've never heard anything like that.'

'Yes, I think I'd rather have had a punch on the nose,' he said.

'So I'm guessing you haven't remained friends,' Sarah said.

Lloyd looked at her and laughed. 'You're guessing right.' He took a deep breath and stood up. 'Why are we wasting valuable time talking about such people, when there is this beautiful city to explore?'

'Because you said you wanted to know all about me, and I wanted to know about you too.'

'Well, I think we've had quite enough revelations today, don't you?'

Sarah nodded. 'I do,' she said.

'How about some lunch? I've found the perfect place. It is clean, quiet, and the tablecloths are straight.'

'And the food?'

'Not sure.'

'Well, as long as the tablecloths are straight, that's the main thing.'

'Exactly,' Lloyd said. 'You know, it's so refreshing to meet somebody who understands these things.'

⁓

Mia was still on edge with the whole lavender incident and couldn't get her sister out of her mind. She was quite sure Sarah had been there, and it was more than the scent of lavender—it was a *feeling*, a prickling of the skin, a certain *frisson*.

'Are you okay, sweetie?' Shelley asked, seeing her friend's pale face. Mia nodded.

'I know what we need,' Shelley announced. 'A wonderful cream tea! How about the Pump Room?'

Mia blinked in surprise. 'Isn't that a bit expensive?'

'It's my treat. I've been saving up.'

'Oh, Shelley, I can't.'

'You can and you will. Come on,' she said, linking her arm through Mia's. 'I absolutely insist.'

They walked toward the Pump Room together, and Mia felt a little excited by the prospect of eating there. With its beautiful windows, columns, and arches, it was the most refined way to eat out.

Joining a small queue, Mia marveled at the great chandelier that sparkled high above the diners. This was the room used in the 1995 adaptation of *Persuasion*, and Mia could just imagine Anne Elliot and Captain Wentworth there now.

'You're picturing it, aren't you?' Shelley said.

Mia nodded. 'This is where they all used to parade, isn't it?'

'Just imagine all those amazing dresses,' Shelley said, 'and all that fan fluttering. I'm so glad we wore our dresses today, but I do wish we could travel back in time and see it all for real.'

They were shown to their seats and were soon ordering home-made scones with clotted cream and fruit preserves and a pot of tea. Waiters wearing green-and-yellow-striped waistcoats buzzed between tables, and there was a pianist playing soft music above the chatter of the diners.

'Isn't this lovely?' Shelley enthused.

Mia nodded. 'Life should be like this all the time.'

'Yes,' Shelley said. 'Life should be a permanent holiday with sunny weather, Regency costumes, and cream teas.'

Mia laughed.

'It's good to see you smiling,' Shelley said. 'You've not been doing a lot of that since you got here.'

'I'm sorry,' Mia said.

'It's okay,' Shelley said, fingering her napkin. 'Well, it's not okay, actually. It's far from it. I want to know what's bothering you.'

'I know you do.'

'Then why won't you tell me?' Shelley's voice sounded urgent, and she reached out across the table and grabbed Mia's hand. 'I want to try to understand. You seem to have changed.'

'I haven't.'

'Yes, you have,' Shelley insisted. 'You're not the girl I used to share a flat with, the one who always had a sunny smile and a funny quip for every situation. Where's she gone?'

'I don't know what you're talking about. She's right here,' Mia said.

'Then perhaps it's time I wore glasses, because I don't recognize you anymore.'

There was a pause as their waiter returned with the tea and scones.

'I've ruined this now, haven't I?' Shelley said. 'I shouldn't have said anything.'

'Don't be daft,' Mia said. 'You haven't spoiled things.'

For a moment they stopped talking and got on with the serious business of spreading their scones with butter, jam, and cream.

'I shall have to run a marathon to make up for this,' Mia said.

'You're still running then?'

'Of course,' Mia said.

'Where do you go?'

'Just around the streets.'

'I hate to think of you living in London on your own,' Shelley said.

'I'm not on my own,' Mia said.

Shelley frowned. 'What do you mean? You've got a new flatmate?'

Mia paused before answering. 'No, I mean I see my neighbors all the time.'

'Oh,' Shelley said, taking a sip of tea. 'And how's the job going?'

'It's fine,' Mia said. 'I'm doing more hours now.'

'Really? Why?'

'What do you mean, why? To make more money, of course.'

'But what about your auditions? I thought the whole point of a crappy job at a café was so that you could have time to go to auditions.'

'Yes, well, I just have to juggle more things at the moment.'

Shelley put down her cup. 'You *are* still going to auditions, aren't you?'

Mia took a bite of her scone, as if to delay answering the question straightaway.

'Mia?' Shelley persisted.

Mia sighed. 'I haven't had an audition for some time now.'

'Why not? You're still putting yourself forward, aren't you?'

'Not really,' Mia said quietly.

'Mia!' Shelley said, with so much shock in her voice that she caused Mia to drop her knife on the floor.

Bending down to retrieve it, Mia wondered if she could crawl right underneath the table and hide for a while, but she knew that Shelley had to be faced.

Sitting back up in her chair, Mia faced her friend. 'I had a bad experience a while ago.'

'We all have bad experiences. It's part of the business. You can't let it put you off.'

'But it was more than that.'

Shelley paused for a moment, waiting for Mia to continue. 'What happened?' she said at last.

Mia pushed the remains of her scone around on her plate and shrugged. 'I think I just lost my nerve.'

'But that happens to us all. Remember the time when I couldn't even walk out on to the stage? I just turned right round and bolted.'

Mia nodded. 'Yes, but you went to an audition the very next day, and you got the job.'

'But you can do that too.'

'No,' Mia said, and the word sounded so final that Shelley blanched. 'That was my last audition.'

'Can't you just talk about it? Maybe you need to tell somebody about it, and then it'll be okay.'

'I'll tell you what happened, but it won't do any good. I'm never going to walk onto a stage ever again.' Mia drained her teacup.

'Okay,' Shelley said, 'so what happened?'

Mia cast her mind back to the day she'd been trying to forget. It had been an audition for a new musical, and she'd been put forward for one of the main roles. Ordinarily it would have been enough to send her heart rate soaring with excitement, but she turned up at the theater feeling strangely numb.

She remembered the line of girls waiting to audition before her, and they all looked miserable. If they weren't pale with nerves, they were pale with fatigue and from not having eaten properly.

'Why do we do it ourselves?' she asked Shelley now. 'We put ourselves through absolute hell for the merest chance of success. You were sensible. You gave it up ages ago.'

'Yes, but that's because I've never had your drive and determination.'

'Well, I don't seem to have it anymore either. Anyway, I certainly didn't have it that day. I waited my turn. Normally I would have been shaking with anticipation from head to toe, but I was calm. It seemed, for the first time, I knew what I was doing. When my name was called, I walked out onto the stage and nodded at the people in the seats below. I knew the song well. I'd been practicing all week, but when the music started, I opened my mouth, and nothing came out. There was no voice there anymore. It disappeared.'

Shelley put down her teacup with a clatter. 'Where had it gone?'

Mia frowned. 'I don't know, but do you know what? I didn't care. I really didn't care!'

Shelley looked at her as if she were quite mad. 'You weren't worried?'

'No.'

'Or upset?'

Mia shook her head. 'I just couldn't help thinking that there were more important things to do than stand on a stage and sing a song.'

'But you love singing! It's your whole life!'

'Not anymore.'

'I don't understand. How can all that passion have just evaporated?'

Mia swallowed hard. It was the one question she didn't want to answer, but Shelley was looking at her so beseechingly that she wondered whether she should tell her the truth. Surely her friend deserved no less.

'Shelley,' she said. 'I have something to tell you.'

'Yes?' Shelley sat forward in her seat, her eyes wide and her mouth open in anticipation.

'I haven't exactly been honest with you, but I want to tell you now. It's time.' Mia took a deep breath, but then something caught her eye. Standing by the entrance to the Pump Room was a tall, dark-haired man, the man Mia hoped she'd never, ever see again.

Chapter 26

Barton Cottage

'D BETTER NOT COME IN,' ALEC SAID AS THEY REACHED THE garden gate at Barton Cottage. It was dark then, and the only light was the moon, which kept slipping behind the clouds.

'No, perhaps you'd better not,' Mia said, 'although I don't think I'm ready to say good night just yet.'

He smiled at her. 'You are an amazing girl.'

Mia frowned. 'I'm not a girl; I'm a woman.'

'Of course,' he said, reaching out to tuck a long, dark curl behind her ear. 'How could I have made such a mistake?'

'I really don't know,' Mia said coyly. 'Especially after—'

Alec placed a finger on her lips.

'Don't you want me to talk about it?'

'It's not that,' he said, 'but I do think it should be our little secret, don't you?'

Mia smiled. 'You mean not tell Sarah?'

He nodded. 'I don't think she'd be too delighted, do you?'

'No,' Mia admitted, 'although I don't see why she shouldn't be. It's up to me who I'm involved with, isn't it?'

'Of course it is.'

'And she can't expect to tell me what to do for the whole of my life.'

Alec cocked his head to one side. 'Are you saying she warned you against me?'

Mia sighed. 'She was just being her usual overcautious self, that's all.'

'What did she say?'

Mia reached up and stroked his shoulder. 'Does it really matter?'

'I should like to know.'

'Well, I don't remember exactly; she was just moaning on about not knowing you very well, which is ridiculous, because I feel as though I do know you, even though we've been together for only a few days. I tried to explain that to Sarah, but she just doesn't understand these things. You feel the same way though, don't you?'

Alec's gaze seemed to penetrate deep into the garden. 'Yes,' he said at last. 'I feel like I've known you both all my life.'

'Well, Sarah's so stuffy about these things. She thinks you have to be formally introduced by a mutual acquaintance and have known somebody for years before you can even contemplate having a relationship with them.'

'That must make life rather difficult.'

'Exactly. It does. It's why she never sees anyone.'

'But she must have had relationships in the past.'

'Oh, yes, but they've all been complete disasters.'

'Dear Sarah.'

'Yes, poor Sarah. I do feel sorry for her, but she's her own worst enemy.'

They stood in silence for a moment. Mia gazed down toward the estuary, drinking in the beautiful sight of the reflected moon.

She didn't often get to feel like a heroine in a novel, but right then, no author could have improved on the moment, not even Jane Austen.

'I could walk you to the door,' Alec said at last.

'No, Sarah might see.'

'What are you going to tell her about today?' Alec asked as the moon dipped behind a cloud.

'As little as possible.'

'She'll know you've been with me.'

'Yes,' Mia said.

'And you're sure I shouldn't come in with you?'

'Quite sure.'

'Good night then,' he said, bending forward to kiss her cheek.

Mia frowned, grabbing hold of his shoulders and kissing him on the mouth. 'Good night,' she said, watching as he disappeared into the darkness down the lane.

She crossed the lawn, the moon emerging from a bank of clouds to light her way. She'd never known how completely dark the countryside could be. Cities were constantly lit, and it was almost impossible to see the heavens, but at the cottage, they were all-pervading. For a moment, Mia stood in the middle of the lawn, gazing up at the sky above her and feeling that it could swallow her whole at any moment. What if it did? Would she care? She had never felt so at peace in her life. If some mystical force took her away right then, she would have been happy, because she had lived that day fully and beautifully.

Opening the front door, Mia slipped out of her shoes but didn't have time to do anything else before a question was fired at her from the living room.

'Where have you been?'

Mia groaned. It was time to face big sister.

'On the estate. Where do you *think* I've been?'

'With Alec?'

'Well, of course with Alec. There isn't anyone else around here for miles.'

'It's late,' Sarah said. 'I was getting worried about you.'

'But you've been out all day.'

'I've been back for hours. I tried to call you, but your mobile's switched off.'

'Sorry,' Mia said, sitting down on the sofa opposite Sarah. 'But I thought you wanted to get away from me. I didn't think you'd want me ringing you every five minutes. Where have you been, anyway?'

Sarah pursed her lips. 'I told you, I went into Tavistock.'

'And was it nice—Tavistock?'

'It was pretty. I think you would have been bored there.'

'Which is why I stayed here. We can't always be with each other, Sarah.'

'But this week was so that we could do exactly that.'

'We *have* been together. I don't understand what you mean.'

'I mean, you seem to be spending more time with Alec than with me.'

'No, I'm not. Don't be so silly.'

'I'm not being silly. I'm being serious.'

'Well, don't be. There's absolutely no reason to be serious about this. I'm sorry if you think I've been spending more time with Alec, and I'm sorry that you don't trust him.'

'I didn't say that.'

'You don't need to. Your face says it all. You made up your mind not to like him the moment he entered Barton Cottage, and nothing's going to change your mind, is it?'

'I don't dislike Alec. I don't know why you think that.'

'But you don't trust him, do you?' Mia was beginning to sound angry.

'I just think you should slow down with all this. You know you have the naïveté of Catherine Morland and the recklessness of Marianne Dashwood, and that's a lethal combination.'

Mia's mouth dropped open at the Austensian insult. 'Yes, well you have the conservatism of Elinor and the prudishness of Fanny Price, and that's a pain in the arse!'

Sarah's eyes widened. It was like Elizabeth and Darcy in the scene where they both say too much and wound each other almost beyond repair.

Sarah got quickly from the sofa. 'I don't want to fight with you, Mia. I'm going to bed.'

Mia watched as Sarah left the room. She really knew how to spoil a perfect day, but Mia was determined not to let it get to her.

Marianne Dashwood, indeed! She was nothing like her! Okay, so she sometimes let her heart rule her head, but what was wrong with that? She was a passionate person and believed in spontaneity and saying what she thought. Sarah's problem was that she was so shut off and set in her way of thinking and anybody who didn't respond to the world as she did was rash and wild.

As she got up to switch the lamps off in the living room, she looked out the window and across the moonlit lawn. This really was the most perfect place, she thought, and she'd fallen in love there. Life just couldn't get any better.

❦

Sarah had taken hours to get to sleep that night and had given up completely at one point, getting up to read a few chapters of

Sense and Sensibility. It didn't relax her, though, because it was the part where Willoughby was discovered to be a scoundrel, and Marianne's heart was broken.

Alec isn't Willoughby, though, she told herself as she got back into bed. You're just being paranoid.

But he's flirting with both you and Mia!

Yes. No matter which way she looked at it, she couldn't get around that. She wasn't imagining it.

But perhaps that's just his affable personality, and he doesn't mean any harm in it. He's just naturally friendly.

Sarah shook her head. Why didn't she believe that?

Closing her eyes, she imagined herself back on Dartmoor with the wind in her hair and the realization dawning on her that she was in love with this man. It was all so ridiculous. How could she possibly be in love with him, when she'd known him such a short time? She was behaving like Mia—*worse* than Mia, because this went against the very grain of her being. She was a rational woman who was always in control of her life.

But you're not in control now, are you?

Sarah sat up and thumped her pillow. Why couldn't love be rational like everything else? What right did it have to bulldoze through your reasoning and leave you spinning?

She opened her eyes and stared up at the ceiling, knowing that falling in love wasn't the real issue here; it was the fact that Mia was so obviously falling in love as well.

And what are you going to do about that?

It was an impossible situation. Two sisters in love with the same man. How on earth could that have happened?

With so many questions whirling around her head, Sarah didn't manage to get to sleep until after three in the morning. After an appalling nightmare in which both she and Mia were chasing Alec across the tors of Dartmoor, she slept soundly, not waking until nine o'clock, which was horribly late for her, and she spent the rest of the morning trying to catch up with herself.

She was just about to take a book out into the garden when there was a knock on the door. Sarah froze, knowing that it could be only one person. What should she do? Ignore it and hide in the depths of the house?

There was a second knock and then a voice.

'Sarah? It's Alec. I need to talk to you.'

She swallowed. She really didn't want to talk to him. She wanted to banish him from her mind and move on, but it was clear she wasn't going to be able to do that until they left Barton Cottage.

'Come on!' he called through the door, knocking again. 'Let me talk to you.'

She could ignore him no longer, realizing that it would just be postponing the inevitable.

Opening the door, she stared at Alec. 'What do you want?'

'That's not very friendly,' he said, his eyes twinkling mischievously.

'Mia's out. At least I think she's out. Her trainers have gone, anyway. You're very good at timing it for when Mia's out jogging.'

'I saw her go up the lane. I hid behind a tree so she wouldn't see me.'

Sarah gasped at his subterfuge.

'Well, you know what she's like. She'd be linking arms with me and marching me off for the whole of the day, and I wouldn't be able to get to see you.'

'But you're meant to be her friend, not mine,' Sarah said.

'Who says?'

'I do. Mia's the one you met first.'

Alec let out a loud laugh. 'I'm not for sale to the first person who claps eyes on me! I think I should have a say in this, don't you?'

'But I'm busy,' she said, not sounding very convincing, even to her own ears.

'So I see,' Alec said, nodding to the paperback in her hand. 'A busy day of immersing yourself in fiction. You couldn't possibly squeeze in a quick conversation with a real person.'

'That's right,' Sarah said. 'I'm on holiday, and I can do precisely what I want.' She retreated into the house and shut the door in his face. Her heartbeat was racing wildly. She wasn't used to being so rude, but it had seemed the only thing to do.

'Sarah?' he called through the door, banging on it with his hand. '*Sarah!*'

She stood perfectly still for a moment. She couldn't go in either of the front rooms, because the curtains were open, and he would see her.

Stay calm. If you ignore him, he will leave.

The next thing she heard told her that he had no intention of leaving.

'Alec?' She walked through to the sitting room, and her eyes widened in surprise at the sight that greeted her. Alec had taken full advantage of the window Sarah had opened earlier that morning and was in the process of climbing through it.

'What are you doing?' she screamed.

'What does it look like?'

Sarah flapped her hands as Alec pushed his body through the window frame and came tumbling down onto one of the sofas.

'You impossible man!' she cried, but then she laughed at the sight of him crumpled in an ungainly heap among the cushions.

Alec laughed too as he pushed himself back into a shape that vaguely resembled a man. 'I'm nothing if not resourceful,' he said, running a hand through his disheveled hair.

'You should have just knocked again,' Sarah said.

'You mean you would have opened the door?'

'No,' she said.

Alec frowned at her. 'Looks like I had no choice if I wanted to talk to you.' He smiled at her, and it was such a heart-melting sort of a smile that Sarah couldn't remain angry with him. He was like a naughty puppy that would completely wreck a room but then sit in the middle of it looking totally adorable and beyond reproach.

'Won't you listen to me?' he asked her, his eyes pleading.

'I don't know what you can possibly have to say to me.'

'I just want to get a few things straight.'

Sarah sighed and sat down opposite him. She was still holding her book, her fingers tightened around it anxiously, as if she were holding onto a lifebelt.

'Before you begin,' she said, 'I want to say that I don't like what you're up to.'

Alec frowned. 'What exactly am I up to?'

'If this is some weird kind of seduction game of yours, it won't work—not this time.'

'Sarah, I don't know what you're talking about.'

She shook her head. 'I know what you're up to. You're playing me off against my sister, aren't you? Is that how you get your thrills? Have you done this sort of thing before?'

'No!' he said in protest. 'You've got me all wrong.'

'Have I?'

'Yes,' he said, leaning forward, his eyes beseeching her.

'I'm not worried for myself, you understand, but when some-body messes around with my sister—'

'I'm not messing around with Mia.'

Sarah's eyes narrowed at him. 'Because if you try to trick her—'

'I have never tried to trick your sister,' he interrupted again.

'You promise?'

'I promise. But I can't be held responsible if she flings herself at me.'

Sarah shook her head. 'You must understand this about her: she's young and she's recklessly passionate, and it would be wrong to take advantage of that. You do understand me, don't you?'

'Yes, I do,' he said, and he was suddenly on his feet crossing the room toward her. He knelt down in front of her and took her hands in his. The book she had been holding fell to the floor.

'Leave it,' Alec said when she made to retrieve it. 'Listen to me. You can't just shut yourself off from this, Sarah. I know how you feel about me.'

'How do you know? I haven't told you how I feel at all.'

'You don't need to. I can see it in your eyes.'

'That's rubbish,' she said, instantly lowering her gaze.

'No, it isn't. Why do you keep running away from this? What's so wrong about it?'

'It's wrong because of Mia.'

Alec sighed. 'Can we just stop thinking about Mia for one second?'

'No,' Sarah said.

'If Mia didn't exist—'

'But she does exist,' Sarah said in her matter-of-fact way.

'If it were just you and me here, are you telling me I still wouldn't stand a chance with you?'

'There's no point talking like this.'

'No, you're right,' he said, his hands reaching up to cup her face. 'No point in talking at all.'

Sarah gasped at his touch and didn't move when he lowered his lips to hers and kissed her. A few brief moments of bliss followed, but then Sarah broke away. 'I can't do this,' she said. 'It's so wrong.'

'But it isn't. Can't you feel it? This feels right.'

Sarah closed her eyes and he kissed her again, and there was no denying that it felt wonderful, but that didn't make it right, did it? Wonderful things weren't necessarily good for one. Sitting in the sun for hours felt good, but it was likely to leave one with horrible sunburn. Eating a whole tub of chocolate ice cream felt good, but that wasn't good for you either.

'Sarah, admit it. This is meant to be. You know it is.'

She shook her head. 'I… I have to think about this,' she said.

There was the sound of a key scraping in the door. The two of them sprung apart just in time, as Mia ran into the hallway. Her face was flushed from her jog, but Sarah suspected that it wasn't nearly as red as her own face.

Sarah waited for realization to dawn on Mia, feeling quite sure that it would, but it didn't. Mia merely looked from one to the other with an innocent smile on her face when she saw Alec.

'Were you waiting for me?' she asked.

'Yes,' Sarah said. 'Of course he was.'

Chapter 27

'WHAT IS IT?' SHELLEY SAID, HER MOUTH HALF STUFFED WITH scone. Mia didn't respond, but her face had drained of all color, and she was staring into the middle distance as if she'd seen a monster there. Shelley followed her gaze, and her eyes settled on a tall, dark-haired man who was staring right back at Mia.

'Mia?' Shelley tried again, grabbing her friend's hand and squeezing it. At first, Mia didn't seem to respond. There was a brief flicker of something in her eyes, but it passed quickly. She merely got up, slowly and calmly, and walked through the maze of tables and chairs where people were enjoying their afternoon tea.

Shelley watched, spellbound. What was Mia doing? Who was the man?

'Alec?' she whispered to herself. Was this the mysterious Alec Mia refused to talk about? He was certainly handsome, with his dark hair and intense gray eyes, but what was he doing here in Bath?

A few words were exchanged, but Shelley couldn't hear them above the mutterings of the tea crowd. What was being said? It didn't really matter, because of what happened next.

It was as if everything were in slow motion. Shelley watched as Mia's hand rose in the air and slapped the dark-haired man across his cheek. The sound seemed to echo around the Pump Room, and teacups clattered in saucers and the pianist stopped playing. Shelley almost choked on her scone and was on her feet in an instant, as if ready to spring to her friend's defense, but there was no need, and she watched as Mia pushed her way through the sea of tables back toward Shelley.

'Are you okay?' Shelley asked.

Mia sat down, but then stood straight back up again. Her eyes looked glazed and she seemed to be twitching with restlessness.

'Mia, talk to me for goodness sake! Who's that man? Is it Alec?'

Mia didn't respond.

Shelley looked back toward the dark-haired man. 'He's coming over,' she said.

There were a few gasps from the tea crowd as the man pushed his way urgently through the tables and chairs.

'Stay away from me, Alec!' Mia cried.

So it was Alec, Shelley thought.

'I just want to talk,' Alec said.

'Well, I don't want to talk to you!'

'I came all this way, Mia. Please, just listen to me.'

'Get your hands off me!'

One of the waistcoated waiters sidled over to their table. 'I'm sorry, but I'm going to have to ask you to leave,' he said, his tone polite but firm.

Shelley's mouth dropped open in surprise, and she realized that the whole of the Pump Room was watching them.

'But we haven't finished our tea yet,' Shelley said.

'If madam would accompany me.'

Shelley couldn't remember having ever been called madam in her life. She tried to catch Mia's eye, but she was still arguing with Alec as a second waiter did his best to escort them out of the Pump Room.

'My scone!' Shelley suddenly said, doubling back to pick up the scone loaded with jam and cream. There was no way she was going to pay for something she hadn't finished.

By the time she was outside, Mia had vanished into the crowds and Alec was nowhere to be seen either. Where had they gone? Shelley sighed. This isn't what she'd expected when they went for tea in the Pump Room.

∽

Mia ran through the streets of Bath, tears blinding her vision. What was Alec doing in Bath, and why had he sought her out?

She looked back over her shoulder and saw him running after her. He was gaining on her.

'Mia!' he cried. She could hear the anguish in his voice, but she didn't stop running.

I have to get away from him, but where? It was hard to run in a nineteenth-century costume, and she wasn't sure how long she could keep it up. She thought about diving into a shop, but then she would be cornered. An idea occurred to her. The Jane Austen Centre. She could hide in the ladies room there. It was tucked away downstairs and might be the perfect hiding place. Even if he found it, he wouldn't dare follow her in, would he?

Mia picked up her pace as much as she could in her long dress and turned the corner at the end of the road that led to the Jane Austen Centre. If she was quick enough, she could make it inside before he saw where she'd gone.

Charging past a Regency-clad gentleman standing in the doorway, she dashed through the hallway, ignored the shop for the first time in her life, and charged down the stairs to the toilets, thanking her lucky stars that they were empty, because her face was streaming with tears.

She pulled a tissue out of her handbag and did her best to mop up her face. It was then that she saw the portrait of Mr Darcy on the opposite wall. It was a representation of Colin Firth in his famous role and was from one of the most romantic scenes from the 1995 adaptation of *Pride and Prejudice*, the moment where Darcy is watching Elizabeth at the piano and a look of total love fills his face.

Mia gazed at it for a moment. 'Oh, Colin!' she cried. 'What am I going to do?'

Chapter 28

Barton Cottage

'Don't forget your DVD,' Mia said to Sarah from the hallway. 'It's still inside the machine.'

'Of course it's not still inside the machine. I took it out last night,' Sarah said, wondering why Mia still perversely thought that a person with OCD could possibly forget anything. She walked through to the hallway and saw Mia standing in the open doorway, looking out across the lawn to the estuary. It was a perfect May morning. A blackbird's rich song could be heard from the hedge and a light breeze carried the sweet scent of spring.

'I don't want to go,' Mia said as Sarah joined her.

'I'm afraid we have to.'

'Do we? Can't we hide away somewhere on the estate? There are acres and acres. I'm sure we wouldn't be discovered for weeks.'

'What, pitch a tent in the wood somewhere?' Sarah said.

'Why not?'

Sarah laughed, quite sure that Mia was crazy enough to do such a thing.

'Maybe we can come back again,' Mia said.

Sarah nodded.

Half an hour later, the car was packed and Sarah had vacuumed, dusted, and cleaned every surface in the house, even though she didn't need to. Mia had stopped telling her off for such things, having experienced enough holidays with her in the past to know that Sarah couldn't leave a place without making sure it was spick-and-span.

Finally, it was time to leave.

'Wonderful holidays are always laced with sadness, because one knows that they can't last forever,' Mia said as they closed the door of Barton Cottage for the last time.

'That's very poetic,' Sarah said.

Mia sighed. 'It is a bargain we make when we book them. We expect perfection, relaxation, beauty, and inspiration. Only then will we be content to go back to our humdrum lives.'

'Oh, dear,' Sarah said, 'that does sound depressing.'

Mia's face did, indeed, look a little longer than usual. Her eyes weren't quite as sparkly as normal, and her pretty mouth was down-turned as she looked along the path by the estuary.

Suddenly her whole face lit up, and Sarah knew why, without even looking. Alec was there.

'Good morning!' he called up from the path as he picked up speed to join them at the garden gate.

'I thought we'd missed you,' Mia said, running to greet him and flinging her arms around him.

'You didn't think I'd let you go without saying good-bye, did you?'

'Of course not,' Mia said. 'But you nearly missed us!'

'I can't believe you're going. You've only just arrived,' he said, directing the statement at Sarah.

She nodded and looked away.

'I can't believe you've got another whole week here,' Mia said. 'I'm sure there must be room for me in your cottage.' From the tone of her voice, she was joking, but Sarah knew that she was hoping for a last-minute reprieve so that she could stay with Alec.

Alec laughed lightly but didn't offer to let her stay.

'We'd better get going,' Sarah said.

'Then I'd better say good-bye properly,' Alec said. Mia immediately launched herself into his arms and kissed him passionately on the mouth.

'I don't want to go,' she said.

Alec cleared his throat. 'But you have your life in London to go back to.'

She glared at him as if he'd said the worst thing imaginable, but he didn't seem to notice, because he was looking at Sarah.

'Good-bye, Sarah,' he said quietly, moving toward her and kissing her. Sarah took a step back, shocked that he had kissed her on the mouth in front of Mia. 'Keep in touch,' he said.

'Of course we will,' Mia answered.

Sarah didn't say anything but grabbed Mia's hand and dragged her away from Alec before she could launch herself at him again.

'I can't believe he kissed you!' she said. 'I suppose he didn't want you to feel left out.'

'It was just a quick kiss,' Sarah said, feeling herself blush.

'He's a great kisser, isn't he?'

'I—I wasn't really thinking about it.'

'What else could you possibly be thinking about when he was kissing you?'

Sarah panicked. 'I was thinking that we should get going.'

Mia laughed. 'Oh, Sarah! You're the least romantic person I know. It's a good job Alec's fallen for me and not you, isn't it?'

Sarah didn't answer, and the two of them got into the car. Mia instantly fell silent as if the reality of leaving was finally hitting her. She glanced quickly at her sister and could see tears brimming in her bright eyes, and at that moment, she hated Alec. Why did he have to be there that week of all weeks? And why did he have to make them both fall in love with him? He had spoiled everything, and she would never forgive him for it.

Sarah started the engine and drove the car out onto the drive that would lead them to the end of the estate and out into the real world once again. Being at Barton Cottage had been like living in a beautiful, safe bubble, but that bubble had burst, and it was back to normality.

'Ready?' she said to Mia as Alec appeared behind them to wave them off.

She nodded, which caused her tears to spill down her face. Opening her window, she madly flapped a hand out of it.

'Wave to Alec,' she told Sarah, but Sarah chose to ignore her. She merely lifted her eyes briefly to the rearview mirror and saw him standing there. He was looking right at her.

∽

Sarah was very good at getting over the holiday blues. She threw herself into her work, talking to new clients, sorting out accounts, and dealing with the endless muddles people seemed to get themselves into when trying to keep their own books balanced.

She would have worked right through the whole weekend, if it hadn't been for Mia's arrival. She'd popped down on the train from London to get away from a party that was taking place in the flat above hers.

'I don't know what they've got to party about,' she said, taking a sip of tea out of one of Sarah's white china cups, 'but they always seem to be having them, and it always sounds as though my ceiling is about to come down at any moment.'

'Can't you complain to the landlord?'

'He seems to leave town whenever they happen. He's probably got some luxurious country estate to retreat to that his tenants are paying for.'

'I wouldn't be surprised.'

Mia sighed and flopped dramatically into a chair, looking as if she were about to spout a speech from a Shakespearean tragedy.

'It's not just the party,' she said. 'I've had a crappy week. I went for an audition for a dreadful play that I didn't even want to be in, and I didn't even get a callback.'

Sarah frowned. 'Well, isn't that a blessing, if you didn't even want to be in it?'

'That's not the point,' Mia said with a gargantuan sigh. 'But that's not the worst of it. Alec hasn't called me. Don't you think that's strange?'

'It hasn't been that long.'

'Sarah, it's been over two weeks,' she said, twisting around in the chair, her forehead wrinkled in consternation. 'I gave him my number. I gave him *all* my numbers—even my neighbor's number. I thought he would have called by now.'

'Maybe he's been busy. His job's pretty stressful, you know.'

'Did he talk to you about his job?'

Sarah bit her lip. 'Erm—not really. Just, you know… that he's always kept busy.'

'But a phone call doesn't take long, does it? He should have called me by now. It's really mean of him to keep me waiting like this.'

'Do you want another cup of tea?' Sarah asked, escaping into the kitchen. She felt awful because Alec had been calling her every day since they left Devon. At first the calls had been one a day, but the number slowly increased, and just yesterday, he'd called her four times. In fact, she was a little worried that the phone might go whilst Mia was there.

Last night, they'd been on the phone for hours. In fact, Sarah had just started watching the 2005 adaptation of *Pride and Prejudice* when Alec rang, and the film was long finished before they hung up.

How easy it was to talk to him! They never seemed to run out of subjects. Sarah hadn't had such an easy relationship with a man for ages. 'Not ever,' she corrected herself.

'What?' Mia called from the living room.

'Nothing,' Sarah quickly said. 'I'm just talking to myself again.'

Mia appeared in the doorway. 'I've called his home number and his mobile and I've left a message everywhere, but he hasn't called me back. What's going on?'

Sarah hated hearing the pain in her sister's voice, but more than that, she hated hiding the truth from her. She could offer no words of comfort for her sister, because if she did, they would be lies, and she couldn't do that. 'How's your job?' she asked instead.

'Sarah! I don't want to talk about my job. I want to talk about Alec.'

Sarah switched the kettle off and turned her full attention to her sister.

'I can't stop thinking about him,' she said. 'We got on so well. I found it so easy to talk to him, do you know what I mean?'

Sarah nodded, knowing *exactly* what her sister meant.

'It sounds corny, but I really felt like we'd connected, and that doesn't happen very often, does it?'

'No,' Sarah said, 'it doesn't.'

Mia threw her head back and groaned at the ceiling. 'Why are all men so horrible?'

'Not all men are. Just most of them are.'

Mia gave a tiny smile. 'It must be genetic. Perhaps they don't even know they're all horrible.'

'Perhaps.'

'It's so unfair. No matter how hard I search, I always end up with a Wickham or a Willoughby rather than a Darcy or a Wentworth.'

'That's the unwritten law of love,' Sarah said. 'We all have to suffer our share of cads before we find our hero.'

Mia looked at Sarah for what seemed like an age.

'What is it?' Sarah asked.

'I don't know what I have to complain about. I mean, you've never found your hero, have you? And you're so much older than me.'

'Well, thank you, dear sister. I can always rely on your honesty.'

'Oh, you know what I mean.'

'You mean my chance of happiness has long passed, and I'll remain an old spinster like Miss Bates from *Emma*.'

'I don't mean that at all. Oh, I don't know what I mean.'

'I think you mean that you're impossibly impatient and that you expect to fall in love with the perfect man and to find your dream job before you reach the old age of twenty-two.'

'That's not so unreasonable a request, is it?' Mia said with a little laugh.

There was a pause, and Sarah wondered what to say next. Part of her wanted to end the masquerade right there and then, but the other part—the greater part—wanted to keep it a closely guarded secret for as long as possible. It was prolonging the agony, of course, but she was kind of hoping for a miracle to come along. What that miracle was, she had no idea, but she was hoping it would solve the problem of their both being in love with the same man.

Just then, the telephone rang.

'I'll get it,' Mia said, seeing that it was right next to her.

'No, don't!' Sarah said, but it was too late. Mia had lunged for the phone and picked it up.

'Hello?' she said.

Sarah swallowed hard and looked at the clock. Alec had never called this early before, but there was a first time for everything, wasn't there? She watched Mia's expression and saw her frown. Was it Alec? What was he saying to her? How would he explain ringing Sarah? Perhaps he would say that he'd lost Mia's contact details—*all* of them—and was ringing her sister in order to get in touch.

The agonizing seconds ticked by, and finally Mia replaced the phone in its cradle.

'Who was it?' Sarah blurted.

'I don't know,' Mia said. 'It was all silent, and then they hung up.'

Sarah breathed a sigh of relief. Her secret was safe—for now.

Chapter 29

WHERE HAD SHE GONE? SHELLEY HAD RUN DOWN MORE streets than her dainty shoes were really capable of and was standing in front of the Pump Room again. She'd tried ringing Mia's mobile, but it was obviously switched off, and Shelley had been forced to leave an angst-ridden message for her.

'If only she told me what was going on,' she said quietly to herself. 'I might have been able to help.'

How could you possibly have helped? a little voice inside her asked.

'I don't know,' Shelley said. 'Perhaps I could have slapped Alec too!'

She certainly wanted to slap him now for having scared her friend off like that. What was she going to do?

She dialed a number on her mobile and waited.

'Pie? It's Shelley. Is Mia there? Are you sure? Have you looked upstairs? I don't mind waiting. This is important.' Shelley sighed as she listened to the huff, puff of Pie walking up the stairs. 'Oh,' she said a moment later. 'Well, if she comes back before me, tell her to give me a call, okay?'

Shelley tried a different number. 'Gabe? It's Shelley. Is Mia with you? Yes, something is wrong, except I'm not quite sure what.'

Mia knew that she couldn't hide in the ladies toilets in the Jane Austen Centre forever, no matter how kindly Mr Darcy was looking after her. Splashing her red face with cold water, she looked at her reflection in the mirror. She could handle this. What was she getting so worked up for? Hadn't she'd moved on from this ages ago? If so, why had she responded the way she had?

It was just the shock of seeing him again, she told herself. It had brought everything all back to her. She hadn't been prepared; she'd just been enjoying tea and scones. She hadn't expected her past to walk in on her like that.

Venturing forth from the restroom, Mia slowly walked back up the stairs, passing the gift shop before braving the great outdoors once again. She paused on the steps beside the Regency gentleman who nodded at her as she looked up and down Gay Street. A good number of people were around, but luckily she could see no sign of Alec. Taking a deep breath, she turned right, walked up the street that had once been home to Jane Austen, and entered the splendor of The Circus.

She needed to walk. She couldn't go back and face Shelley just yet. She had to think things through.

You knew this was going to happen, a little voice inside her said. *You're going to have to face this properly sooner or later.*

'I know. But can't it be *later*?' she whispered.

She followed the curve of The Circus around to the right, aware that the sun had disappeared behind thick, dark clouds and that the temperature had dropped. Mia wished that she were wearing jeans and a proper coat rather than her flimsy Regency gown and shawl, which were no protection against the autumn elements.

She entered Brock Street. It was an impressive street lined with beautiful three-story Georgian houses and linked The Circus to The Royal Crescent, but it was often overlooked by tourists en route from one place to the other. Mia had a vague idea of where she was going, knowing there were benches by the green that overlooked The Royal Crescent. Perhaps she could sit there for a while and gather her thoughts.

She didn't get that far. As soon as she entered The Royal Crescent, she saw him. He was standing by the railings, shielding his eyes as if that might help him in his search for her.

Mia stood frozen for a moment, not knowing what to do, and in that instant, he spotted her.

'*Mia!*' he shouted, causing a group of tourists to turn around.

Mia turned and ran but, despite her years of jogging, she knew she couldn't outrun Alec, not when wearing such a restricting dress. How on earth had heroines managed to outrun heroes in Jane Austen's time? she wondered briefly. Not that you'd want to outrun most of them, she thought, but it wasn't Mr Darcy or Henry Tilney who was chasing her; it was Alec.

Chapter 30

'Y ou shouldn't have rung me so early,' Sarah told Alec as he entered her house.

'How was I to know Mia would answer the phone?' he said. 'Anyway, don't you think it's time we told her?'

'No.'

'You've got to face it sometime.'

'Why?'

'Because I want the whole world to know how I feel about you, Sarah.'

Sarah walked away from him. This was all happening too fast, she thought, and her head was spinning. Everything was new and strange. She wasn't used to being in a relationship, and she certainly wasn't used to having a man in her house. She watched as Alec paced the front room. He didn't really look at home there, and she felt anxious about the possibility that he might want to move in with her; however, *not* having him there was equally scary.

'Everything's so neat,' he suddenly said.

Sarah swallowed hard and nodded. This was usually the deal breaker. Once he realized what she was like, he'd run a mile.

'You don't mind?' she asked tentatively.

'No, I like it,' he said.

Sarah smiled, relief filling her.

'I could do with a bit of organization in my life,' he said.

'Could you?'

'Yes,' he said, moving toward her. 'And I think you're just the woman for the job.'

Before she could respond, he was kissing her, and all thoughts of incompatibility vanished. How easily our worries fade when we're being kissed, Sarah thought. She was no longer thinking about the fact that she'd never seen Alec's own house and didn't know how tidy he was; neither was she thinking about her sister and the problem still lurking out there in the future that would have to be faced.

At least she wasn't thinking about those things until they stopped kissing. Then, all her worries and concerns flooded her mind once more. 'This is all wrong,' she said.

'Why? Tell me why.'

'Because you're meant to be in love with Mia.'

'Why?' Alec said, his forehead etched with bemusement.

'Because she's the one who met you, and she cares for you so much.'

'Mia's a child,' he said. 'You're the one I love. *You*, Sarah. And I want you to tell me that you feel the same way, because I know you do.'

Sarah shook her head. 'This shouldn't be happening.'

'Stop punishing yourself! Why won't you let yourself have a bit of fun?'

'Because it will be at the expense of my sister.'

'She'll get over it. She's a grown woman, for goodness' sake.'

'But it's my job to protect her.'

'Why?'

'Because I always have.'

Alec groaned and flopped down into a chair. 'Do you want to be with me or not?'

Sarah sat down next to him and picked up his hands gently. 'Of *course* I want to. There isn't anything else that I want more.'

'Well, then,' Alec said simply.

'We have to tell Mia.'

Alec shook his head. 'No. *You* have to tell Mia.'

Sarah closed her eyes, knowing he was right. 'Okay,' she said.

'You're going to tell her?'

'Yes.'

'When?'

'I don't know.'

'Do it tomorrow. Don't put it off. Just get it over and done with.'

She nodded.

'She needs to know if she's going to have a brother-in-law.'

Sarah's eyes widened, and Alec smiled at her before reaching into his pocket for a small blue box. He handed it to Sarah. 'Open it!' he said.

Sarah's fingers were shaking as she opened it up, and tears welled up in her eyes when she saw the diamond solitaire, perfect in its simplicity.

Alec took it out and placed it on her ring finger. 'You're shaking, Mrs Burrows.'

'Kiss me,' she said, so he did, and it was the first time in Sarah's life that she wasn't worried about a man wearing shoes in the front room.

Her happiness was short-lived, however, because she knew she had to tell Mia. She might have been able to hide an affair from her sister, but she couldn't hide a marriage.

'Just get it over and done with.' Alec's words echoed through her brain. He'd made it sound so simple and easy, but she knew it would be the hardest thing she should ever have to do.

How was Mia going to respond? Would she realize that Alec and Sarah were the better match and that it had been wrong of her to think she had a future with him? She'd be absolutely delighted with the news, and Sarah would be flabbergasted at Mia's offer to be her bridesmaid.

She shook her head. That wasn't going to happen, was it? It would most likely end in carnage with faces being slapped and noses being punched.

Picking up the phone later that evening, Sarah rang her sister's mobile.

'I'm coming into town tomorrow. Do you want to meet me for lunch? It's my treat.'

'Oh, dear. I was so looking forward to the moldy lettuce in my fridge,' Mia said. 'Of course I'll come to lunch. I love it when my rich sister treats me.'

'You'll be on time, won't you?'

'I'm always on time.'

'No, you're not. You're always late.'

'Early, late—what's the difference?'

'Be on time, Mia.'

Sarah heard her sister laugh. 'All right,' Mia said. 'What's all this about? Have you met someone?'

'We'll talk tomorrow.'

'You *have* met someone, haven't you?' Mia said. 'Oh, tell me about him! What's he called?'

'I've got to go.'

Mia laughed again. 'Rather talk to a row of numbers than your sister?' she teased.

'I'll see you tomorrow.'

Tomorrow always comes much faster when you're dreading it. Holidays take an absolute age to come around, but deadlines and days for breaking bad news rush in upon one.

Sarah left for London first thing in the morning, even though she didn't need to. She simply couldn't stay at home, so she walked the entire length of Oxford Street, Regent's Street, and then down Piccadilly before finding a bench in Green Park. It was a warm May morning, and the park was full of bare-armed tourists. Sarah sat watching them for a while, wondering if they were about to have lunch with sisters they had betrayed in the worst manner possible.

By the time she reached the restaurant, she was a nervous wreck, not that she was very good at relaxing at the best of times— somebody with OCD never really relaxed—but that day was worse. Having rushed itself upon her, time seemed to have slowed down now, and the hands on the clock were creeping at an intolerably slow pace.

Sarah had chosen a table at the back of the restaurant in the little corner that she hoped was private enough to tell Mia the truth. She sat perfectly still, a glass of water between her hands, as she watched the restaurant slowly filling up. Lucky, lucky people, she thought. They were here for nothing more than a lovely lunch. Did they realize how blessed they were?

Finally Mia arrived. As ever, she was late, and, as ever, she was full of apologies and excuses.

'You wouldn't believe the trouble I had on the tube! Honestly, whichever line I got on, there seemed to be essential maintenance works, signal failures, or some trespasser on the line intent on ruining everybody's day. But I'm here now,' she said, pulling out a chair and flopping into it.

'Yes,' Sarah said.

'You look nice,' Mia said. 'Is that a new dress?'

'Oh. Yes,' Sarah said. 'I suppose.'

'What do you think of this?' Mia said, getting up and giving a theatrical twirl in the middle of the restaurant to show off her new skirt. 'I found it in a charity shop. Isn't it marvelous?'

'It's very short.'

'Of course it is. It's a skirt, and I'm not an old woman yet, although you'd have me dress as one.'

'Look, I didn't ask you here to talk about clothes.'

Mia blanched at her sister's words and sat down again.

Sarah swallowed. 'I'm sorry,' she said. 'It's just, I want to talk to you.'

'I know. You said. So what's all this about? Is it about a man?' Mia asked, leaning forward conspiratorially.

'Yes,' Sarah said. 'It is.'

'Well, I'm listening.'

Sarah began fiddling with her cutlery. 'I really don't know how to tell you this, so I'm just going to say it.' She swallowed and took a deep breath. 'I'm in love with Alec.'

Silence filled the space between them, and neither of them spoke for a moment. Then Mia smiled. 'Is this a joke?' she said with a little giggle. 'I didn't know you told jokes. Is this a new Sarah? I rather like it.'

'I'm not telling a joke, Mia.'

Mia's smile faded slowly and was quickly replaced with a frown. 'But I don't understand. You're *in love* with Alec?'

'Yes,' Sarah said in a tiny voice.

There was another long, drawn-out silence between them, and then Mia spoke. 'But I thought—I thought he loved me. It was me he was talking to all the time at Barton Cottage. You didn't spend any time with him at all.' She spoke the words as if talking to herself, as if trying to work things out in her own mind. 'You don't even like Alec,' she added, looking up at Sarah once again.

'That's not true. It never was true. Only you thought I never liked him. I was simply trying to hide my feelings from you, because I knew they were wrong, and I knew how much you liked him.'

'Okay,' Mia said slowly, her hands hovering over the table as if she could control the situation that way. 'Let's get things into perspective here. You're in love with Alec. And I'm in love with Alec.'

Sarah nodded.

'So we've got a bit of a problem here,' Mia continued. 'Although,' she said with a little laugh, 'I'm not really sure we can do anything about it seeing as he's not bothered to call or see us since Devon.'

Sarah grimaced.

'What?' Mia asked.

'That's not quite true.'

'What isn't quite true?'

'That he hasn't called us,' Sarah said.

'What do you mean? He hasn't called me once, and I've left no end of messages for him.'

'I mean, he's called me,' Sarah said.

'Did he lose my number?' Mia asked, confused.

'No, he hasn't lost your number.'

'Then why hasn't he called me?' Mia asked. 'This is all too confusing. What's going on?'

'I'm trying to tell you.'

'You're scaring me, Sarah.'

'I don't mean to scare you,' Sarah said, grabbing her sister's hands and holding them tightly. 'Just listen to me for a moment.'

'Okay,' Mia said. 'I'm listening.'

Sarah took a deep breath. 'Alec and I have been talking every day since we came back from Devon. I told him a thousand times that it shouldn't be happening, but it has happened—it *is* happening—and there isn't a lot I can do to stop it, even though I've tried. I've *really* tried.'

'What's happening? For goodness' sake, just tell me!'

'He's asked me to marry him,' Sarah blurted out.

Mia sat stunned for a moment, and then she slowly withdrew her hands from Sarah's. 'What?'

'Alec asked me to marry him, and I said yes.'

'Alec? Asked you?'

Sarah nodded.

'When?'

'Yesterday.'

'Why didn't you tell me?'

'I am telling you.'

Mia shook her head. 'No! Why didn't you tell me that all this has been going on? I've been waiting for him to call me, Sarah. You knew that, but instead, he's been talking to you!'

'I didn't know what do for the best. I kept putting off telling you, because I thought it might all just go away. I didn't want things to turn out like this. I didn't think they *would*.'

Mia's eyes filled with tears. 'How could you do this to me, when you knew how I felt about him?'

'I didn't want it to happen,' Sarah said, desperation in her voice. 'You've got to believe me. I tried to stop it so many times, but you've got to try to understand how I feel. I've never felt like this before in my life.'

'But—' Mia stopped.

'What?'

'I—I—'

Sarah leaned across the table, but Mia pushed her chair out from behind her and stood up and her face hardened suddenly. 'You've told me what you came here to tell me.'

'Mia—sit down. Let's talk about this properly.'

'I've got to go.'

Before Sarah could stop her, Mia left the restaurant. Sarah ran after her.

'Mia! Please!' she shouted.

Mia had vanished, though, and Sarah knew she had lost her.

Chapter 31

*M*IA!' Alec's voice cut through the noise of tourists and traffic in Bath.

Mia kept running, not daring to turn around to see how close he was.

'Mia, *please*!'

She wasn't listening to him. She would shut him out from her mind and just keep running, as if she were running somewhere else, anywhere else. But where could she go? Back to the Jane Austen Centre toilets? She knew she wouldn't be able to make it in time, because he was gaining on her.

Suddenly an arm grabbed her from behind.

'Mia!' he rasped, his chest heaving with the efforts of his running. He seemed out of shape. Perhaps he'd stopped running since becoming an old married man, she thought. 'Why didn't you stop? You heard me shouting.'

Mia shook his hand off her arm, but she didn't reply.

'Talk to me!' he said. 'Sweetheart!'

'Don't call me that. You have no right to call me that!'

'Finally… a response,' he said with a laugh.

'I've already given you my response in the Pump Room,' Mia said.

'Yes, and my face is still stinging,' Alec said. 'But I daresay I probably deserved it.'

Mia stared at him. 'You *probably* deserved it? You made me fall in love with you, and then you married my sister!'

Alec held up his hands as if in defense. 'I know, I know. And I can't tell you how sorry I am for that. It's what I need to talk to you about now. Mia, listen—'

Just then the heavens darkened and it started to rain, great fat drops turning the pavements slick and wet in a matter of seconds. Alec grabbed Mia's arm and propelled her toward a covered porch that was filled with the first leaves of autumn.

'Will you stop manhandling me?' she cried out.

'I didn't want you to get wet,' he said, looking down at her white dress. 'Is that a paw print on your shoulder?' He reached out to touch it, but Mia was too quick for him and moved away, covering up the offending paw print with her shawl.

'Alec, what are you doing here?' Mia demanded.

'I remembered you liked Jane Austen. You said you used to come to the festival, so I thought I'd find you here. Wasn't that clever of me?'

Mia frowned. It was as if he wanted to be congratulated for having found her.

'I need to talk to you,' he said, obviously realizing that he'd receive no praise from her.

'You have nothing to say that I want to hear,' Mia said.

'How can you say that?' Alec asked. 'After all that's happened between us, don't you want to talk about it at all?'

'You got me thrown out of the Bath Pump Room, for goodness' sake! What on earth would Jane Austen think of such a thing?'

Alec laughed. 'Now there's the Mia I remember! You always were able to make me laugh.'

'I wasn't put on this planet for your entertainment,' Mia said. Her eyes narrowed in fury and her fingers itched to slap him again.

'I know, I know,' he said. 'But... God, I've missed you. I've missed you so much. You don't know how often I think about our days together in Devon and how stupid I was to have messed everything up.'

'You used me.'

'That's not fair,' Alec said. 'You wanted to be used.'

'I didn't want to be used. I wanted to be *loved*.'

Alec sighed. 'Look—'

'What did I ever see in you?' Mia interrupted. 'I'm really trying to think now.'

'You saw something special, just as I did in you, although I foolishly chose to look away.'

'You chose to look at my sister,' Mia cried.

'Yes,' he said, looking at the ground and at least having the decency to look ashamed for a moment. 'And I regret it so much. I can't say what I was thinking of, except that I wasn't thinking properly at all. It was just something about her—I don't know—but what I do know now is that it was fleeting. It didn't last. But *we* had something special.'

'No,' Mia said, shaking her head.

'Yes, we did, except I couldn't see it at the time. What can I say? I made a huge, huge mistake, Mia. I was never meant to be with Sarah.' He shook his head. 'You just don't understand how difficult she can be,' Alec said. 'I mean, the woman is nuts! She drove me mad, Mia! I've never known anyone like her in my life.'

'I don't want to hear this, Alec.'

'One morning, when we were in bed—'

'Alec, don't!'

'I thought things were—you know—getting romantic,' he continued, unabashed, 'and she jumped out of bed to straighten a bloody curtain. I mean, that's not normal behavior, is it?'

'It's normal for Sarah,' Mia said. 'You must've known about her OCD!'

'Yes, but I didn't realize it affected absolutely everything she does. She can't even leave the house without a crazy long list of things to do, and everything's got to be immaculate all the time. It's just madness, and I couldn't stand it any longer. She's so different from you, Mia. She's so—so tightly wound. Not like you. You're so free. I don't know how I didn't see it before.'

'You mustn't talk to me like this. You're married to Sarah, not me. It's her you should be talking to. You should be trying to work things out with her, not running back to me when you hit your first problem.'

'But it's you I love.'

'How can you say that?'

'Because it's true.'

'No, it isn't.'

'How can you be so sure about that?'

'Because I've changed. I'm not the girl you met down in Devon.'

He looked puzzled for a moment. 'I can't believe you'd ever change. You'll always be the delightful young woman I met on holiday.'

Mia shook her head. 'You don't know me. You might think you do, but you don't.'

'Well, then let me get to know you all over again. We can do things right this time. I know I messed up. I should never have let you out of my sight, but I'm only human. I make mistakes.'

'Listen to yourself,' Mia said. 'Don't you realize how ridiculous you sound? You married my sister, and yet you make it sound like you did nothing more than flirt with somebody. I might have been able to forgive you if you just flirted with Sarah a little, but you *married* her. Does that mean nothing to you? Did you think, well, if it doesn't work out, I can always go back to the other sister?'

'No,' he said. 'I didn't think that at all.'

'Because I'm not a consolation prize, Alec.'

'I never thought of you like that. God! You're not listening to me. I love you! I made a huge mistake, and I want to put things right.'

She looked at him, and for the briefest of moments, almost felt sorry for him. He looked exhausted, as if he'd not slept for a week. His dark hair was disheveled, and his eyes were red. What had been happening between him and Sarah? How long had they been separated? She was tempted to ask, but she didn't want to talk to the man. He had broken her heart.

'We had something special, Mia,' he said. 'You can't just throw that away.'

Her eyes widened. '*I* didn't throw it away; you did.'

'I know,' he said, 'and I've paid the price ever since.' He sighed, and they were silent for a moment, the sound of the rain pattering on the pavements. In any other circumstances, Mia thought, sheltering from the rain with a handsome man in a Georgian porch whilst wearing her favorite Regency gown would be wildly romantic. Instead she was itching to get away. Everything inside her was telling her to go.

'Mia,' Alec whispered, daring to take a step closer to her, 'you're the most amazing girl I've ever met. That week we had together was magical, and I've never stopped thinking about it. It's what got me through some pretty rough times recently. I've wanted to talk to you for so long, and I thought you'd understand why things haven't worked out with Sarah and me. I know how you must feel about everything, and I know you can probably never forgive Sarah, but can't you find a little place in your heart for me?'

Mia looked at him, not quite knowing how to respond to such a declaration.

'You think I'd forgive you but not my own *sister*?'

'Well, come on, Mia, you've not spoken to her for over three years.'

'And that's my business. It has nothing to do with you.'

'Oh, really? Nothing to do with me?'

'You know what I mean,' she cried.

'So you're going to forgive Sarah too?'

'I didn't say that, and I certainly didn't say I was going to forgive you. I don't even want to talk to you. This shouldn't be happening, Alec. Please, just leave me alone.'

Mia left the shelter of the porch.

'Mia, don't go!' Alec said, running after her. 'I came all this way to see you. I had to take time off work.'

'I didn't ask you to,' Mia said without looking back.

'I wasn't blaming you,' he said quickly. 'Sorry, I shouldn't have said that.'

'That's your problem, Alec,' Mia said, stopping briefly to look back at him. 'You say and do these things without any thought.'

'But I'm thinking now. I can't stop thinking about you.'

'But it's too late, Alec. It's much too late.'

Mia started to run, and this time, she didn't look back. She would rather run through the streets in the rain than stay for a moment longer in that man's company. She couldn't believe the nerve of him. First, he'd made love to her, then he'd married her sister, and now he expected to be able to win her back. What was going on in that head of his? Did he really think that she'd allow him back into her heart so easily?

She could hear him running behind her, but she was determined to lose him once and for all, this time. Just then, a double-decker bus pulled up in front of her, one of the tour buses that toured the city, and if she was quick enough, she could jump onto it.

She dared to look back behind her and saw Alec hopping in rage as he had to wait for traffic before crossing a road. Mia got on the bus, paid for a ticket, and sat down next to a white-haired woman.

'My dear,' the lady exclaimed. 'How wet you are!'

'Yes,' Mia said. 'I'm afraid I am.' She laughed as the bus pulled away.

'What's so funny?' the woman asked.

Mia nodded toward the window, and the woman turned to see a dark-haired man running alongside the bus.

'Is he with you?'

'No,' Mia said. 'He most certainly is not with me.'

Chapter 32

W HEN THE RAIN STARTED, SARAH AND LLOYD WERE JUST coming out of the abbey.

'I love rain in cities,' Lloyd said, getting his camera out again. 'I love the reflections in the pavements and the jostle of umbrellas.'

Sarah nodded, but she wasn't really listening. 'I'm divorced,' she suddenly blurted.

'What?' Lloyd looked at her, a surprised expression on his face.

She looked up at him and gave a tiny smile. 'It seems so strange to say that. I guess I'm still getting used to it.'

'Were you married long?'

She shook her head. 'Not long at all. It was all a terrible mistake, and I'll never forgive myself for it.'

'But surely you weren't to know at the time.'

'I should have known. Everything was pointing it out to me and yet, like a fool, I went ahead anyway. I've never done anything so rash in my life.'

'Do you keep in touch with him?'

Sarah gave a little laugh. 'No,' she said. 'It was the man I was telling you about, the one my sister was in love with.'

'Ah!' he said. 'I see.'

They stood for a moment in the shelter of the abbey, wondering whether to venture out into the rain.

'I still can't believe it,' Sarah said. 'I used to think that I'd never ever get married—I just wasn't that type of person. I'm far too… complicated. I didn't think anyone would want to bother.' She laughed. 'But Alec did, and it took me so much by surprise that I said yes without thinking about anything else. I mean, I thought about my sister—of course I did—but I just got so swept along by the idea of somebody loving me enough to want to spend the rest of his life with me that everything else seemed unimportant.'

'Does your sister know you're divorced?' Lloyd asked.

Sarah shook her head. 'We haven't spoken for years, not since I told her I was engaged. I tried hard to reach her, but she moved house and changed jobs, and I couldn't trace her.' There were tears in Sarah's eyes, and Lloyd reached out a hand and squeezed her shoulder.

'You're both Jane Austen fans, aren't you?'

Sarah nodded.

'Then she might be here in Bath.'

'I'd thought of that,' Sarah said. 'There's a part of me that is praying that she's here somewhere. I so long to talk to her, but another part of me is dreading seeing her again. I keep looking out for her. I've imagined seeing her a dozen times already since I've been here. It's driving me mad.'

'Surely we can find out if she's here,' Lloyd said.

'How?'

He looked thoughtful for a moment. 'Well, where's she likely to stay?'

'I don't know. Somewhere cheap. She never did have very much money.'

Lloyd pursed his lips. 'That doesn't really narrow things down, does it? What about the events? Do you know which ones she's likely to attend?'

'She usually loves anything involving dancing,' Sarah said.

'Okay, well, let's have a look at the program.'

Sarah took the festival program out of her handbag and scanned the events. 'There's a dance demonstration tonight.'

'Have you got a ticket for it?'

'Yes,' Sarah said, and then she swallowed. 'Do you think Mia will really be there?'

'If she's in Bath, there's a very good chance she could be, isn't there?'

Sarah took a deep breath and then slowly exhaled. 'I guess there is,' she said.

⁓

Mia knew that she couldn't sit on the tour bus forever. For a start, she was still soaking wet and was beginning to get funny looks from the other passengers. Then there was the fact that it kept going around in circles, and Alec could leap onto it at any moment, so at the next stop, she hopped off.

It was still raining, but she wasn't thinking about the weather as she walked down a street she didn't recognize. She managed to calm down a little on the bus, because the sweet woman sitting next to her had talked almost nonstop, which had helped Mia to take her mind off things for a little while.

'A girl like you shouldn't be having problems in love,' the woman had said when Mia confessed that she'd been running away from the dark-haired man. 'Why, you're so young and beautiful! You should be attracting the very best of young men.'

Mia had blushed. 'That's very sweet of you, but I'm afraid I just seem to be attracting rogues!'

'Then you must keep looking until you find the right man. Isn't that what Jane Austen tells us?'

'You're a Jane Austen fan too?'

'Of course. That's why I'm here in Bath,' she said, a big smile lighting up her sweet face. 'Ah!' she said a moment later. 'This is my stop. I'm afraid I have to leave you. Will you be all right?'

Mia assured her that she would be fine.

'Oh, how very rude of me—I didn't introduce myself. I'm Doris Norris,' she said, shaking Mia's hand. Mia smiled at the funny name.

'I know,' Doris said. 'My name always makes people smile, but that's nice, don't you think?'

Mia did, indeed, think it was nice, and she'd been sorry to lose her company.

Now she felt horribly alone, and nothing could stop her thoughts from crowding in on her. Foremost was the fact that Alec had never really been in love with Sarah at all, or if he had, it had been so fleeting an emotion as to be almost nonexistent. Mia was quite sure that he'd made no effort to understand Sarah, and that just wasn't fair.

Mia had many emotions flooding through her. Although she hadn't spoken to Sarah for years, she couldn't help siding with her, and even though her sister had betrayed her in the worst possible way, she still felt sad that her marriage was over.

Like Sarah herself, Mia had always found it hard to imagine her sister getting married. It wasn't that she wasn't lovable, only that she needed to be understood for the person that she was. It would take a loving, patient, and kind man to live with Sarah for the rest of her life, and Alec obviously wasn't that man.

'He wasn't right for either of us,' she whispered to herself, 'and yet we both thought he was perfect.' She looked up and down the street, anxious that just thinking about him would conjure him up before her.

'Mia!'

Mia stopped. Someone had called her name.

'It's not Alec,' she told herself, but her heart was still racing as she tried to locate the owner of the voice.

'Mia!' it called again.

'Gabe?' she said, spotting him leaning out of a taxi window on the other side of the road.

'Come on and get inside!' he called.

She crossed the road and hopped into the back of the taxi, her dress clinging around her legs and her hair plastered to her face.

'What on earth happened to you?'

'I got caught in the rain.'

'So I see.' Gabe unbuckled his seat belt and took off his jacket, handing it to Mia.

'Oh, you don't need to do that,' she said.

'It's no problem. I'm not even wearing it properly,' he said, motioning to his sling.

'But it'll get all wet,' she said.

'That's okay, just put it on. We don't want you getting a chill.'

'Isn't that an old wives' tale?'

'I don't care if it is,' Gabe said. 'I'm not taking any risks.'

The taxi pulled out and joined the Bath traffic.

'Where were you going?' Mia asked a moment later. 'I mean, when you saw me.'

'To find you,' Gabe said. 'Shelley called round. I've never seen her so worried.'

'Oh,' Mia said, remembering that she'd left her friend hours before and hadn't even bothered to ring her to tell her what was going on.

'Are you okay?'

'Of course I'm okay,' Mia snapped. 'I don't need to be rescued. I'm not some feeble heroine.'

'I know,' Gabe said calmly. 'So are you going to tell me what's been happening?'

'Nothing's been happening.'

'Well, something's obviously happened. Shelley said you slapped some man in the Pump Room.'

'I don't want to talk about it.' She turned to stare out the taxi window and bit her bottom lip to stop it from trembling. She was *not* going to cry!

'It might do you some good if you talk about it,' Gabe said.

'It won't.'

'Okay,' Gabe said with a sigh.

They sat in silence as the taxi drove through the wet streets before crossing the river and heading up the hill toward Shelley's.

'I've been reading *Northanger Abbey*,' Gabe said.

'You've got a copy already?'

'I'm reading it on my Kindle,' he said.

'Oh, I don't like those. A book should be something you can feel in your hands. You should be able to smell it and hear the pages turn.'

'Yes, but there weren't any bookshops open late last night,' he said.

Mia sniffed. 'Well, I still don't approve.'

'But you should. Surely anything that makes books more accessible is a good thing.'

'But a book is a physical thing. It should be held, and then it should be placed lovingly on a shelf where you can see it, not switched off like an emotionless computer.'

'Well, I love books too, but I think there's room in the world for new technology too,' Gabe said. 'Anyway, what I was trying to say to you was that as I was reading, I kept imagining you as Catherine Morland.'

'Catherine Morland?' Mia said in horror. '*Me?* But she's so naive and—well—not very intelligent.'

'I didn't mean *that* side of her,' Gabe said quickly. 'I meant the liveliness of her, her love of life, and her passion for books. It reminded me of you.'

'Oh,' Mia said.

The taxi pulled up outside Shelley's house, and Gabe leaned forward to pay the driver before struggling to open the door and get out with his bandaged arm.

'I'm not like Catherine Morland, you know,' Mia said when she joined him on the pavement.

'Okay,' Gabe said. 'You're not like Catherine Morland.'

They stood awkwardly for a moment before Mia spoke again. 'I'm sorry I sounded so cross in the taxi. It's been a rather unusual day.'

'You don't need to explain.'

'But I do. I don't want you thinking I'm rude. I'm not. I'm just—'

'Unhappy?' Gabe suggested.

Mia nodded.

'Listen,' he said, 'if you ever need anyone to talk to—'

He didn't get a chance to finish what he was about to say, because Shelley came bounding out of the house with Bingley tearing after her.

'Mia! I was so worried about you! Where have you been all this time? Oh, you're soaked to the skin. Just like Jane in *Pride and*

Prejudice when Mrs Bennet made her ride over to Netherfield in the rain.'

'I'm fine,' Mia said. 'And I'm *not* just like Jane Bennet *or* Catherine Morland!'

Shelley looked confused. 'What happened? The last thing I saw was Alec pursuing you through the streets. Did he catch you?'

'So to speak.'

'Well, what did he say?'

'Don't you think you should get Mia inside, Shelley?' Gabe said. 'I think she could do with some dry clothes and a hot drink.'

'Oh, yes, of course,' Shelley said, ushering her friend indoors, followed by Bingley, whose nose was finding the wet folds of Mia's dress most interesting.

'I hope you thanked Gabe,' Shelley said, once the door was closed. 'He was in the middle of a heap of work when I interrupted him, and he dropped everything to try to find you.'

Mia bit her lip. She hadn't thanked him, had she? She'd been rude and ungrateful, and she wouldn't be surprised if he wanted nothing more to do with her.

'Why didn't *you* come to find me?' Mia asked. 'Why send Gabe?'

Shelley looked shifty, but then replied, 'I couldn't leave Bingley. He was in a funny mood and looked like he might wreck something. Anyway, I thought it best if I stayed here in case you came back.'

Mia wasn't convinced by her argument but didn't have time to challenge it, as Shelley bustled her up the stairs to get changed.

'Why don't you have a warm bath, and I'll get you a cup of tea?'

It sounded like bliss. Mia nodded. 'I think I'm just going to write off today and curl up with a book,' she said.

Shelley looked horrified. 'You can't do that! We've booked to go dancing tonight. We can't miss it.'

'But just look at the state of my dress,' Mia complained.

'That's okay. I've got my old one from last year. You can wear it. I put a new ribbon on it, and it looks as good as new.'

'Oh, Shelley, I really don't know if I'm in the mood for dancing.'

She tutted. 'You sound just like Mr Darcy at the Meryton ball. Of *course* you're in the mood for dancing, or you will be once you get there. You know you will be. "There is nothing like dancing after all,"' Shelley said with a big grin, and then she disappeared downstairs before Mia had the chance to think up another excuse.

Closing her bedroom door, Mia got undressed quickly, her pretty white gown lying in a sodden heap on the carpet. She felt completely drained—physically, emotionally, and every way that it was possible to be drained. She could quite happily hide herself away under the duvet, but perhaps Shelley was right. If she stayed in, she'd only mope and dwell on things, wouldn't she? And that never did anyone any good. Perhaps dancing would cheer her up.

She nodded to herself, determined that she would approach dancing in the manner of Mr Bingley rather than Mr Darcy.

Chapter 33

THE BAROQUE DANCE DISPLAY WAS BEING PERFORMED AT THE Chapel Arts Centre, and the seats were filling up by the time Sarah arrived. She'd asked Lloyd if he'd accompany her, and they managed to get him one of the few remaining tickets for the event.

'As long as you don't expect me to dance,' he said as they walked inside. 'You've heard of people having two left feet? Well, I've got at least six, and they're all bound to tread on yours if I take to the floor.'

'I promise you won't have to dance,' she said. 'I'm just grateful you're here. I'm not sure I could've gone through this alone.'

'Where do you want to sit?'

Sarah pointed to a dark corner where she knew she would be hidden but would have a good vantage point of the rest of the room.

'You mustn't panic, Sarah. Mia might not even be in Bath.'

'I know,' she said, but she couldn't stop her hands from twitching in her lap.

'You mustn't be disappointed if she's not here,' Lloyd went on.

She nodded, but her gaze fixed itself to the door as more people entered. Most were wearing the very finest of Regency gowns in a rainbow riot of colors. There was a very pretty girl wearing a dress the color of summer sunshine and another in the palest pink, which reminded Sarah of the inside of a shell. They were all finished beautifully too, with pretty ribbons, beads, and bows.

Sarah looked down at her own modest dress. She'd never been one to overdo things when it came to accessories, but she felt quite bare next to her peacock-like companions.

'What's the matter?' Lloyd asked her as she examined her simple white gown with the blue sash.

'I feel…' she paused, 'a little plain.'

'You look great,' Lloyd told her.

'You're sure I'm not too white?'

'White?' he said quizzically. 'You mean white like a swan? Or a perfect summer cloud? Or the first snowdrop of the year?'

Sarah laughed. 'Well, when you put it like that.'

'White is the most desirable of colors,' he said with a wink that made Sarah blush. He was right too. White had, indeed, been a favorite color in the time of Jane Austen. You couldn't go wrong with white. It was the color of modesty and femininity and always looked pretty and fresh.

She glanced toward the door again, eager not to miss a single soul. A woman with a huge bosom entered, her face stony, as if dancing were the very last thing on her mind. Sarah watched as she grabbed ahold of a woman checking the tickets and instantly recognized her from one of the talks she'd attended. Hadn't she been disagreeable there too, complaining about something that didn't warrant complaining about at all? How such a woman could be a Jane Austen fan beggared belief. Austen fans were usually amiable and enthusiastic, but this woman seemed to be on a permanent mission to make everybody's lives miserable.

Sarah looked away, determined to find somebody happier to watch.

That's when she saw her. Wearing a simple cream gown with a square neckline, not dissimilar to her own, Mia looked around the room.

'That's her!' Sarah blurted, grabbing Lloyd's arm.

'Are you sure?' he said.

'Of *course* I'm sure!'

'I mean, all these gowns make everyone look the same. Which one is she?'

'The one with the dark curly hair.' Sarah couldn't help smiling when she saw her little sister. She hadn't changed at all, at least not from the outside, although Sarah could see there was a certain sadness in her eyes, and she looked unsure about being there.

'Right!' Lloyd said. 'The one who's looking over here now?'

'Oh, God! Do you think she saw me?' Sarah asked, ducking her head.

'Well, isn't that the whole point of being here?'

'But I'm not ready yet.'

'No, I don't think she saw you,' Lloyd assured her. 'And she's moving away now, but what's your plan?'

'I don't have a plan,' Sarah said, surfacing again, 'which is highly unusual for me, but this is a highly unusual situation.' For a moment she made a mental list of how the evening might go.

1. See sister from afar.

2. Contrive to meet sister.

3. Apologize to sister for having stolen and married the man she loved.

4. Run out of room in tears after being slapped by sister.

Sarah sighed. Perhaps it was better that she not make that particular list.

'I really don't know what I'm going to do,' she confessed to Lloyd.

He took her hand and squeezed it, and her eyes opened wide with pleasure at his sudden touch. 'Why don't you let the evening pan out naturally? Just see what happens? Don't try to force anything.'

'Okay,' she said with a nod, half expecting him to release her hand, but rather thrilled when he kept hold of it.

༄

'Are you sure I let out the dress enough?' Shelley asked as they entered the arts centre.

'The dress is fine, Shelley. Don't fuss. Where shall we sit? There aren't many seats left.'

'Over there, in front of the stage. Isn't that where you like to be?'

Mia gave a little smile but didn't answer. 'How many men are there?' she asked as they found the two last remaining seats together.

'Not enough,' Shelley said, quickly eyeing up the men on offer. 'And most of them are *ancient!*'

'That's always the way,' Mia said, and then they both fell silent as the dancers entered the room.

The first half of the evening was delightful, with the dancers performing for the audience. The music was soft and sweet, and the costumes were mesmerizing, their pretty fondant colors swirling across the floor. A little earlier than Jane Austen's time, the women's dresses were more Marie Antoinette than Elizabeth Bennet. Curly white wigs were worn, and everywhere, there was an abundance of lace and bows.

'Make me a dress like that one,' Mia whispered to Shelley, pointing to a resplendent dress in pink. It was the sort of dress that would have forced the wearer to walk through most doors sideways, because it was so wide.

'I love the lacework,' Shelley said, and Mia nodded, looking in envy at the frothy lace at the end of the sleeves. 'They just don't make clothes like that anymore.'

'Yes, but imagine running for a bus in a dress like that, or trying to find a seat on the tube!'

'But the romance of it all!' Shelley said.

'Yes, modern life is definitely lacking something, isn't it? I suppose that's why events like this are so popular.'

'But I'm not sure I like the men's clothes so much,' Shelley said.

'No, lace doesn't work so well on a man, does it?'

'They all looked like fops,' Shelley said and then giggled.

'No, Mr Darcy's clothes were much more manly,' Mia said.

Shelley nodded. 'You couldn't stride across a muddy meadow in that poor excuse for a pair of shoes,' she said, nodding to the feminine footwear that one of the men was sporting.

Shortly thereafter, things got lively, with the audience being encouraged to join in. The room was soon filled with willing volunteers. This was what a lot of the Austen fans had come for, to dance, to feel the same giddy delights that Catherine Morland and Jane Bennet might have experienced when dancing with the men they loved.

One of the women from the dance group walked up onto the stage and began giving detailed instructions for the participants.

'I'll never remember all that,' Mia said to Shelley.

'Don't worry; nobody ever does, and it's much more fun when it all goes wrong. Just keep moving!'

Mia kept on moving, and sure enough, before long she was moving totally in the wrong direction, with arms twisting left instead of right and her feet tumbling over each other. It wasn't as bad when she partnered with Shelley, because they just laughed, but when they had to cross over and switch partners, Mia was paired with a very sour-faced woman who tutted and shook her head in disapproval.

'Other way, girl!' the woman bellowed above the music, her huge bosom shaking alarmingly in disdain.

'Oh, you poor thing,' Shelley said afterwards. 'Trust you to have to dance with that dreadful Mrs Soames.'

But worse was to come, much worse.

'Come on, then,' Lloyd said at the other side of the room.

'But I thought you weren't dancing,' Sarah said.

'Well, I can't have you being a wallflower all evening, can I?'

Sarah smiled, glad he'd decided to give it a go, because it wasn't much fun sitting and watching everyone else have all the fun.

'But what about Mia?' she asked as he led her to the floor at the start of the next dance.

'She's on the other side of the room,' Lloyd said.

Sarah looked uncertain for a moment and glanced down the length of the room as if trying to gauge the distance between them both.

'It'll be fine,' Lloyd said. Sarah gave in, and five minutes later, she was glad she had. Together they slipped some circles, got two-hand turns down to perfection, and cast each other down the outside. Sarah felt sure that Lloyd had grossly misrepresented himself when he told her he couldn't dance. He was a wonderful partner, and Sarah was proud to get several envious glances from the female dancers around her.

'I haven't had such a good workout in ages,' Lloyd said as they came to the end of yet another dance. 'You don't mind if I sit the next one out, do you? I think I'll take a few shots with the old camera.'

Sarah nodded, not sure what to do. Part of her wanted to join Lloyd on the sidelines, but the other half wanted to continue dancing.

'Take your partners,' the organizer called from the stage.

Sarah looked around the room and caught the eye of a kind-looking woman who was also searching for a partner.

'I know I'm not exactly Mr Darcy,' the lady began, 'but I generally move in the right direction.'

Sarah laughed, and her fate was sealed. She hadn't realized it, but she was now in the middle of the room and ever closer to her sister.

Chapter 34

MIA HADN'T LAUGHED SO MUCH IN AGES, AND IT FELT GOOD. Shelley had been right to insist on her going out that night. The memory of Alec was fading fast, each dance step taking her further away from her encounter with him. He was consigned, once more, to the past. He had broken her heart once, but she wasn't going to let him do it again. She would dance him out of her system once and for all.

'You look happy,' Shelley told her as they met in the middle of their dancing quartet.

'I am,' Mia said, smiling at her friend. 'I really am!'

The dancing went on, and Sarah was impressed with her new partner. Her name was Doris Norris, and despite her age, she seemed inexhaustible.

'One has to keep active at *any* age,' she told Sarah in between dances, and Sarah agreed.

During a long set dance called 'Irish Lamentation,' it happened. Somebody somewhere in the room turned the wrong way and caused absolute mayhem, because everybody seemed to lose their partner at the same time. Sarah wandered around trying desperately to find Doris Norris once more, but she didn't find Doris. She found Mia.

Suddenly, after three years of being apart, Sarah and Mia were dancing together, their arms intertwined and their fingers locked. There was no escaping for either of them, as everybody had partnered up again.

At first Sarah couldn't believe it. How had it happened? She hadn't planned it. She hadn't meant to be on that side of the room at all. Lloyd had told her everything would be all right, and it wasn't, but at the same time, wasn't this what she wanted?

'Mia!' she began tentatively as they moved across the floor together. Her sister's face was stony and shocked. Her eyes looked empty and haunted, and Sarah's vibrated with tears at the sight of them. It hurt her more than she could ever have imagined that her sister was not pleased to see her, but what had she expected, open arms and all to be forgiven? 'Mia, talk to me. *Please.*'

They circled around each other, hands locked together, but each of them distant.

'I'm sorry,' Sarah said simply. 'I can't tell you how sorry I am. If you knew how many hours I've spent regretting what I did.'

Mia said nothing.

'I so wanted to talk to you,' Sarah went on, undeterred by the lack of response. 'You're my darling little sister, and I've always taken care of you, and I couldn't bear being apart from you, not knowing where you were or what you were doing.'

Sarah was interrupted as the dance forced them apart for a moment. Sarah panicked, thinking Mia would escape her, but a moment later, they were back together again.

'*Please*—talk to me,' Sarah begged her.

'What do you expect me to say?' Mia asked at last.

'Anything. Anything at all.'

'What are you doing here?'

'I hoped to find you,' Sarah said, raising her voice above the music. 'I know how much you loved dancing, and I thought you might be here tonight.'

Mia gave a funny little laugh. 'So you're both here to try to find me, are you?'

'What do you mean?'

The two of them were parted for a brief moment as the dance continued.

'Mia? What did you mean?'

'Nothing,' she said abruptly.

'Then tell me how you are,' Sarah tried again, once they were linking arms. 'I've tried so hard to find you.'

'I didn't want to be found,' Mia said abruptly.

'No, I guessed. But you're okay?'

'What do you think? Did you imagine I'd be lying at the bottom of the River Thames by now?'

'Mia—'

'You did the very worst thing you could possibly do to a sister, but I'm a fighter, Sarah. You should know that about me. I don't give up easily.'

'I know,' Sarah said, wounded that Mia thought she knew her so little. 'I'm glad. I mean—you *know* what I mean, don't you?'

'I don't know anything about you anymore,' Mia said, her voice cold and monotonous. 'You're a stranger to me. Worse than a stranger, for I never want to become acquainted with you.'

The reference to *Persuasion* cut Sarah at the very bone. It was the cruelest thing her sister could have said to a fellow Jane Austen fan.

The dance came to an end, the two sisters stood opposite one another for a protracted moment, and then Sarah watched as Mia turned and disappeared into the crowd.

'Mia!' she shouted after her. Where had she gone? She didn't want to lose her again. Not when she'd only just found her. '*Mia!*'

'Sarah?' Lloyd was beside her in an instant.

'She was here. Lloyd—help me find her.'

'Okay, okay!' he said, placing a hand on her shoulder.

'Don't let her get away!' Sarah said, desperation making her voice high and unnatural.

'I won't let her get away,' Lloyd said, and the two of them separated in search of Mia.

~☉~

The air outside felt cold and crisp after the claustrophobic atmosphere of the Chapel Art Centre, and Mia stood for a few moments breathing deeply. What had just happened? She closed her eyes. It didn't feel real. Had she imagined it?

'Mia!' A voice called her name, and Mia turned around to see that it was Shelley. 'What's going on?' she said, handing Mia her coat. She put it on, feeling the eighteenth-century Mia being abruptly replaced by the twenty-first-century one.

'Why did you leave me?'

'When?'

'On the dance floor. Where did you go?'

'I'm sorry, some idiot stepped on my foot, and when I looked up, you were gone.'

'It's all your fault!' Mia said.

'What's all my fault?'

'Sarah!'

'Sarah's here?'

Mia nodded.

'Well, where is she?'

'I don't know. I needed to get away from her.'

Shelley frowned. 'But don't you think you should talk to her?'

Mia shook her head.

'Just say, *hello*. You can't go wrong with *hello*.'

'But I did go wrong.' Mia bit her lip. She couldn't believe what she'd actually said to Sarah, and she was far too embarrassed to confess it to Shelley.

'Let me go and find her for you,' Shelley said.

'No, don't!'

'But you might not get another chance like this.'

'I don't want to talk to her.'

'She's your sister, Mia—*please* talk to her.' Shelley reached out to touch her arm, but Mia flinched and then broke into a run. She couldn't stay there a moment longer. She needed to get away.

'Mia!' Shelley shouted after her.

Mia didn't stop. She wanted to get away from everyone. It seemed as if the whole world were after her that day.

⁓

'I can't see her,' Lloyd said as he and Sarah left the arts centre.

'I can't lose her. We have to find her!'

'Who was the girl she was with when she came in?'

'Shelley,' Sarah said. 'She attended drama school with Mia.'

'Do you have her phone number?'

Sarah looked at him and nodded. 'I've got her mobile number, but when I tried to get in touch with Mia before, Shelley didn't know where she was.'

'She does now.'

'We don't need to ring her,' Sarah said, nodding to where Shelley was standing on the curb. 'Shelley!'

Shelley turned around and gasped. 'Sarah!'

'Where's Mia?'

'I don't know. We were talking, and she just ran off. It's the second time today she's done that to me.'

'Which direction did she go in?'

'You won't catch her, and I think it's best if you don't try,' Shelley said.

'But I've got to talk to her.'

'I know,' Shelley said. 'I wanted Mia to talk to you too.'

Sarah felt her eyes fill up with tears again and then felt the comforting weight of Lloyd's hand on her shoulder.

'We'll find her,' he told her. 'You'll talk to her, and it will be fine.'

'How can you say that? How can you know that?'

'She's staying with me,' Shelley suddenly said.

'Then I can see her tonight?' Sarah asked, desperation in her voice.

'I don't think that's a very good idea,' Lloyd said. 'You're both so wound up tonight. I think both of you need some time to think this through.'

Sarah shook her head. 'No, no, she'll run away from me again. I know she will.'

Shelley took a step forward and picked up Sarah's cold hands. 'I'll make sure she stays,' she told her.

'Will you?'

Shelley delved into her handbag for a piece of paper and scribbled her home phone number on it. 'You've got my mobile number, haven't you?'

Sarah nodded. 'Don't let her leave before I've seen her.'

'I won't,' Shelley said. 'I promise.'

Chapter 35

IT WAS COLD, DARK, AND LATE BY THE TIME MIA REACHED Shelley's home. It had been silly to walk the whole way in her dainty little dancing shoes, but she'd needed to clear her head, and although the shoes were probably ruined, the walk had calmed her and given her time to think.

As she climbed the last steep hill and approached Southville Terrace, she saw that the light was on in Gabe's front room. She paused for a moment, peered inside, and spotted him by one of the bookcases. He had his back to the window and was reaching up to take a book down, and Mia wondered which book he chose. Was it a dry and dusty book on architecture or a fabulously engaging novel?

Just then, he turned around, and Mia gasped, moving along the path quickly, so that he wouldn't spot her staring. Whatever would he think of her?

She rang the bell on Shelley's door, and when Shelley opened it a moment later, Mia was almost bowled over by an excited Bingley. Shelley's eyes were wide and wild, and Mia soon found herself in the tightest embrace of her life.

'Don't keep running away from me like that,' Shelley said.

'I'm sorry,' Mia said, feeling like a naughty child.

'I waited for you for ages. I was worried!'

'I just needed to walk for a bit,' Mia said. 'I didn't mean to worry you.'

'Why didn't you ring me? I thought you'd been abducted by some mad Austen fan who likes a woman in costume.'

Mia shook her head. 'I was fine.'

'Well, come on in and have a hot drink. You must be frozen.'

'I must go and apologize to Gabe.'

Shelley frowned. 'What?'

'I was rude to him earlier, and I feel awful. At least I can do one thing right today.'

'Can't it wait until tomorrow? It's so late.'

'His light's on,' Mia said. 'I won't be long.'

'But I want to talk to you!'

But Mia was already retracing her steps down the path.

It felt funny knocking on Gabe's front door, having previously squeezed through the fence and gone in the back door the last time. It felt so formal.

When he opened the door, he stood looking at her for a moment.

'Hello,' she said. 'Can I come in?'

'Of course,' he said. 'Are you okay?'

'I wanted to apologize for earlier. I was rude.'

'Do you want a coffee?' he asked as he showed her into the front room.

'No, thanks,' Mia said. 'Coffee makes me hyper at night, and I'm already wound up enough.'

'I make a mean hot chocolate,' Gabe said.

Mia couldn't help smiling. 'Okay,' she said in a little voice.

'Good.'

He disappeared into the kitchen, and Mia was left to look

around the front room. It was lit by a couple of enormous lamps and looked wonderfully cosy. It was the kind of room you could easily settle into and never want to leave. Mia could quite imagine curling up in one of the big armchairs with a book and a cup of tea and whiling away many a happy hour.

Suddenly Mia was swept by a tide of sadness as she remembered Andrea. Had she sat in this very chair, thinking of the happy days ahead with Gabe, only to have her life cruelly cut short by her illness? Mia swallowed hard, realizing that her own problems were petty in comparison.

Gabe appeared with her mug of hot chocolate. It was funny— Gabe was forever making her hot, comforting drinks.

'Thank you,' she said.

'You're welcome.' He winced as he set down her mug.

'Are you okay?' she asked, looking at his bandaged arm.

'Just a twinge,' he said.

'When does it come off?'

'Next week, so not long now.'

'It must be very annoying,' Mia said. 'How have you been coping?'

'Slowly,' he said with a grin. 'I've been living at half speed, but it could have been worse. Just imagine if I'd broken my leg.' He went to get his own mug of hot chocolate from the kitchen and then took a seat opposite her. 'I like your dress,' he said at last. 'It really suits you.'

'Oh, it's Shelley's. I ruined mine.'

'Yes, I noticed.'

'It's been a strange day,' she said, taking a sip of hot chocolate.

'Did you want to tell me about it?'

She leaned back in the chair and then turned around. 'Is this a cardigan?' she asked, picking it up from the back of the chair.

'Yes,' Gabe said.

Mia pulled a funny face. 'I thought only grandfathers wore cardigans.'

Gabe laughed. 'You really don't mince your words, do you?'

'I don't think men should wear cardigans.'

'Oh, you don't, do you?'

'They're mumsy.'

'I thought you said only grandfathers wore them.'

'You know what I mean.'

Mia pulled the cardigan around her shoulders. 'What?'

'I thought you didn't approve of cardigans,' Gabe said. 'But you don't object to wearing them yourself?'

'It's rather comforting,' she said, settling back in the chair.

He smiled at her. 'A cup of hot chocolate and a cardigan around your shoulders.'

'Do I look ancient?'

'No,' he said. 'Far from it.'

'Well, I *feel* ancient,' she said. 'I've never felt so old in my life.' She sighed and closed her eyes for a moment, knowing she was in danger of falling asleep in Gabe's front room. 'Sorry,' she said a moment later, opening her eyes and looking at him. 'You must think I'm so rude.'

'Not at all.'

'I don't mean to be rude,' she said. 'It's just—' she paused. 'I keep running into my past, and it's… unnerving me.'

'Then your past isn't a happy one?'

'Not the last few years,' Mia said. 'Before that, everything was fine. Well, apart from our mother walking out on us.'

'And who is "us"?' Gabe asked.

'My sister—Sarah—and me.'

'And she's here in Bath?'

'I met her this evening at the dance.'

Gabe nodded.

'Tell me more about Andrea,' Mia said.

'But I want to know more about Sarah,' he replied.

'You go first.'

He shifted in his chair. 'What do you want to know?'

'Did you ever argue?'

'Of course,' he said.

'What was the worst argument about?'

Gabe looked thoughtful for a moment, and Mia wondered if he was going to tell her the truth or just tell her to leave. 'It was shortly after we got married,' he said. 'I got offered a job here in Bath. We were living in London at the time. Andrea had always lived there, and her friends and family had always been on her doorstep. We had a big fight about leaving. I loved London too, but I wasn't tied to it as much she was.'

'So what happened?'

'We had a weekend here in Bath and wandered around together, soaking it all in. We stayed in a little bed and breakfast in a village just outside Bath. The views were breathtaking, and one morning we set out walking. We really didn't know where we were going, and we even got lost at one stage.' He laughed at the memory. 'But something changed, that day. We spent the whole day together—*really* together—and it wasn't like our life in London, where things were always rushed and time was always short. We felt as though we'd stumbled across a different way of living here. We both discovered this new place, and there were no ties from either of our backgrounds, no preconceptions or previous commitments. We were free to make a brand new life that would be completely ours.'

Mia smiled. 'That's really romantic.'

'I guess it is,' he said. 'Anyway, shortly after, we found a house about a mile from here and left London for good.'

'I can't imagine leaving London.'

'Have you always lived there?'

'No, just since I was a student.'

'So you like it?'

Mia looked at him and then slowly shook her head. 'No,' she said. 'I don't think I do. At least, not anymore. When I was a student, I got a real buzz from being there. Everything seemed so exciting. I thought it was the center of the whole world.'

'But not anymore?'

She shook her head again. 'Please don't tell Shelley. She still thinks I'm going to make it in the West End.'

'And you're not?'

Mia looked at him. His bright eyes looked so kind and understanding and she felt as if she could tell him everything, which was an experience she'd had only with her sister in the past.

'I can't imagine leaving London, but there's a part of me that would love to.'

'Then why don't you?'

'I don't know where I'd go,' she said.

'Doesn't Shelley have a spare room? She told me she was looking for another lodger.'

'It's not that simple,' Mia said.

'You've not fallen out with Shelley, have you?'

'Oh, no—I don't think that would ever happen.'

'Then what?'

Mia's hand clasped her warm mug. 'It's a long story,' she said slowly.

Gabe shrugged casually. 'I'm not going anywhere.'

Even though she'd only known the man for a short time, and even though she didn't know him all that well, she began to tell him what happened to her from the heavenly holiday in Devon to Sarah's confession that she was in love with Alec and they were to get married.

'And tonight was the first time you've spoken to her since then?' Gabe asked.

Mia nodded. 'And I was horrible. It was like all the hatred I have ever felt in my life came pouring out of my mouth. I shouldn't have said anything,' she said, hiding her head in her hands.

'But she hurt you.'

'I know, but I didn't want to hurt her back. I feel just awful.'

'Well then, talk to her again. There must be a way through this.'

'I don't know. I just can't see it. We'll always have this *thing* between us.'

'Do you want to sort out things?'

'I obviously didn't this evening.'

'But you were in shock then. What if you could meet up again and just talk, would you?'

Mia sat in silence for a moment. What did she want to do? It seemed like it was up to her now. 'All I know is that I don't want things to be as they are right now.'

Gabe nodded. 'Then we'll have to make sure that they change, won't we?'

'That sounds scary.'

'Change usually is.'

Silence descended between them again, and Mia heard the comforting tick of an old carriage clock on the mantelpiece.

'Okay,' Gabe said at last. 'What was this afternoon about? Who were you running away from then?'

Mia blinked. She'd almost forgotten about the events of the afternoon.

'Alec,' she said.

'He's here in Bath?'

'He said he came to find me. He thought I'd be here for the festival.'

'Did Sarah ask him to find you for her?'

'No,' Mia said. 'They've broken up.'

Gabe shook his head. 'I don't understand. Why did he want to see you, then?'

Mia gave a little laugh. 'He wanted to tell me that he'd made a terrible mistake and that he wanted me back.'

'My God!' Gabe said. 'I don't believe it.'

'Neither did I.'

'And what did you say to him?'

'I told him I never wanted to see him again.'

'And you slapped him?'

'Only once,' Mia said. 'Although he deserved several, really.'

'I wish I'd seen it,' Gabe said, risking a tiny smile.

'It's a shame you didn't. I think half of Bath saw it.'

'I should have bought an evening paper. Perhaps it was reported.'

Mia gave the tiniest of smiles.

'Do you think he's gone?'

'I hope so,' Mia said.

Gabe took a deep breath. 'You've had quite a day.'

Mia gave a little laugh. 'I wouldn't want to live through it again.'

Gabe looked at her. 'But that's not the whole story, is it?'

'What do you mean?'

'You've not told me everything, have you?'

Mia looked at him and wondered how he seemed to know her so well. 'No,' she said. 'It isn't the whole story.'

Chapter 36

SHELLEY DIDN'T NORMALLY EAVESDROP. WELL, NOT VERY OFTEN, anyway. It wasn't polite, was it? Of course, there'd been that time she eavesdropped on her parents when she'd been seven years old. They'd been discussing Christmas presents, and it totally ruined her surprise, because she then knew she was getting the doll's house that she'd been begging for since the summer holidays. Perhaps that was the day she decided to become an actress, because she'd been very good at feigning surprise when opening her present that year.

Then there had been the time she eavesdropped on one of her friends at school. Well, Shelley thought the girl was her friend, until she eavesdropped on the girl and heard what she *really* thought of Shelley.

If only she lived by the maxim that eavesdroppers never heard anything good, but the problem was that Shelley was worried about Mia and thought it was time for her to come home. What on earth could she have to talk to Gabe about, anyway? Mia was *her* friend, not his.

She left the house by the back door and slipped through the gap in the fence and walked down Gabe's darkened back garden, tripping over a football that he'd bought for Bingley.

Gabe usually left the back door open until late and was quite used to her popping in and out. Sure enough, she found that it was still unlocked, and she sneaked into the kitchen. A faint aroma of hot chocolate lingered in the air, and Shelley grimaced. Things were obviously getting cosy pretty quickly between Mia and Gabe.

It would have been plain common courtesy to shout a quick hello at that point, but Shelley didn't. Instead, she hid in the shadows of the kitchen and listened in silence to the conversation taking place next door.

'You really want to hear all this?' Mia said.

'I'd like to try to understand what's going on, but please don't think you have to tell me. It's just that you look so sad, and I know that something's troubling you.'

'It's okay,' Mia said. 'I like talking to you. You're like—'

'I know, an affable grandfather.'

'I wasn't going to say that,' Mia said. 'No, you're like a dear friend who I know won't pass judgement.'

There was a pause, and then Mia began. 'When I got back to London after the holiday in Devon, I started feeling really unwell. I put it down to depression and tried to carry on, but it wasn't long before I realized I was pregnant,' she said, her eyes sparkling with tears. She quickly blinked them away, hoping Gabe hadn't seen them. 'I was so shocked. It was the last thing I expected to happen. I'd been on the pill, you see, but I'd forgotten to take some. It was stupid, but I'd been so busy that I'd simply forgotten.'

She paused, remembering the day she found out she was pregnant. 'It was a pretty dark time, and I really didn't know what to do.'

'Did you ring your sister?'

'No. How could I? She was getting married to the father of my baby!'

'Good point,' Gabe said. 'So what happened?'

'I got on with things. I'm quite good at that. It's usually the only option, isn't it?'

'You had the baby?'

'Of course! How could I not?' Mia said, her eyes large and glittering with tears. 'But it was the scariest time of my life.'

'Wasn't there anyone to help you?'

Mia shook her head. 'I thought I could get through it on my own. I didn't feel I had the right to burden anybody with it. It had been my own stupid fault.'

'What about Shelley? Why didn't you tell her?'

'She was leading her own life. We were speaking on the phone every now and then, but I never wanted to worry her. She had her own worries. Anyway, I'd kind of been adopted by a woman in one of the flats in my apartment block. She was amazing. She had three children of her own that had all grown up and left home, and I think she was looking around for somebody else she could help. She was like a mother, and I couldn't have got through it all without her.'

There was a pause.

'So, I'm dying to know,' Gabe said at last. 'What did you have, a boy or a girl?'

Mia smiled. 'A boy. He's two years old now. I can hardly believe it. He's quite the little man.'

'Have you got a picture of him?'

'Of course. I never leave home without it.' Mia opened her little bag and took out her purse. Inside it there was a photograph of a small boy with cherry-red cheeks and a tumble of dark curls just like his mother.

'He's gorgeous,' Gabe said.

'Well, I might be just a little bit biased, but I think he's the most wonderful little boy in the world.'

'I'm sure he is. What's his name?'

'William,' she said.

'And here was me thinking he'd be called Darcy.'

Mia laughed. 'Well, I was tempted for a while, and I even thought of Fitzwilliam, but you can't burden a child with that, can you? So I named him William Fitz instead, but he usually just gets called Will.'

'He's cute,' Gabe said, 'and he's very lucky to have such a devoted mother.'

Mia bit her lip. 'I wish I could spend more time with him. It breaks my heart, but he lives with the woman I was telling you about. She takes care of him when I'm working. She works as a curtain maker from home, and I envy her, because she gets to spend all day with my little boy.'

'But that won't be forever, will it?'

'It feels like forever at the moment, and I can't see a way out of it. I have to work, and I've got a crummy job in a café that I can't seem to get out of, to pay for a flat that I hate, and I'm not even bothered about going for auditions anymore, which was why I took on the crummy job in the first place. It was meant to be only temporary and allow me time to pursue my singing, but now William is the only thing that's important to me.'

'You're not auditioning anymore?'

'I haven't done it for ages,' Mia said. 'And the last audition was so awful that I don't think I'll ever bother again. I feel sad sometimes, because I put so much time and energy into it all, and I really thought that's all I wanted to do with my life.'

'But life has a way of throwing us all curveballs, doesn't it?'

'Yes. I'd never have predicted the position I'd be in, but I wouldn't want to change it now that I'm in it.'

They sat in silence for a moment.

'Did you ever want children?' Mia asked at last.

Gabe nodded. 'Andrea and I were about to start a family,' he said.

'Oh,' Mia said. 'I'm so sorry.'

He sighed sadly. 'We both come from big families and wanted one of our own.'

'Of course,' Mia said. 'But there's still time, isn't there?'

'For me?' he said.

'Yes. Men can have children into their eighties, can't they? It's not like being a woman.'

He laughed. 'Yes, but I wouldn't want to be chasing my kids around on a walker!'

'They are exhausting,' Mia said. 'I think it's best to do it when you're young.'

'It's a pity you don't live here in Bath,' he said. 'I could baby-sit for you.'

'Really? You'd do that?'

'I work from home a lot,' he said. 'And I've lots of experience bringing up my own brothers and sisters. I'm the eldest of five.'

'Goodness!'

He smiled. 'I might look like an old grandfather—'

'I didn't say that!'

'But I know how to handle kids.'

They smiled at one another.

'Have you never thought to tell Alec?' Gabe said quietly a moment later. 'I mean, he's no longer with your sister, is he?'

Mia shook her head. 'It's the last thing I want.'

'Don't you think he has a right to know he's got a son?'

Mia blushed. 'You think I'm wrong? You think I should tell him?'

'No,' Gabe said, and then he sighed. 'I don't know. I guess it's up to the mother of his child.'

'You're right. It is,' she said, 'and I'm in no mood to tell him.' She looked at Gabe. 'What that's expression for?'

'I'm just thinking how sad it all is. How this beautiful baby boy exists and how very different it could have all been.'

'I often think that too,' Mia said. 'I really loved him, and I'm sure we could've been great together, but I guess he wasn't my Mr Darcy after all.'

Gabe scratched his chin. 'It seems to me that this Mr Darcy causes a lot of problems for young women.'

Mia frowned. 'How so?'

'Well, he sets an impossibly high standard, and real men can't possibly be expected to live up to that.'

'But it's important to have high standards,' Mia said.

'Yes, but you also have to be realistic about things.'

Mia sighed. 'That's what Sarah always says, and it drives me crazy.'

'Brothers and sisters have that written in their job description, I'm afraid.'

'You really think I should tell Alec about William?' Mia said after a moment.

'I don't know. Only you can answer that, but if I had a child, I should like to know.'

Mia sat looking thoughtful, and then quite suddenly, the weight of the whole day seemed to fall upon her and her eyes began to close again.

'I should go,' she said. 'It's late, and it's been a very long day.'

Gabe stood up, and they walked to the front door together.

'Thanks for listening,' she said as he opened the door for her.

'Thanks for talking.'

She smiled. 'You're a good listener.'

'You're a good talker.'

Mia laughed.

'And if you ever need to talk again—'

'I know where you are,' she finished for him.

He nodded and then leaned forward very slowly, bending down to kiss her cheek. Mia caught her breath. She hadn't expected it, but it felt rather nice.

Not until she reached Shelley's did she realize she was still wearing his cardigan.

Chapter 37

SHELLEY LEFT AS SOON AS SHE HEARD MIA GET UP, SNEAKING out of the kitchen and running the length of the back garden before squeezing back through the gap in the fence. She could hardly believe what she'd heard, and her eyes smarted with tears at Mia's revelation.

Why hadn't Mia confided in her? Weren't they friends? How had she managed to hide such a secret from her for all these years? And why pour it all out to Gabe, whom she'd only just met? It didn't seem fair.

She closed the back door behind her and locked it. Bingley came trotting into the kitchen and gave his owner a quizzical look, as if to ask what she'd been doing out in the garden in the middle of the night. He shoved his wet nose into the palm of her right hand when she didn't respond to his presence, and she smiled down at him, pulling one of his funny stubby ears.

'Mia has a little boy, and she never told me about him,' she told Bingley. He looked up at her with his big brown eyes as if in total sympathy with her, but then he did a typical Bingley thing and leapt up on her, his great fat paws on her shoulders.

'Not now, Bingley. Get down!'

There was a knock at the door. Shelley dabbed her eyes with a tissue. She had to act normally.

'Hi,' Mia said as she came in. 'I'm sorry I was ages.'

'Yes, you were,' Shelley said. 'You seem to spend more time with Gabe than you do me. Why don't you go and stay in his spare room instead?' She hadn't meant to snap like that, but the words tumbled out before she had a chance to stop them.

'Shelley!' Mia said, resting a hand on her shoulder. 'What's wrong?'

'Nothing. Why should there be something wrong?'

'Because you sound so angry, and that's not like you.'

Shelley sighed and tried to calm herself. 'It's just been a very trying day, hasn't it?'

'You can say that again.'

Shelley bit her lip. 'Mia?'

'Yes?'

'You know you can talk to me about anything, don't you?'

'Of course.'

Shelley looked at her. 'Because I'd like to do all I can to help you.'

'That's really lovely of you, but right now all I want to do is go to bed.'

Shelley clenched her fingers into fists lest she reach out to physically shake Mia until she spilled the truth. 'But we'll talk in the morning?'

'What about?'

'Everything,' Shelley said. 'We've hardly talked properly since you arrived, and there's so much I want to know.'

Mia frowned at her. 'But there's really not that much to tell, Shelley.'

'Are you sure?'

Mia's eyes narrowed at her friend's words. 'Why don't you just tell me what's on your mind?'

Shelley could feel a blush creeping up on her and felt her heartbeat racing. Should she tell Mia she'd been eavesdropping next door and heard her confession? Mia would never trust her again. 'I know you,' Shelley said at last, deciding not to confess to subterfuge, 'and I know you're not telling me everything.'

'Yes, so you keep saying. What is it you think I'm hiding from you, Shell—'

'Stop lying to me, Mia, for God's sake! I don't know how much more of this I can take. Just tell me what's going on!'

Mia blanched and bit her lip, looking chastened, but then her face softened. 'I think we'd better sit down first.'

Only then did Mia tell her everything. Shelley had heard it all a moment before in Gabe's kitchen, but she felt relief surge through her that her friend had, at last, decided to confide in her, even though Shelley had to resort to shouting to prize the truth from her.

'Why didn't you tell me before?' Shelley asked, when Mia showed her the photograph from her purse.

Mia sighed. 'You seemed so far away, and we were both leading different lives.'

'But I could have helped. I could have been with you.'

'I'm sorry,' Mia said. 'I really am, but it just felt like something I had to get through on my own.'

'But you don't ever need to be alone. Isn't that why you have friends?'

'I suppose,' Mia said, and she looked so young in that moment that Shelley could hardly believe that she was a mother.

'I'm guessing Sarah doesn't know anything about all this,' Shelley said.

Mia shook her head. 'How could I tell her?'

'But you can tell her now, surely. Now that Alec's out of the picture, it'll be easier, won't it?'

Mia's forehead furrowed into deep lines. 'Will it?'

'And he has a right to know too, Mia,' Shelley said, well aware that Gabe had just told her exactly the same thing. 'He has a child. Don't you think he'll want to know?'

'I don't want anything from him.'

'I didn't say you did,' Shelley said. 'You've obviously been coping, and I really admire you for that, but I think he should know, all the same.'

Mia took a deep breath and sighed slowly. 'I can't believe how this trip's turning out,' she said and then laughed. 'I thought I could leave all my troubles behind me in London. I didn't realize I was heading into even more trouble here.'

'Bath isn't immune from trouble,' Shelley said. 'Fine architecture and a Jane Austen connection can't cancel out your problems, I'm afraid.'

'I've been a fool, haven't I?' Mia said. 'I thought I could get through this on my own and nobody ever needed to know a thing.'

'You've not been a fool,' Shelley said, 'but I wish you wouldn't be quite so independent.'

'What do you mean?'

'I don't like thinking of you struggling along on your own.'

'I haven't been strugg—'

'No? Are you sure?'

Mia relented. 'Well, I might have been struggling a bit, but I've always got by.'

'Getting by isn't much fun,' Shelley said. 'For goodness' sake, Mia! I've got a spare bedroom here desperately in need of another lodger, and I'd love to have you and William here with me. I could even baby-sit him, or he could join in at Tumble Tots. And you could help me out with all my dressmaking. You were always so much more organized than me, and I think things could really take off if we worked at it together. It would be brilliant! *Do* say yes!'

'That's kind of you, Shelley, but my life's in London.'

'Is it? Is it really?'

'My flat—'

'That you're always complaining about.'

'And my job.'

'The badly paid one in the crummy café? You can get any number of crummy jobs here in Bath if you want to.'

There was a moment's silence.

'What's keeping you in London, Mia? You've said you're no longer auditioning.'

Mia gazed at her friend. 'I'm afraid I've given up on that. I'll never be one of the leading lights of the London stage, and do you know what? It no longer bothers me. I used to think that my singing was the only thing that kept me going, and that if I ever stopped, my whole world would crumble, but it hasn't. In fact I've never been happier. I mean, I know I've been pretty miserable over the last couple of days, but my life is a good one.'

Shelley smiled at her. 'You're amazing.'

'No, I'm not.'

'You are! I don't think I'd have coped half as well as you.'

'Yes, you would. You have to. You just keep getting up in the mornings and doing the very best that you can.'

Shelley laughed. 'Boy, we've not done very well as drama school graduates, have we?'

Mia smiled. 'Maybe not as well as we could have done, but I wouldn't change anything. I'm through trying to set the world on fire, and I no longer want to see my name up in lights. Do you know what makes me happy now?'

'What?'

'Spending an evening at home watching William on his play mat. Or taking a walk with him to the duck pond with a crust of stale bread.'

Shelley laughed.

'I think I've entered middle age before I'm even out of my twenties,' Mia said.

'No, you haven't,' Shelley said. 'You've just calmed down a bit.'

'I sometimes worry that I'm unrecognizable now. I feel I've changed so much.'

Shelley looked thoughtful. 'Not that much,' she said. 'You're still my best buddy.'

Mia smiled. 'But are you absolutely sure about William and me moving in with you?'

'Of *course* I'm sure,' Shelley said with a grin. 'I can't think of anything more wonderful!'

Mia laughed. 'I don't deserve a friend like you.'

'No, you don't,' Shelley said. 'You deserve *much* better!'

Chapter 38

Lloyd had insisted on walking Sarah back to her hotel, even though she told him she was perfectly all right and could manage on her own. She was wearing her coat over her Regency gown, but even so, she couldn't stop shivering.

When they reached the river, she stopped, leaning on the stone wall and looking down into the dark swirl of water below.

'Sarah?' Lloyd said, his voice gentle. 'Are you okay?' He placed a hand on her shoulder, and it felt warm and comforting.

'I can't stop thinking about Mia,' she said. 'The look on her face! I'll never forget it. She looked horrified to see me.'

'It was just shock,' Lloyd said.

'No,' Sarah said. 'She hates me.'

'She doesn't hate you.'

'You didn't see her.'

'You're her sister, Sarah. She couldn't hate you.'

'But she does. I'm sure of it.'

'You've got to talk to her. That's the only way to sort it out.'

'But she doesn't even want to see me.' She felt Lloyd's hand squeeze her shoulder, and she turned around to face him. 'I'm sorry to drag you into all this. It's not fair to you, is it?'

'I don't mind,' he said.

Sarah shook her head. 'I wouldn't blame you if you wanted to walk away from all this right now. Really, I wouldn't.'

'I'm not going anywhere.'

'Are you sure? Are you really sure you want to put up with all this? Everything's such a mess, and even if it weren't, you really don't want to get involved with someone like me.'

'What do you mean?'

'I'm a nightmare. I really am.'

'What—the OCD?'

Sarah nodded.

'You keep forgetting that I'm a nightmare too.'

'Yes, but I have a tendency to steal my sister's boyfriends and marry them.'

'Well, I can't lay claim to that particular fault myself,' Lloyd said with a little smile.

Sarah took a deep breath. 'But you didn't come to Bath to become involved in a family feud.'

'Maybe not, but I'd like to become involved with you, and if that means a few family feuds along the way, then so be it.'

Sarah looked at him. 'What on earth did I do to deserve you?'

'Let's discuss that over coffee, shall we? I'm absolutely freezing.'

Sarah nodded, and the two of them walked across Pulteney Bridge, crossing Laura Place into Great Pulteney Street. The lamps were lit, and it was easy to imagine that one was no longer in the twenty-first century but rather in the nineteenth.

She felt a little strange inviting a man back to her hotel room, but it was probably preferable to going back to his.

When they arrived, they went straight up to her room.

'Two coffees, then?' Sarah asked as soon as the door closed

behind her. 'I'm afraid it's just that packet stuff, but they've left me a jug of real milk.'

'That's fine,' Lloyd said.

'You're sure it won't keep you up all night?' Sarah asked and then blushed. 'Sorry. That was an insensitive question.'

'Not at all,' he said. 'I doubt very much if I'll sleep tonight.'

'Me either,' Sarah said, 'so I might as well enjoy a coffee.'

She watched as Lloyd looked around the room. Was he taking everything in? she wondered. It must be hard to gauge a person from her hotel room, because there was so little of her in it, but he immediately spotted something that gave much of her away—a little pile of books that she'd brought with her.

'Jane Austen, of course?' he said, taking the top one in his hands and examining it. '*Persuasion*,' he read. 'I'm afraid I've never read it.'

'It's set in Bath,' Sarah said. 'Well, the second half of it is.'

'And it is your favorite?' he asked.

'No,' she said. She crossed the room to join him and picked up the next book from the pile. 'This one is.'

'*Sense and Sensibility*?'

She nodded.

'Tell me about it.'

'You didn't come here to talk about Jane Austen.'

'But I'd like to know.'

'Well,' Sarah began, 'it's about two sisters and their troublesome love lives.'

Lloyd looked surprised. 'Sounds familiar,' he said.

'You have no idea! I'm afraid Mia and I bear more than a striking resemblance to Elinor and Marianne in the book. Elinor is ruled by her head, whilst Marianne is ruled by her heart, and it almost costs them both the loves of their lives.'

'What happens to them?'

'Oh, they get a happy ending. Jane Austen wouldn't allow anything else.'

'Is that why you're a fan?'

'One of the reasons, but it's so much more than that.' Sarah looked out of the window onto the street below. 'Jane Austen's always been there for me. She brightens every dark moment with her stories. I've only to think of a favorite scene from *Pride and Prejudice* or a favorite character from *Emma*, and I'm smiling again.' Indeed, she was smiling as she remembered the joy the books gave her.

'You and Mia are like these sisters?'

Sarah took a copy of *Sense and Sensibility* from him and nodded.

'And I'm guessing you're like the one ruled by the head?'

'Yes,' Sarah said. 'At least I was, and Mia was always the one ruled by the heart. I used to worry about her all the time. She was always impetuous and lived life by her emotions. There's a lot to be admired about that, but for someone like me, it's a constant worry too. The strange thing is that it was I who was impetuous—it was *I* who was ruled by the heart down in Devon. Of course, Mia was too, but that was perfectly normal.' Sarah twisted her hands together in an anxious knot. 'I don't know what happened. I was like a different person, and no matter how many times I told myself to snap out of it, I couldn't.'

'I suppose the heart really does win out in the end, then,' Lloyd said.

'That doesn't make any sense,' Sarah said. 'I need to be in control of things.'

'But we can't always be,' Lloyd said. 'And I don't think you should drive yourself mad trying to be in charge all the time.'

'Yes, but the one time in my life that I didn't feel in control led to disaster.'

'That's all over now,' he said.

'Except for Mia. I still need to sort that out.'

'Of course.' Lloyd sat down on the window seat, and Sarah thought how comfortable he looked there. She returned to making the coffee. 'How do you like it?' she asked.

'A tiny splash of milk. No sugar.'

'The same,' Sarah said.

'So,' Lloyd began, 'when am I going to hear exactly what happened between you and Alec?'

She looked across the room at him. She didn't particularly want to talk about Alec, but Lloyd was surprisingly easy to talk to, and she felt as if she owed him the truth after what he'd been through that day.

'I mean, I know how you met him, and I know about him and your sister, but you've not told me much more.'

'There isn't much more to tell. We were a disaster from day one.' Sarah paused. 'No,' she added. 'That's not strictly true. It was amazing to begin with. I'd never experienced anything like it before. For the first time in my life, I felt free. I can't explain it, but it was like I was a different person.' She paused for a moment before continuing. 'I can't really remember when it started going wrong, but we did disagree about the wedding. It was a quiet one. Alec didn't want a fuss, and neither did I, really, although I would have liked something a little more romantic than the local registry office. I kept feeling that a Jane Austen heroine would have disapproved of such austere surroundings. Still, I told myself that marriage was more than a wedding day, and at least there'd been flowers, even if it was only the tiny bouquet I bought for myself.'

She shook her head at the memory. 'I had to pluck one of the flowers to make a buttonhole for Alec, because he'd forgotten one. I was a little disappointed about that. I know there aren't many men who pick flowers for women. I can't expect everyone to be like Willoughby or Colonel Brandon, but I thought—'

'For your wedding day, at least,' Lloyd said.

'Exactly. But he did look handsome,' Sarah said. 'I'm afraid I forgave an awful lot because he was handsome. How silly is that?' She sighed. 'I suppose the cracks started when he moved in. He still kept his own home and stayed there for work, but weekends were always at mine, and that's when the problems started. He moved a lot of stuff in, and I was fine with that—I really was—except he wasn't very tidy, so I'd tidy everything for him. I thought I was doing him a favor. I knew how busy he was during the week at work, and I didn't think he'd want to bother with such things during his time off, so I put everything away for him, but then he said he could never find anything, and even when he could, he complained about it. He didn't like the way I folded T-shirts or color coded his socks. He found it all rather strange. I tried to explain to him that it was part of my OCD, but he told me to snap out of it.'

Lloyd laughed. 'That's the typical response by someone who knows nothing about OCD. If only one could snap out of it.'

Sarah nodded. 'At least you understand, but Alec made no attempt to. At first he made a joke about things, as though humor might break the OCD spell I was under, but then he just became frustrated and angry and shouted at me, and I was quite glad when the weekend was over and he'd return back to his own home. We did have some good times, but they were usually when we went away together, and I made a sincere effort not to fuss over things, but there was this one time when he caught me cleaning the cutlery in a restaurant. I tried to hide what I was doing under the table, but he spotted me and made a big scene. I've never been so embarrassed in my life. After that, he spent more and more time at his home and made excuses that he couldn't get down to stay with me. It wasn't much of a marriage after that.'

Sarah sat down on the end of the bed. 'So that's my marriage,' she said with a hollow laugh. 'It was everything I dreamed it would be.'

'Jane Austen let you down,' Lloyd said.

'No, only life let me down. After all, Jane Austen had already warned me that "Happiness in marriage is entirely a matter of chance."'

'You don't really believe that, do you?'

Sarah shrugged. 'I'm beginning to.'

'You were just unlucky the first time.'

'The first time?' Sarah said. 'You make it sound like I'm going to risk it again.'

'Aren't you?'

She looked at him. What was he suggesting? 'I don't have any immediate plans.'

'You mustn't give up. I mean, you're far too young to turn into an old cynic, and there are many ways that you can make sure that happiness isn't just down to chance.'

'Like how?'

'Like good old-fashioned getting to know somebody. People don't make time for it anymore. Everyone is always in such a rush, and I don't think marriage is taken seriously. It seems that a wedding day is just an excuse for a big party, and nobody really thinks about what it means, and divorce is so easy.'

'Do I detect an old-fashioned romantic here?'

'If you mean do I believe in the sanctity of marriage, then yes.'

Sarah smiled. It was nice to meet somebody who believed in such values, and it made her feel inexplicably miserable. 'I can't believe I'm divorced.'

'I didn't mean that divorce is wrong,' Lloyd added quickly.

'I know,' she said. 'But I never imagined it playing a part in my life. I thought that if I ever married, it would be for life. I'd never have done such a thing to my sister if I'd known it was going to last only a short time.'

'But you can't live like that, Sarah. All of us make what we think is the right decision at the time. You can't live your life by *if onlys*.'

She nodded. 'But if only Mia would let me talk to her,' she said with a sad smile.

'I'm sure she will.'

'What if she leaves Bath and I never see her again?'

'Sarah, you've got to stop worrying. I know that's easier said than done, but you can't control this, and you're driving yourself crazy trying to.'

She twisted her hands and nodded. He was right, of course.

'Look, I'd better be going,' Lloyd said at last. 'It's getting late.'

Sarah nodded. It had been the longest day she'd ever known, yet she didn't want it to end. She crossed the room toward the door with him.

'Thanks for being so... tolerant.'

He blanched at the word. 'Tolerant?'

She nodded. 'I've never known anyone to tolerate quite so much in one day.'

He laughed. 'I had no idea Bath would be so very surprising.'

'No,' Sarah said, 'neither did I.'

They looked at each other for a moment, and Sarah wondered if he was going to kiss her. Would it be the right moment? She wanted him to kiss her, but her head was so full of emotional jumble that she wasn't sure that a kiss would be right at the moment.

'Good night,' she said.

'I'll call you tomorrow, okay?'

Sarah nodded, deciding that his promise was as good as any kiss.

Chapter 39

MIA WOKE UP, AND FOR A FEW BLISSFUL MOMENTS, FELT perfectly contented with the world. The morning light streaming in through the pink curtains gave a warm, rosy glow to the room that felt typically Shelley-like. She was such a romantic when it came to soft furnishings, and rosy pinks and baby blues adorned every room of the house. Was this going to be her new home? Mia wondered. It was a strange feeling that, in a few weeks' time, she could be living there with little William.

She felt wonderfully relieved for having told Shelley the truth the night before. It was a huge weight off her shoulders, but something else was weighing her down, and that was the fact that she hadn't yet told Sarah.

There was a gentle knock on the door, and Shelley's tousled head peeped in. 'I've brought you a cup of tea,' she said, entering the room. 'A proper cup of tea. Not one of my dad's strange concoctions.'

'What time is it?' Mia asked, sitting up in bed.

'Gone nine.'

'Goodness!' Mia said. 'I was out for the count.'

'I'm not surprised, after the day you had. How are you feeling?'

'Like yesterday was just a dream—or rather a nightmare—and I'm not even sure if it happened, now.'

'Oh, it happened, I'm afraid,' Shelley said, 'but it wasn't all bad, was it? I mean, you haven't changed your mind about moving here, have you?'

Mia swung her legs out of bed. 'No, I haven't changed my mind. I think it's an amazing idea.'

Shelley's smile stretched across the whole of her face. 'I can't tell you how excited I am.'

'You might change your mind after the first week. You've no idea how much mess a toddling boy makes,' Mia warned her.

'You think I'll notice a little bit more mess?' Shelley said with a laugh.

'It's so kind of you, Shelley.'

Shelley shook her head. 'I want to do this more than anything else in the world.' She looked pensive for a moment as if she were about to add something.

'What is it? I'll pay you rent, if that's what's worrying you.'

'It's not that.'

'What, then?'

'Sarah rang.'

'What, this morning?'

Shelley nodded. 'She was anxious that you might have fled Bath in the dead of night.'

'What did she say?'

'That she wants to see you.'

Mia sighed.

'Please see her, Mia,' Shelley begged. 'It's the only way.'

'I know. I know.' Mia got out of bed and started searching through her suitcase for something suitable to wear.

'So you'll see her?'

'Do I have a choice?'

'Not really,' Shelley said.

Mia looked at her. 'You've already arranged something, haven't you?'

Shelley bit her lip. 'Kind of.'

'What?'

'It was Sarah's idea. She wants to meet you at twelve.'

'Where?'

'In the Georgian Garden. She said you know where it is.'

'Of course I do,' Mia said. 'We've been there before.'

The Georgian Garden was one of Bath's many hidden gems. The entrance was by way of the pretty Gravel Walk down which the promenaders walked during the opening of the Jane Austen Festival, but it was often overlooked by tourists hurrying to and from the Royal Crescent. It was a simple eighteenth-century design of a small town garden with neat box hedging containing shrubs, roses, and pretty perennials, but the real treat was the magnificent white garden seat. A replica of an eighteenth-century original, it was possible to imagine Jane Austen herself sitting on it, chatting merrily to her sister, Cassandra, before heading to the shops to buy ribbons and muslin.

The thing that was really special about the Georgian Garden was the view it provided of the back of The Circus. Story after story of fabulous windows rose up into the sky, and there was the most fabulous spiral fire escape that Mia had ever seen.

Mia and Sarah had discovered the Georgian Garden on their last trip to Bath, just a few months before their fateful holiday to Devon. They visited it in the full Regency costume, sitting on the bench together and bemoaning the lack of fine young gentlemen to keep them company.

'I don't think I'll *ever* meet anyone,' Mia had said with a dramatic sigh.

'You will, just don't be in such a hurry,' Sarah told her.

'Is he really out there?'

'Of course he is. Just remember what Jane Austen said. "Do not be in a hurry: depend upon it, the right Man will come at last."'

'He never comes to Bath,' Mia said.

'No. I don't think we're ever going to meet anybody suitable in Bath.'

'I wonder where, then.'

'Probably when we least expect it, when we're not looking at all.'

'But I'm always looking.'

'Then you should stop. There are more important things to think about,' Sarah said.

'Well, I can't think of any.'

Sarah laughed.

'If only I knew when I was to meet him,' Mia said. 'I'd be more settled then.'

'You'll never be settled. You're always in a state of flux.'

'I am not.'

Sarah shook her head and then closed her eyes, tipping her head back toward the sky. 'It will happen. You just have to keep the faith, like Elizabeth Bennet. She knew it would be wrong to settle for life as Mrs Collins, didn't she? We mustn't settle, either. We must wait for our own Mr Darcy to come along, because Mr Darcy is forever.'

How romantic they'd both been back then! How full of optimism! How sure they had both been of a happy ending!

'How very long ago that was,' Mia said with a sigh.

Twelve o'clock at the Georgian Garden. Mia's heart was already racing at the thought of it, but there was no backing out. She knew she had to go through with it.

Having showered and breakfasted, Mia went downstairs and met Shelley in the kitchen.

'You ready?' Shelley asked.

'As ready as I'll ever be.'

Shelley walked across the room and wrapped her friend up in a big hug. 'You'll be fine,' she said.

'I wish I felt as sure as you. I feel like I'm auditioning for the biggest role of my life.'

'You're sure to get the part,' Shelley said. 'Sarah loves you so much, and she wants to make things right.'

Mia nodded.

'You do too, don't you?' Shelley added.

Mia paused before answering. 'Of course I do.'

'Well, then, there shouldn't be any problems, should there?'

'I'd better get going,' Mia said, extricating herself from Shelley's second hug.

'Call me as soon as you can, and don't run away this time.'

Mia left the house, and as she was walking down the pathway, Gabe called over.

'Hey!' he said.

She waved to him.

'Got a minute?' he called.

'Not really,' she said.

'I wanted to ask you about this Darcy guy.'

'I'm in an awful hurry, Gabe. Can it wait?' she snapped and hurried toward the waiting taxi before he could reply.

Chapter 40

SARAH WAS THE FIRST TO ARRIVE AT THE GEORGIAN GARDEN. She'd walked into town from her hotel, crossing Pulteney Bridge before wending her way through the streets to reach the Gravel Walk.

She smiled as she saw the large ornate bench, remembering it from her last visit there with Mia, but she was too anxious to sit down. Instead, she paced the length of the neat pathways, her gaze darting continuously to the entrance in the hope that Mia would arrive on time. She didn't expect punctuality from her sister, even after their years of separation, but she hoped that Mia would respect the clock for once in her life.

As the taxi crossed the river into town, Mia wished it would slow down. It was going too fast. She wasn't ready. Staring out of the window at the Georgian buildings that passed by in a blur, she thought how easy it would be to leave Bath right then. She could just tell the taxi driver to keep going, hit the M4, and keep going until they reached London. Okay, so she wouldn't be able to pay him, but at the moment, she'd rather face that problem than have to face Sarah.

As much as she loved Bath, it had brought her nothing but trouble on this trip. At that moment she felt close to Jane Austen, who had many unhappy times in Bath. Her father had died there, and her family had been forced to take cheaper accommodations. It must have been a difficult time for her.

Jane Austen loved Bath as a visitor, but had no wish to live there. She was a girl of the countryside, and life in a city must have been difficult for her. In her letters, she described Bath as being 'vapour, shadow, smoke and confusion,' and Mia could well understand where the author was coming from.

Mia thought about how Bath was portrayed in the novels. In *Northanger Abbey*, the first novel Austen wrote, the young heroine, Catherine Morland, reveled in its bustle, enjoying her first foray into society, but then there was Austen's last completed novel, *Persuasion*, where its heroine, Anne Elliot, loathed the city, finding it 'disagreeable.' Mia remembered the moment when Anne first arrives in Bath with Lady Russell. "'She persisted in a very determined, though very silent, disinclination for Bath,'" Mia recited. She'd often wondered at these two contrasting portrayals of Bath and how they showed a change in Jane Austen herself.

How did *Mia* feel about it? Wasn't it going to be her new home?

'Okay, here, love,' the taxi driver said, pulling up by the Gravel Walk.

Mia paused a moment before answering, looking down the length of the pathway that would lead her to her sister.

Sarah looked at her watch for the fifth time in as many minutes. She tried sitting on the bench at one point, drumming her fingers on her knee, but she was soon up again, pacing the length of the small garden.

Where was she? Had Shelley not been able to persuade Mia to come? Would Sarah be pacing up and down in the garden forever? She thought about ringing Shelley, but she didn't want to worry her. Shelley had sounded anxious enough when Sarah called that morning, and she didn't want to put any more pressure on her. The situation was between herself and Mia now.

Please let her come, she whispered to herself. *Please!*

Suddenly Mia was there, standing in the sunlight like some kind of mirage. Sarah blinked hard, to make sure she wasn't imagining it, but there was her little sister. No longer wearing the pretty Regency dress of the night before, she looked surprisingly grown up in blue jeans and a crisp white shirt. Her hair was as wild and wonderfully tumbly as Sarah remembered it, but her face looked drawn, and her eyes had lost some of their youthful sparkle.

'I wasn't sure if you'd come,' Sarah said at last as they walked forward to meet each other.

'Neither was I,' Mia said.

'I'm so glad you did. Shall we sit down?'

Mia nodded, and they walked over to the big white bench.

'Remember when we were here last time?' Sarah said.

'Yes, I do.'

'I was thinking about it before,' Sarah said. 'How romantic we both were then.'

'That was a long time ago,' Mia said.

Sarah bit her lip, feeling chided. 'I know.'

A few moments of silence passed between them before Sarah dared to speak again. 'It's all over between Alec and me,' she said. 'It was all over before it really began. I tried to let you know, but you were pretty hard to contact. Did you move?'

'Yes.'

'I thought you must have. Well, I hope you've got a nicer flat these days.'

'Not really.'

'Oh.'

There was another awkward silence.

'Mia,' Sarah began again, 'I'll never forgive myself for what I did to you. I still can't believe I let a man come between us.' She twisted her hands together in her lap, willing herself not to burst into tears. She wanted to be in control of things. 'I've never regretted anything more in my life,' she continued. 'I can't explain what happened in Devon. It was like some awful kind of madness, but I tried so hard to control it. I thought I could forget about Alec, and I really did try, but I just couldn't.'

An elderly couple entered the garden and stopped by an information board next to them. It was like one of those annoying moments when a waiter interrupts a conversation to ask if you're ready to order. The sisters waited for the couple to move on before Sarah continued.

'I feel so ashamed of myself when I think about what I did to you. I know how you felt about Alec, and—'

'It doesn't matter,' Mia said.

'What?'

'I said it doesn't matter anymore. I don't want to keep thinking about the past,' Mia said. 'I've agonized over it enough, and I think it's time to move on now.'

'I need to apologize to you,' Sarah said. 'We can't ignore what happened.'

'I know,' Mia said. 'That's why I came here today, and there's another reason too.'

'What is it?' Sarah asked gently, observing her sister closely. She was avoiding eye contact which pained Sarah. Mia looked as if she were being interrogated by an enemy rather than talking to her sister, and Sarah was desperate to reach out and hold her hands in her own.

Mia swallowed hard. 'I didn't know how to tell you,' she said. 'I still don't, so I'll show you, instead.' She reached into her handbag and brought out a photo of a young boy and handed it to her sister.

Sarah looked at it for a moment without speaking. The resemblance was startling, from the mass of dark curls to the beautiful bright eyes and rosy cheeks. 'You've had a baby?'

Mia nodded.

'Oh, my goodness!' Sarah said, realization dawning on her. 'I'm an auntie?'

'Yes,' Mia said. 'You've been an auntie for two years.'

Sarah gasped and a hand flew dramatically to her mouth in the sort of gesture that was far more common for Mia. 'I can't believe it.'

'It's true,' Mia said. 'Look, I've got another photo of him somewhere when he was a baby. You'll love it.' She delved into her handbag and brought out a little notebook with a silhouette of Jane Austen on the cover. Opening it up, she took out a tiny photograph of a baby boy.

'This was taken just after he was born.'

'Oh!' Sarah said, seeming to have lost the power of speech.

'And this one was taken a few days ago,' Mia said, handing her a third photo. This one was of him on a swing in the park. He was wearing a scarlet hat and his cheeks matched the hat perfectly.

'What's his name?'

'William,' Mia said. 'William Fitz Castle.'

Sarah nodded and smiled. 'A lovely variation of Fitzwilliam,' she said.

'I couldn't burden him with Darcy's real name.'

Sarah sat looking at the three photographs. Here was a lovely little boy—her very own nephew—and she had missed seeing him being born. She hadn't been there when he'd learned to crawl or taken his first steps or spoken his first words, and that knowledge tore into her heart as keenly as a knife.

Mia seemed to realize what her sister was thinking. 'You would have loved him as a baby. He was always laughing. I've been so lucky with him.'

'How do you take care of him? What about your auditions?'

'They've had to take second place. Third place, really. I have a neighbor who takes care of William when I'm working. She adores him.'

'I had no idea,' Sarah said.

'Of course you didn't. How could you?'

Sarah felt a strange fluttery feeling in her stomach.

'He's Alec's, isn't he?'

There was a pause before Mia answered. 'Yes,' she said.

Sarah nodded. 'Does he know?'

Mia shook her head. 'I wondered if I should tell him, but I didn't feel it was right. He's here in Bath, you know.'

'What?'

Mia nodded. 'He said he wanted to see me.'

Sarah frowned. 'What did he want to see you about?'

Mia sighed.

'Tell me, Mia. Now's not the time to hide anything.'

'He wanted us to have another go.'

'*What?*'

'I know. I couldn't believe it either.'

'What did he say?'

'I—'

'Tell me! I need to know.'

Mia sighed. 'He said he'd made a mistake. He said he wanted to be with me.'

Sarah felt hot tears pricking her eyes.

'I told him what I thought of him and how he obviously hadn't given things with you a proper chance.'

'You told him that?'

Mia nodded. 'He hasn't been fair to you.'

'How can you be so understanding after all I've done to you?'

'Because you're my sister,' Mia whispered.

'Oh, God!' Sarah said at last. There was a pause for a moment when they both sat looking at each other. 'Everything's such an awful mess, isn't it?'

'Yes,' Mia said, 'but I think we might be able to work a way through it, don't you?'

Sarah nodded, and her first tears spilled down her cheeks. 'I hope so. I really hope so.'

'Don't cry! You'll make me cry too.'

'You should have told me, Mia,' Sarah cried. 'Why didn't you tell me?'

'I so wanted to, but it didn't seem right.'

'It would have changed everything.'

Mia sighed. 'I didn't want it to. Alec chose you, not me.'

'But that was wrong of him. He had no right to marry me, not when—'

'It doesn't matter,' Mia interrupted. 'Not now.'

'How can you ever forgive me, when I'll never forgive myself?'

'You must try to forgive yourself, Sarah. We've got to try to put all this behind us.'

'You were so mad at me last night, though. You didn't want to speak to me at all.'

'I know,' Mia said. 'I'm sorry. I think I was just shocked to see you there, but I've been thinking about everything. My head hurts from thinking so much.'

'Mine does too.'

'And I just...' she paused.

'What?'

'I just want my sister back.'

Suddenly they embraced and tears flowed freely down both their faces. They didn't even notice the young family that entered the garden, nor did they see the baffled little girl pointing a stubby finger at them crying on the garden seat.

'I can't believe we let somebody come between us,' Sarah said when the tears finally stopped. 'I've missed you so much.'

'I've missed you too. I've felt as though I've been only half here.'

'Me too,' Sarah said. 'That's *exactly* how I've felt.'

'There's been so much I've wanted to share with you,' Mia continued, 'and I don't just mean the big things, like having a baby, but silly little things too, like the first time I dressed William and took him out for a walk. It felt like the biggest adventure in the world, and I really wanted to share it with you.'

'When can I see him?' Sarah asked.

'Whenever you want to.'

'Gosh! I want to seem right now. He's not here in Bath with you, is he?'

'No. He's in London.'

'We have so much time to make up,' Sarah said.

'I know,' Mia said, 'but we can start straightaway, can't we?'

Sarah nodded, her eyes full of tears once again.

'I'm leaving London,' Mia said.

'Really?'

Mia nodded. 'It's time. I've been miserable there. I thought it was what I wanted, but when William came along, everything changed. I'm not the person I used to be. I want different things now.'

'Where will you go?'

'Here.'

'Here? Bath?'

'Yes. Shelley's said I can have her spare room. She's been looking for a tenant for ages.'

'And she knows about William?'

'She does,' Mia said. 'I can't believe it, but she can't wait for us to move in.'

'What about your singing and your auditions? Are you really giving up on everything?'

'I gave up on those some time ago.'

Sarah looked sad. 'But your singing was your whole world.'

'Not anymore.'

'Gosh,' Sarah said, 'I'm just trying to imagine my little sister as a mother. I always assumed that would be my role first.'

'And it will happen. I'm sure of it.'

'Just not with Alec,' Sarah said.

'No, not with Alec.'

During a pause they watched as a young couple walked around the garden together. They were holding hands, and the two sisters watched their progress.

'I've met someone,' Mia said suddenly.

'Really? When?'

'This week, here in Bath,' Mia said.

'You have? So have I!'

'Really? Oh, God! He isn't called Gabe, is he?'

'No, Lloyd.'

Mia breathed a sigh of relief. 'It wouldn't do for us to fall in love with the same man again, would it?'

'Er—no. Let's not do that again.'

They left the Georgian Garden and walked the length of the Gravel Walk toward the city centre.

'Did you hear they've made a new version of *Persuasion*?' Sarah asked.

'Yes!' Mia said. 'And Oli Wade Owen was right here in Bath. I can't believe I missed him.'

'I read he's getting married,' Sarah said. 'To that director woman, Teresa Hudson. Apparently they have a daughter.'

'I read that too.'

'There seems to be a lot of secret children about,' Sarah said.

Mia blushed.

They stopped at the top of some steps, and Sarah linked Mia's arm. 'I think you should tell Alec,' she said in a low voice.

Mia bit her lip and then nodded. 'Everybody thinks I should.'

'Will you?'

'I wish that I didn't have to have anything more to do with him, but I think it would be unfair of me to make that decision for my son too.'

'Is Alec still here in Bath?'

'I'm not sure. I saw him yesterday, but he might have left by now.'

Sarah reached inside her handbag and scribbled a phone number on a piece of notepaper. 'This is his number. Give him a call.'

Mia took a deep breath. 'Okay.'

'It's the right thing to do.'

'I know it is.'

They hugged, and Sarah felt a tumultuous mix of emotions.

'Call me, won't you?'

Mia nodded, and a tear rolled down her left cheek.

'I don't want to leave you,' Sarah said. 'I'm so scared I won't see you again.'

'You will,' Mia said. 'I promise.'

'Send William my love.'

'I don't need to. You can give it to him yourself when you meet him.'

Sarah smiled. She'd never felt happier in her life.

Chapter 41

S HELLEY WAS PACING UP AND DOWN THE KITCHEN WHILST PIE was trying to make a cup of tea in the corner of the room.

'She said she'd ring as soon as she could. Why hasn't she rung? I've tried her phone, but it just goes to voice mail.' She put her phone down on the kitchen table. 'I know she's got a lot to think about now, but I wish she'd remember me too. I'm worried about her, and I wish she knew that I cared so much. I sometimes wonder if she knows that.'

'You're stressed,' Pie said from the other side of the room.

'You're damned right, I'm stressed,' she said, and then registered that Pie hadn't just grunted as usual but had spoken real words.

'Come on,' he said, walking across the room.

'Come on where?'

'Upstairs.'

Shelley frowned but followed him upstairs. 'What are we doing?'

'Come in here,' he said, opening his bedroom door.

She looked up at him. His face was dark and serious, but there was nothing unusual in that. She stepped into his room. It was the first time she'd been invited into it. She had taken a few sneaky peeks into it when Pie was out, but it was quite a different experience to be invited in.

She looked around the room. It was stark, as rooms went, apart from the feminine touches Shelley had placed there, such as the blue floral curtains and matching lamp shade. Everything was pretty much in its place. There were no clothes on the floor or drawers spilling out their contents. There was also a curious smell.

'What *is* that?' Shelley asked.

'Ylang-ylang.'

'Pardon?'

'Take your shirt off.'

'What?'

'And sit on the bed.'

'Pie!' Shelley's hands were firmly on her hips and her forehead crinkled in bemusement.

'Go on,' he said.

'I'm not taking my shirt off. I'm not wearing anything underneath.'

'I'll turn away,' he said. 'Take your shirt off and hug it to your chest.'

Something in the tone of his voice reassured her that he wasn't up to anything suspicious.

'Ready?' he said a moment later.

Shelley was sitting on the edge of the bed and almost leapt right off it when she felt his hands on her shoulders.

'What are you doing?' Shelley asked in alarm.

'Sit still and relax,' he said, and once again, she smelled the warm and exotic scent. He was massaging her!

'Oh, my God!' she exclaimed.

'Stop talking.'

Shelley heard a sudden crack in her shoulder. 'Oh! Was that me?'

'I'm just ironing out your kinks. You have quite a few.'

'Yes, I'm very kinky,' she said with a giggle.

'Shush,' he said.

'You're good. You should do this for a living.'

'I do,' he said.

'Oh,' Shelley said. '*Oh!*' Suddenly all of Pie's mysterious comings and goings made sense. He always smelled sweet. He worked the most peculiar hours. There were always women leaving messages on the house answering machine.

Shelley closed her eyes and sighed in bliss as Pie worked his way down her spine.

'Oh, that's so good. Hey! You're not going to charge me for this, are you?'

Pie laughed. It was the first time she'd ever heard him laugh, and it was a delightful sound. 'I'm sure we can work something out.'

Shelley smiled. She really hoped they could.

By the time Mia returned, Shelley was completely blissed out from her massage and had calmed down to such an extent that she didn't feel it necessary to leap on Mia as soon as she walked through the front door.

'You look happy,' Mia said. 'What's that smell, more tea bags?'

'No, it's ylang-ylang. Pie gave me a massage.'

'Really?'

'It's his job.'

'Oh,' Mia said.

'Never mind about that *now*. How did it go with Sarah?'

They went through to the living room together and sat down.

'It was… it was… strange,' Mia said.

'Good or bad strange?'

'Good, I think,' Mia said. 'We cried a lot.'

'And you told her about William?'

'Of course.'

'What did she say?'

'She wants to see him.'

'Well, of course. So do I,' Shelley said. 'What else did she say? Did you tell her about Alec in Bath?'

'Yes.'

'*And?*' Shelley said in exasperation.

'I think she guessed he was Alec's as soon as she saw the photos, and she thinks I should tell him about William too.'

Shelley nodded. 'It's the right thing to do.'

'I know it is, but it's not going to be easy or pleasant.'

'Nothing concerning that man is ever likely to be pleasant,' Shelley said, 'but you've done an amazing thing today, Mia. I'm proud of you.'

Mia nodded, and her eyes were brimful of tears once more.

'I couldn't bear it when you and Sarah weren't speaking. You guys used to be the *best* of friends. I've never seen anyone closer. Boy, I'd *kill* to have that closeness with anyone, and I know how much it must have hurt you when you fell out like that.'

'It's been like walking around with an open wound for three years,' Mia said, pushing her hair out of her face and mopping it with a tissue. 'I've missed her so much. Even when I hated her, I loved her too.'

'But it's going to be all right now, isn't it?'

'I think so,' Mia said. 'I wish I didn't have to see Alec again, though.'

'Yes,' Shelley said. 'There's no easy way of getting out of that, is there? Let's not worry about that now. I think you've had more than enough angst for today. I'm going to make us a slap-up lunch, and then we're going to get dressed up and go into town. I've got us tickets for the Dame Pamela Harcourt recital, and wait until you see the dresses I've lined up for us to wear!'

Dame Pamela Harcourt was one of England's greatest actresses.

She had played all the great Shakespearean roles, from Lady Macbeth to Juliet, but among the Janeites, she was more famous for her roles as Marianne Dashwood in *Sense and Sensibility*, and more recently, Lady Catherine de Bourgh in *Pride and Prejudice*.

That afternoon, she would be reading extracts from Jane Austen and taking questions from the audience.

The room was packed with enthusiastic fans. 'I used to think I was going to be a huge star of the stage and screen, like Dame Pamela,' Mia said as they took their seats three rows from the front.

'You would have been one of England's greats,' Shelley assured her.

'Yes, like Lady Catherine de Bourgh would have been "a great proficient" if only she'd learned to play the piano.'

'No! I've seen you act, and you would have been fabulous.'

Mia smiled at her friend's reassurances. 'I guess we'll never know now.'

'Nonsense! Who's to say you won't go back into singing and acting later on? Maybe when William's at school.'

'William's my priority now,' Mia said.

'Of course,' Shelley said, 'but you've got to have some Mia time too.'

Mia thought about it for a moment. For the last few years, she'd put herself on hold and had been quite happy to do it, but maybe—just maybe—Shelley was right, and Mia could allow a little bit of the old Mia to resurface again one day.

As she was beginning to daydream about William cheering her on from the front row of a West End theater, Dame Pamela Harcourt entered the room. She was wearing a fabulous chiffon dress in the prettiest cherry-blossom pink. Around her neck she wore three rows of delicate pearls, and there were what looked like mini diamond chandeliers dangling from her ears. Her hair, which was the color of the moon, was swept up in an elegant chignon, and a diamond clasp sparkled from within its wispy depths.

A huge round of applause greeted her, and Mia wondered what it would be like to live her life surrounded by such public adoration. As soon as the thought crossed her mind, she realized that Shelley might be right, and that she could one day tread the boards herself once again.

Dame Pamela began by talking about her lifelong love of Jane Austen. 'Jane Austen has done *wonders* for my career,' she said with a smile. 'She might have written only six books, but I've been lucky enough to star in most of them.'

She started the readings with an extract from *Northanger Abbey*, celebrating Catherine Morland's first ball, and many a knowing glance was exchanged when Dame Pamela read the lines, 'Dress was her passion. She had a most harmless delight in being fine.'

She then read a scene from *Persuasion*, the comic scene where Sir Walter is complaining about Bath. 'The worst of Bath was the number of its plain women. He did not mean to say that there were no pretty women, but the number of plain was out of all proportion. He had frequently observed, as he walked, that one handsome face would be followed by thirty, or five and thirty frights.'

She finished by reading the scene from *Pride and Prejudice* where Lady Catherine visits Longbourn to confront Elizabeth Bennet about a 'report of a most alarming nature.' It was wonderful, as if Lady Catherine de Bourgh and Elizabeth Bennet were in the room with the audience, and nobody wanted it to end. There was many a call of 'encore' when the reading came to an end.

Questions followed. What was Dame Pamela's favorite

Austen role? Answer: Marianne Dashwood, because she was so passionate. Would she have chosen Willoughby or Colonel Brandon? Both, she said, which caused much laughter among the people in the audience.

'Are you going to ask a question?' Shelley whispered to Mia.

'No, I'm too nervous.'

'I think I'm going to.'

'Any more questions?' the organizer asked the audience.

Shelley stuck her hand in the air, feeling like an anxious schoolgirl.

'Yes, the lady in the yellow muslin gown.'

'Dame Pamela, my friend here is a budding singer and actress, and I'd love to know if you have any advice.'

Mia felt herself blush to the very depths of her being as she felt the gaze of Dame Pamela fix itself upon her.

'I am often asked for my advice, and here it is,' she said. 'Never give up. If you have a dream—no matter what that dream is, whether it be to become a great actress or to open your very own sweet shop—never stop dreaming it, because if you do, life becomes one long nightmare.'

Mia and Shelley sat riveted by her words, and then the applause began as Dame Pamela left the stage in a cloud of pink chiffon, her floral perfume scenting the air behind her.

'Wow!' Shelley said. 'There's a part of me that wants to run after her, so I can listen to her forever. Wasn't she amazing?'

'Why did you ask that question?'

'Because I don't think you should give up on yourself so easily, Mia. I know you're a mother now, but you're also a human being in your own right, and I so want to see that old Mia back again. She was fabulous, and I have a feeling there's a little part of you that would like to see her back again too. I'm right, aren't I?'

Mia looked into the smiling face of her friend and realized that she was smiling too. 'You might be,' she said.

Later that evening, in the privacy of her room, Mia rang Alec's number. It rang several times before going to voice mail, and Mia left a message for him to call her back. As she was getting into her bed, her phone rang.

'Mia?' It was Alec. 'How great to hear from you, although, I have to say, I didn't expect to hear from you again.'

'I need to see you. Are you still in Bath?'

'No, but I can get there pretty quickly, if you need me to.'

'I need you to.'

'Then I'm there.'

'Eleven o'clock tomorrow.' Mia gave him directions to a little café that was easy to find, he confirmed that he'd be there, and she hung up. He probably thought that she had forgiven him and wanted to make a go of things together, but that couldn't have been further from the truth.

Chapter 42

I can't believe I'm an auntie,' Sarah said as she walked out of a talk about gambling in Regency times.

'That must have come as a surprise,' Lloyd said.

'It did,' Sarah said.

'You had no idea?'

'No,' Sarah said, her expression pained. 'It's awful. I've missed so much time, not only with William, but also with my sister, and I'm *so* angry at myself.'

'You can make it all up now, can't you?'

'I just wish I hadn't missed it all, and I can't believe I didn't see all this in Devon.' They reached Queen Square and walked along one of the paths to a bench and sat down. It was a favorite spot of Sarah's, because in whichever direction she looked, Georgian architecture greeted her. Three hundred and sixty degrees of beauty. It was like stepping back into the Bath Jane Austen would have known.

'I still don't understand. How could Alec have made love to my sister and still be making a move on me?' she said. 'How can men do that?'

Lloyd cleared his throat. 'Not every man would pull a stunt like that,' he said.

Sarah looked at him. 'I'm sorry. I didn't mean to sound like I was accusing you.'

'Well, I've not met your sister, but I can promise you this right now: I will not fall in love with her.'

Sarah smiled. 'What makes you so sure of that?'

Lloyd's eyebrows rose over his dark eyes, and he smiled back at her. 'Because I'm falling in love with you.'

Sarah's eyes widened at his declaration. 'But we've only just met.'

'Doesn't matter,' he said. 'Haven't you heard of love at first sight? As soon as I saw you, I knew you were the one for me.'

Sarah laughed. 'That sort of thing happens only in books and films.'

'Really? Are you sure? Are you *absolutely* sure that it can't happen in real life too? Because I'm pretty certain I am in love with you.'

Sarah stared at him. He certainly did look sincere, and hadn't she wanted to kiss him the previous night?

'Lloyd, I don't know what to say. You've been wonderful to me, and I've enjoyed your company.'

'I can hear a "but" approaching, can't I?'

Sarah sighed. 'I'm not sure I have it in me to fall in love again— not after Alec.'

Lloyd frowned. 'You really think that? Are you going to let that one bad experience blight the rest of your life? Because that's a rotten way to live.'

'I can't help it. It's just the way I feel.'

'Then you're letting Alec win. You're handing your life over to a man who doesn't deserve it,' Lloyd said. 'Are you sure you want to do that? And are you absolutely sure you don't want to be kissed by the man sitting next to you on this bench?'

'You want to kiss me?'

'I wanted to kiss you last night.'

'You did?' Sarah said. 'Why didn't you?'

'I didn't think it was the right moment; you know, after everything that had happened that day.'

Sarah nodded. 'And is it right now?'

'You need to tell me,' he said, 'because I'm not sure I'd want to waste a kiss on somebody who didn't want to return it.'

'But I do.'

Lloyd looked surprised. 'But you said—'

'I know,' Sarah said. 'I'm confused. My head is telling me one thing, and my heart is telling me another.'

'And you're the sister who's usually ruled by the head, aren't you?'

She nodded. 'The last time I followed my heart, it nearly got broken.'

'That was last time,' Lloyd said, 'not *this* time.' He edged closer to her on the bench and picked her hands up in his. 'What's your heart telling you now?' he asked.

She looked into his dark eyes. What was her heart telling her? It was telling her to kiss him. What was her head saying? It was saying be careful. And what could you do when your head and your heart were at odds with each other? Sarah thought about the books she had read and her beloved collection of Jane Austen novels. They all had happy endings. All the heroes and heroines met their perfect match, even if their journeys toward each other had been fraught with pain and misunderstandings. That was fiction, though. It didn't necessarily follow that Sarah was going to find such a happy ending, did it? What if she was destined to have her heart broken over and over again?

She looked at Lloyd. He didn't look like the heartbreaker type, and as he smiled at her, something deep inside her made her realize that she didn't want to shut herself off from love, and she didn't want to deny herself the chance for a happy ending.

'My heart is telling me…' she paused.

'What?' Lloyd asked.

'That I still believe in happy endings.' Sarah smiled and, despite the tourists strolling by, she leaned forward and kissed him.

∽

Mia wasn't thinking about kisses, although kisses had got her into this situation in the first place. She looked in the mirror for the umpteenth time. She knew that she was no longer the bright-eyed girl that had fallen in love with Alec, and she was glad of that, but she did rather wish she didn't look quite so *old*.

'Do I look okay?' Mia asked Shelley, who walked into the bedroom.

'You look marvelous,' Shelley said, leaning forward to kiss her cheek. Bingley, who had sneaked up the stairs when nobody was looking, tried to get in on the action too and stuffed a nose into Mia's crotch.

'You really must teach this dog some manners, Shelley,' Mia said as she pushed Bingley's head away with a giggle.

'Right,' Shelley said. 'That would be like teaching Mr Collins to become interesting.'

There was a blast of a car horn.

'That'll be the taxi,' Mia said, looking at her watch before running down the stairs.

Shelley and Bingley followed, the former almost tripping over the latter.

'Remember,' Shelley shouted after her, 'no slapping!'

Mia tutted. 'I'm not going to slap anyone,' she said, 'unless they really deserve it.'

'Oh, dear,' Shelley said. 'I wouldn't want to be Alec, then.'

Mia left the house, got into the taxi, and waved good-bye to Shelley. She suddenly felt very alone and half wished that she'd asked Shelley to come with her, but she knew she had to do this alone.

When the taxi dropped her as close to the café as he could get, Mia felt a whole meadowful of butterflies fluttering in her stomach. What was she going to say? How on earth did you tell a man that he has a two-year-old son? Maybe he would slap her for not having told him, or maybe he'd demand to marry her. She shook her head. She couldn't imagine Alec would have marriage on his mind again.

What if he didn't turn up at all? No, that wasn't likely to happen, not if he thought she wanted a reconciliation, which was how she had left things the night before.

Turning off a busy street, she saw the café and made her way toward it. Already it was full of tourists, and the constant chatter was comforting to Mia and might very well disguise any shouting that might occur in the next few moments.

She was still wondering if the whole thing was a good idea, when Alec walked into the café. There was no escaping him; he spotted her straightaway.

'It's good to see you,' he said as he sat down at the table opposite her. 'I was hoping you'd change your mind, because there's something I want to—'

'Alec,' she said, interrupting him. 'You mustn't try to guess why I wanted to see you, because you won't.'

'You've obviously changed your mind from the other day,' he said, reaching across the table to take her hand.

She flinched away from him. 'I haven't changed my mind.'

'Then why are you here?' he asked, a smug smile lifting the corners of his mouth.

'Because I've been persuaded by other people that it's the right thing to do.'

He frowned. 'What do you mean?'

Mia took a deep breath. 'You have a son,' she said, letting the words hang in the air between them for a moment.

'What?'

'After I got home from Devon, I realized I was pregnant, and I had a baby. A little boy.'

'Are you sure it's mine?'

Mia blanched at his words, even though she'd expected them. 'Of course I'm sure he's yours. I didn't meet any other Willoughbys whilst on holiday.'

'What?'

'Never mind,' she said, not bothering to explain the literary allusion. 'Do you want to see a picture of him?'

Alec looked blankly at her. 'I wasn't expecting this.'

'No,' she said. 'I guess not.'

Mia opened her handbag and took out the photo to show Alec. 'He's called William, and he's two years old. I won't stop you from seeing him, if that's what you decide you want, but he's *my* son, and you have to know that there's nothing more important in the world to me now.'

Alec took a moment to study the photograph. 'He's the spitting image of my dad at that age.'

'Is he?' For a moment, Mia thought she saw a softening in Alec's eyes, but he then returned the photograph to her.

'You don't need to worry about me breaking up a happy home,' he said.

'What do you mean?'

'As you said, he's *your* son.'

'You don't want to see him?'

Alec shook his head.

'I don't believe it,' Mia said.

'Come on. Be fair now. I didn't come here for this. I'm not a family man, Mia.'

'Then why did you get married?'

He shook his head. 'Getting married was a mistake. How many times do I have to tell you that?'

'Then we have nothing else to say,' she said, standing up so quickly that her chair fell over behind her.

Alec leapt up and picked it up. 'Mia,' he said, 'don't leave like this. We can work through things.'

'What do you mean? You don't want to see your own son!'

'But I still want to see you.'

'What?'

He smiled at her, and for a moment, she thought she was going to slap him again, but the moment soon passed.

'I guess that's it, then,' Mia said, turning to leave.

'Don't go!' Alec said, making a grab for her arm. She dodged out of the way and glared at him.

'I'm not laying any blame at your doorstep, Alec, and I can't say I'm surprised by your response, but I want you to know that if you ever change your mind, if you want to see William, then I shan't prevent you.'

'It's *you* I want to see.'

'Well, it's like this now: I'm a package deal with my son.' She turned to leave.

'Mia!' Alec called after her. She hoped that he wasn't going to chase her through the streets of Bath again and was thankful when he didn't bother. He was probably thanking his lucky stars that she wasn't demanding more of him in his role as father.

'We've both had a lucky escape,' she said to herself. It was the most unromantic of endings between two people that she could think of, but she also knew that it was the right one.

Chapter 43

SHELLEY WAS TRYING TO FIND MIA AMONG THE BACK STREETS of Bath. She had a pretty good idea of where the café was, but it was almost impossible to steer a direct route, because Bingley kept stopping and starting, pulling and pushing, and generally causing canine chaos.

'I shouldn't have brought you with me, Bingley,' she said, tugging him away from half a hot dog that had been dropped on the pavement. He looked up at her as if to say that he didn't ask for much in life.

Shelley paused in a doorway and reached for her phone, but once again, it went to Mia's voice mail. Shelley sighed. Surely Mia must have said good-bye to Alec by now, unless she'd run away with him. What if she'd had a complete change of heart, had forgiven the rogue, and run away with him?

'Answer your phone!' she shouted, causing a pair of shoppers to turn around and glare at her.

It took her only another five minutes to reach the café, and she peered in through the window in the hope of spotting her friend. Bingley peered in too, his wet nose leaving a long slimy streak across the window, much to the joy of a toddler sitting on the other side.

Mia was nowhere to be seen. Shelley chewed her lip and decided the best thing she could do would be to walk Bingley around for a bit and keep trying Mia's phone.

It had been an extraordinary few days since Mia had arrived. The Jane Austen Festival was always an exciting time, but Shelley had never experienced anything quite like this one before. What with long-lost sisters, dramatic reunions in the Pump Room, and secret babies, Shelley's head was spinning faster than Catherine Morland's after reading her fill of Gothic novels.

And what had all that massaging business been about with Pie? Shelley smiled as she remembered the delicious tingles she'd felt when he touched her. She'd never had a massage before. Well, not a professional one. She'd had a very poor substitute for one from a boy at drama school who knuckled her shoulder blades for a bit and then expected her to kiss him, but Pie had been wonderful, and she sincerely hoped her first massage wouldn't be her last.

Life was intensely interesting at the moment.

Since leaving the café, Mia had managed to get lost—not only in her thoughts, but in the backstreets as well. What was she doing? Had she just made a huge mistake? Should she have pushed Alec more? He was, after all, the father of her son, and surely it was only right that he take an interest in him.

'He doesn't even want to see him,' she whispered to herself. 'How can he not want to see his own son?' She thought about the blank look on his face as he glanced briefly at the photograph of William. It could have been a photo of any young boy in the world, for all he cared. A part of Mia was absolutely furious with Alec, but there was also a part that was relieved. If she was honest with herself, she didn't want Alec in her life. Ever since she found out she was pregnant, William had been her child and her child alone. She had coped through the most difficult years of her life without Alec. She didn't need him now, but at least she'd done the right thing in telling him. She didn't need to feel guilty anymore.

For a moment, she thought about Gabe and how he would have responded if he'd been in Alec's position—not that he would ever be in such a position, because he wouldn't be the sort to become involved with two sisters at once, get one pregnant, and then marry the other one.

She wondered how he'd have reacted when shown the photograph of William, and she could imagine no response other than total delight that he had a son. She knew he desperately wanted a family and had been heartbroken when he lost his chance with Andrea. Life seemed unfair. It was a cruel trick of fate that one man had been denied a child, whilst another had been given one he didn't want.

Mia looked at her watch and gasped when she saw the time. She must have been wandering around for ages, losing all track of time, and Shelley would no doubt be worrying about her.

She reached for her phone and switched it on. Almost instantly, it rang.

'Oh, thank goodness!' Shelley's voice cried into Mia's ear. 'Where on earth are you? I'm here at the café right now.'

'I don't know,' Mia said.

'What?'

'I'm a bit lost.'

'Well, look for a street name,' Shelley told her. 'Bath isn't that complicated.'

Mia searched for a street name. 'Lansdown Road,' she said a moment later. 'And I can see a street called Alfred Street.'

'Good heavens! How did you end up all the way out there?'

'I'm not sure. I've just been walking and thinking.'

'Well, it's time to stop,' Shelley said and proceeded to give her some directions. 'Do you think you can get yourself to the Pump Room?'

'I think so.'

'Good, well get yourself there as fast as you can. I've got a surprise for you.'

By the time Mia reached the Pump Room, a huge crowd had gathered there, and it took a further five minutes before Mia and Shelley were reunited.

'What's going on here?' Mia asked, bending to give Bingley an affectionate tickle.

'I'll tell you about it in a minute. How did it go with Alec?'

Mia sighed. 'About as bad as it could go. He doesn't want anything to do with William.'

Shelley frowned. 'That's a good thing, isn't it? I mean, it's appalling and diabolical and totally unforgiveable, but isn't it also the best thing too?'

Mia nodded. 'I really think it is, but I feel guilty for feeling like that.'

'Don't,' Shelley said. 'You've got absolutely nothing to feel guilty about.'

'I've made such a mess of my life,' Mia said.

'No, you haven't,' Shelley said.

'How can you say that? I'm a single mother with no career prospects who hasn't spoken to her sister in over three years and who, in the Bath Pump Room, managed to slap her ex-lover who, it seems, wants nothing to do with his son.'

'Okay, when you put it like that, it does sound rather a mess.' Shelley gave Mia's shoulder a quick squeeze.

'It serves me right if no man falls in love with me ever again,' Mia said.

'How can you say that?'

'Because I don't deserve it.'

'Men will always fall in love with you, Mia, just because you're you.'

'Shelley, that's a really sweet thing to say, but I'm afraid it isn't true.'

'You mean you don't know?'

'Know *what?*'

'About Gabe.'

'What about Gabe?'

'Gosh, Mia! He's madly in love with you.'

Mia looked baffled. 'He's not interested in me.'

'Oh, no? Then why is he taking part in this appalling Darcy lineup?'

'What lineup?'

Shelley nodded toward the thickest part of the crowd before them. 'Gabe came round when you were out yesterday and asked if I had such a thing as a Darcy shirt. He'd heard about a Darcy lineup for a wet shirt competition run by *Vive!* newspaper, and he thought it would be fun to take part in it, because he knew you'd like it.'

'Really?'

'Yes,' Shelley said. 'It's not part of the official Jane Austen Festival, and the Jane Austen Centre quite rightly didn't want anything to do with it, but... well, you can see how popular it is.'

Shelley was right. It had drawn a huge crowd, and cameras were at the ready.

'We have to try to get near the front,' Shelley said. 'Come on, follow me.'

Chapter 44

M IA FOLLOWED SHELLEY, DOING HER BEST TO KEEP UP WITH her friend, who pushed mercilessly through the endless rows of people.

'Excuse me! Guide dog coming through,' she yelled at the top of her voice. Mia blushed at the blatant lie. Nobody would believe that the boisterous Bingley was a guide dog, but neither did anybody want his persistent wet nose pushed into the backs of their knees, so the crowds parted quickly, and Mia and Shelley soon found themselves at the front.

It was the strangest sight Mia had ever seen: a neat row of Darcy wannabes all lined up together on a small stage, awaiting their watery fate. There were all sorts of men in the lineup, from a teenager who was being egged on by his girlfriend, who was waving a camera excitedly in the air, to an elderly gentleman whose Darcy days were long past.

And then there was Gabe. Mia's breath caught in her throat when she saw him. What on earth was he doing there? He looked out of place, yet the knowledge that he was there for her pierced her very soul.

A man stood with a microphone near a row of buckets of water, like some ghastly television game show on a Saturday night.

'Ladies and gentlemen,' the man at the microphone announced, 'have we any Mr Darcy fans here today?'

The crowd roared in the affirmative.

'And have we anyone who would like to see Mr Darcy in a wet shirt?'

Again the crowd roared in an eardrum-splitting manner.

'Then let the soaking commence!'

A great cheer went up as two men sloshed the first buckets of water over the teenage boy. His hair was instantly plastered to his face, and his white T-shirt clung to him.

Shelley burst into laughter, and Bingley started barking, but Mia wasn't sure how to respond. A part of her wanted to join in with the crowd and laugh, but the whole thing seemed awful and tacky, and she wished that poor Gabe wasn't a part of it.

He's doing this for you, a little voice said. *He knows you adore Mr Darcy. He's trying to make you happy.*

'He's madly in love with you,' another voice said—Shelley's voice. Mia looked at Gabe as he awaited his watery fate further along the lineup. He hadn't spotted her yet, and she had a chance to look at him unobserved. He was wearing a pair of blue jeans and sturdy boots, and most importantly, a Mr Darcy-style shirt in immaculate white. His arm was still in a sling, but Shelley's adept skills as a seamstress had accommodated him, and he looked like the perfect hero, with his dark-blond hair flopping across his face and his eyes bright with laughter. Was he really in love with her? Was he really prepared to humiliate himself just to put a smile on her face?

The old man was the next to get a drenching, and the crowd roared with laughter as his white shirt clung to his bony rib cage.

'Poor Gabe. What on earth was he thinking of?' Mia said.

'You,' Shelley said. 'He was thinking of you.'

Mia watched in horror as the next in the lineup—an unlikely looking man wearing a white shirt and tie as if he were about to walk into a board meeting—got the drenching of his life.

The crowd cheered before the next two men in line got thoroughly sploshed too.

'Gabe next!' Shelley said.

'Oh, I don't know if I can bear to watch,' Mia said.

'You *have* to. He's doing this for you.'

Mia's whole face screwed up in consternation as the two men approached Gabe with their buckets of water.

'Go on!' a middle-aged woman shouted from somewhere behind Mia's shoulder. Mia had the urge to tip a bucket of water over her.

Splash! went bucket number one.

Splosh! went bucket number two, careful to avoid his sling.

The crowd went mad, and Mia had to cover her ears, for fear of losing her hearing completely.

On and on went the men with the buckets until the complete lineup were thoroughly soaked, but Mia didn't see any of that, because her eyes were fixed firmly on Gabe as he stood dripping and laughing on the stage. In that moment, Mia felt a great warmth filling her heart for the sweet man who had done nothing but try to please her. He had listened to her when she needed somebody to talk to; he made her hot chocolate and let her wear his cardigan, and he shared some of the saddest moments of his life with her.

She just told Shelley that she didn't deserve love in her life anymore, but here it was, staring her right in the face.

'And the winner is…' the man announced into the microphone, startling Mia out of her reverie. 'The winner of the Mr Darcy wet shirt competition is…' he paused, dragging out the moment for as long as possible, 'even though he looks more like Napoleon Bonaparte than Mr Darcy, with that bandage… *Gabe!*'

The audience erupted into cheers and some very saucy wolf whistles as Gabe was presented with a white T-shirt emblazoned with the slogan Mr Darcy Forever.

'He won! He won!' Shelley cried, jumping up and down with joy. Bingley gave a volley of excited barks, and then the whole crowd started to disperse and people all got caught up somehow and pulled away from the stage.

'I've got to find Gabe,' Mia said, pushing her way through the sea of people, but he'd disappeared too. She kept thinking she'd spotted him, but it was another of the wet-shirt contestants. Mia sighed in exasperation. Why was it that she spent all her life trying to find Mr Darcy, and then twenty came along at once?

Suddenly he was there, and the crowds seemed to part in one of those magical film-like moments that life rarely throws at you.

'Gabe!' Mia said softly.

He took a step toward here. 'You came!' he said.

'Yes!' Mia said. 'I was in the front row.'

'I didn't see you.'

'No,' she said, feeling inexplicably shy.

'Is this really what girls like?' he asked, his eyes sparkling and his wet hair dripping down his face.

Mia smiled. 'You do look very dashing,' she said.

'Are you saying you'd never have noticed me unless I had a bucket of water chucked over me?'

'I didn't say that,' she said.

Bingley burst onto the scene, and before anyone could stop him, he leapt upon Gabe, leaving a great dirty paw print on his bandage.

'Gabe,' Shelley yelled. 'You were brilliant! I can't believe you won!'

'I know!' he said. 'I thought that man with the funny hat was going to win.'

'Oh, he was dreadful,' Shelley said, 'and his hat was more Dr Seuss than Mr Darcy. *Down*, Bingley!'

'Oh, no! Look at your bandage!' Mia said. 'It's all wet and filthy.'

'Not to worry,' he said. 'It comes off tomorrow.'

'Does it?'

He nodded. 'And then I can wrap both my arms around you.'

Shelley grinned and obviously thought it was a good moment to sneak away and pull a reluctant Bingley with her.

'Listen,' Gabe said, 'I know you've only just agreed to move in with Shelley—'

'She told you?'

'Yes,' he said, 'and I wanted to...' he paused.

'What?' Mia said.

'Well, it seems that it'll be a bit of a crush in there for you and William, what with Pie and Bingley and everything.'

'It'll be pretty luxurious, after the flat I've been living in,' Mia said.

'I know, but, he paused again and then looked directly at her, 'there's far more room in my home.'

Mia swallowed hard. She'd realized what he was going to say, but the actual words struck her so deeply that she thought she was about to cry. What had she done to deserve this man's kindness? She'd never met anyone like him before and couldn't help feeling that she wasn't good enough for him.

'You're offering me a room?' she asked. 'Why? Why would you do that?'

He frowned. 'Why?' he said.

She nodded.

'Because I'm falling in love with you,' he said.

'You hardly know me,' Mia protested.

'That doesn't seem to matter. I'm still falling in love with you.' He gazed at her, and his eyes seemed full of love. 'I know I'm not good enough for you. I know you think I'm way too old, and I know you've been through a terrible relationship, and I really don't want to put any more pressure on you, but I just had to tell you how I feel.'

They stared at each other, their eyes locking, as strangers in the street pushed by them, unaware of the importance of the moment.

At last, Mia spoke. 'I'm glad you did tell me,' she said.

'You are?'

'Yes,' she said. 'Because I think I'm falling in love with you too.'

He looked at her as if she might be teasing him. 'You do?'

Mia nodded, and the wonderfully warming sensation she'd felt when looking at him up on the stage returned.

'If you'd told me that all this was going to happen to me during the Jane Austen Festival, I might have been too scared to come here,' she confessed to him.

'Then I wouldn't have met you,' he said, a frown shadowing his face.

'I know. Isn't that awful?' she said, placing her hands inside his. They felt warm and comforting and *right*, and she knew that, if she placed all her love and trust in this man, it would be returned tenfold.

'But you *did* come,' Gabe said, 'and we *did* meet.'

'Yes,' Mia said with a huge smile. 'Jane Austen couldn't have written it better herself.'

Read on for an excerpt from

A Weekend
with
Mr. Darcy

Now available from Sourcebooks Landmark

Dr Katherine Roberts couldn't help thinking that a university lecturer in possession of a pile of paperwork must be in want of a holiday.

She leant back in her chair and surveyed her desk. It wasn't a pretty sight. Outside, the October sunshine was golden and glorious and she was shut up in her book-lined tomb of an office.

Removing her glasses and pinching the bridge of her nose, she looked at the leaflet that was lying beside a half-eaten salad sandwich, which had wilted hours before. The heading was in a beautiful bold script that looked like old-fashioned handwriting. *Purley Hall, Church Stinton, Hampshire*, it read.

> *Set in thirty-five acres of glorious parkland, this early eighteenth-century house is the perfect place in which to enjoy your Jane Austen weekend. Join a host of special guest speakers and find out more about England's favourite novelist.*

Katherine looked at the photograph of the handsome red-bricked Georgian mansion taken from the famous herbaceous borders. With its long sweep of lawn and large sash windows, it was the quintessential English country house, and it was very easy to imagine a whole host of Jane Austen characters walking through its rooms and gardens.

'And I will be too,' Katherine said to herself. It was the third year she'd been invited to speak at the Jane Austen weekend, and rumour had it that novelist Lorna Warwick was going to make an appearance too. Katherine bit her lip. Lorna Warwick was her favourite author—after Jane Austen, of course. Miss Warwick was a huge bestseller, famous for her risqué Regency romances of which she published one perfect book a year. Katherine had read them all from the very first—*Marriage and Magic*—to *A Bride for Lord Burford*, published just a month earlier, and which Katherine had devoured in one evening at the expense of a pile of essays she should have been grading.

She thought of the secret bookshelves in her study at home and how they groaned deliciously under the weight of Miss Warwick's work. How her colleagues would frown and fret at such horrors as popular fiction! How quickly would she be marched from her Oxford office and escorted from St Bridget's College if they knew of her wicked passion?

'Dr Roberts,' Professor Compton would say, his hairy eyebrows lowered over his beady eyes, 'you really do surprise me.'

'Why because I choose to read some novels purely for entertainment?' Katherine would say to him, remembering Jane Austen's own defence of the pleasures of novels in *Northanger Abbey*. 'Professor Compton, you really are a dreadful snob!'

But it couldn't be helped. Lorna Warwick's fiction was Katherine's secret vice, and if her stuffy colleagues ever found out, she would be banished from Oxford before you could say *Sense and Sensibility*.

To Katherine's mind, it wasn't right that something that could give as much pleasure as a novel could be so reviled. Lorna Warwick had confessed to being on the receiving end of such condescension too and had been sent some very snobby letters in her time. Perhaps that was why Katherine's own letter had caught the eye of the author.

It had been about a year earlier when Katherine had done something she'd never ever done before—she'd written a fan letter and posted it in care of Miss Warwick's publisher. It was a silly letter really, full of gushing and admiration and Katherine had never expected a reply. Nevertheless, within a fortnight, a beautiful cream envelope had dropped onto her doormat containing a letter from the famous writer.

How lovely to receive your letter. You have no idea what it means to me to be told how much you enjoy my novels. I often get some very strange letters from readers telling me that they always read my novels but that they are complete trash!

Katherine had laughed and their bond had been sealed. After that, she couldn't stop. Every moment that wasn't spent reading a Lorna Warwick novel was spent writing to the woman herself and each letter was answered. They talked about all sorts of things— not just books. They talked about films, past relationships, their work, fashion, Jane Austen, and if men had changed since Austen's times and if one could really expect to find a Mr Darcy outside the pages of a novel.

Katherine then had dared to ask Lorna if she was attending the conference at Purley Hall and it had gone quiet, for more than two weeks. Had Katherine overstepped the boundaries? Had she pushed things too far? Maybe it was one thing exchanging letters with a fan but quite another to meet a fan in the flesh.

Just as Katherine had given up all hope, though, a letter had arrived.

Dear Katherine,

I'm so sorry not to have replied sooner but I've been away and I still can't answer your question as to whether or not I'll be at Purley. We'll just have to wait and see.

Yours truly, Lorna

It seemed a very odd sort of reply, Katherine thought. If Lorna Warwick was going to be at Purley, surely the organisers would want to know as she'd be the biggest name and the main pull because she was famously reclusive. In comparison to the bestselling novelist, Katherine was just a dusty fusty old lecturer. Well, *young* lecturer, actually; she was in her early thirties, but she knew that people would come and listen to her talks only because they were true Janeites. At these conferences, anyone speaking about Jane Austen was instantly adored and held in great esteem. In fact, any sort of activity with even the lamest connection to Austen was pursued and enjoyed, from Jane Austen Scrabble to Murder in the Dark which, one year, ended in uproar when it was discovered that Anne Elliot had somehow managed to murder Captain Wentworth.

Katherine smiled as she remembered, and then, trying to put thoughts of Purley out of her mind, she made a start on the pile of papers to her left that was threatening to spill onto the floor. It was mostly rubbish that had accumulated as the term had progressed. It was what she called her 'tomorrow pile,' except she'd run out of tomorrows.

Allowing herself a sigh of relief as she reached the car park, she thought of her small but perfect garden at home where she could kick off her shoes and sink her bare feet into the silky green coolness of her lawn, a glass of white wine in her hand as she toasted the completion of another week of academia.

She'd almost made it to her car and to freedom when a voice cried out, 'Katherine!'

She stopped. It was the last voice—the *very* last voice—she wanted to hear.

'What is it, David?' she asked a moment later as a fair-haired man with an anxious face joined her by her car.

'That's not very friendly. You were the one smiling at me across the car park.'

'I wasn't smiling at you. I was squinting at the sun.'

'Oh,' he said, looking crestfallen.

'I'm in a rush,' she said, opening her car door.

His hand instantly reached out and grabbed it, preventing her from closing it.

'David—'

'Talk to me, Kitty.'

'Don't call me that. Nobody calls me that.'

'Oh, come on, Catkin,' he said, his voice low. 'We haven't talked properly since... well, you know.'

'Since I left you because I found out you'd got married? You're the one who wasn't returning my calls, David. You're the one who disappeared off the face of the planet to marry some ex-student. Nobody knew where you were. I was worried sick.'

'I was going to tell you.'

'When? At the christening of your firstborn?'

'You're not being fair.'

'*I'm* not being fair? I'm not the one who has a wife tucked away in the attic somewhere,' Katherine cried.

'Oh, don't be so melodramatic. This isn't some nineteenth-century novel,' he said. 'That's the problem with you. You can't exist in the real world. You have your head constantly immersed in fiction, and you just can't handle reality anymore.'

Katherine's mouth dropped open. 'That is *not* true!'

'No?' he said. 'So where are you heading now, eh? Purley bloody Hall, I bet.'

'That's my work,' Katherine said in defence of herself.

'Work? It's your whole life. You don't do anything *but* work. Your entire existence revolves around a set of people who've been made up by other people who've been dead for at least a century. It's not healthy.'

Katherine was on the verge of defending herself again but had the good sense to bite her tongue. She didn't want David to launch into his old tirade about how their love affair was doomed long before the arrival of his wife. She knew he'd throw it all in her face—how many early nights had been rejected in favour of the latest Jane Austen adaptation on TV and how often she had burned a much-looked-forward-to candlelit dinner at home because she'd had her head buried in a book. It bothered her when she stopped to think about it long enough because she knew that she was in love with a fictional world. Mr Darcy, Captain Wentworth and Henry Tilney were all creations of a female mind. They didn't exist. Perhaps her obsession with such heroes was because there were so few real heroes, and she was standing looking at a real-life nonhero right then.

'Go home to your wife, David,' she said, getting into her car.

'You know I'd rather go home with you.'

Katherine sighed. 'You should have thought about that before you lied to me,' she said, closing her door and driving off.

Honestly, any man who wasn't safely tucked between the covers of a book was a liability. You couldn't trust any of them. Was it any wonder that Katherine turned to fiction time and time again? Ever since her father had left home when she was seven, she'd hidden from the world around her, nose-diving into the safety of a friendly paperback. Books had always rescued her and remained the one constant in her life.

Acknowledgments

To Helen Wilkinson from the wonderful *Pride and Prejudice* Tours—I highly recommend their holidays. And very special thanks to the Barton Cottage group: Kelli, Kay, Susan, Sharon, Reeba, Asha, Geoffrey, Jim, and not forgetting the amazing Thomas, Betsy, and Toby.

To Joseph WJ Collins and Sara Jackson Kemp, Cally Taylor, Linda Gillard, Ruth Saberton, and Sue Hobbs.

To Annette Green and the whole team at Sourcebooks who have been wonderfully enthusiastic about my Jane Austen addicts trilogy. It's been a pleasure working with you all.

To all at the Jane Austen House Museum in Chawton who have been so supportive of my books.

And it's about time I acknowledged Jane Austen too, because she's been such a huge influence on my life. I adore her books, and when I read *Pride and Prejudice* all those years ago at the tender age of seventeen, I little thought that one day I would be inspired to write three of my own, linked to her wonderful characters.

Finally—as ever—to my husband, Roy, who is my own real-life Mr Darcy!

About the Author

Victoria Connelly was brought up in Norfolk and studied English literature at Worcester University before becoming a teacher in North Yorkshire. After getting married in a medieval castle in the Yorkshire Dales, she moved to London, where she lives with her artist husband and a mad springer spaniel, and ex-battery hens.

She has three novels published in Germany and the first, *Flights of Angels*, was made into a film. Victoria and her husband flew out to Berlin to see it being filmed and got to be extras in it. Her first novel in the UK, *Molly's Millions*, is a romantic comedy about a lottery winner who gives it all away.

Mr. Darcy Forever follows *A Weekend with Mr. Darcy* and *Dreaming of Mr. Darcy* in a trilogy about Jane Austen addicts, which has been a wonderful excuse to read all the books and watch all the gorgeous film and TV adaptations again.

Dreaming of Mr. Darcy

by Victoria Connelly

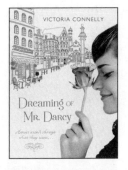

Heroes aren't always what they seem...

Fledgling illustrator and Darcy fanatic Kay Ashton settles in the seaside town of Lyme to finish her book, *The Illustrated Darcy*, when a film company arrives to make a new adaptation of Jane Austen's *Persuasion*. Kay is soon falling for the handsome bad boy actor playing Captain Wentworth, but it's the quiet screenwriter Adam Craig who has more in common with her beloved Mr. Darcy. Though still healing from a broken heart, Adam finds himself unexpectedly in love with Kay. But it will take more than good intentions to convince her that her real happy ending is with him.

Praise for A Weekend with Mr. Darcy:

"Sunshine on a rainy day. A charmingly written slice of warmhearted escapism."—Lisa Jewell, bestselling author of *Roommates Wanted*

"Lively, funny characters... the romances of this novel brilliantly reveal one thing that Miss Austen always knew: true love is often a complicated, but beautiful, mess."—*Luxury Reading*

For more Victoria Connelly, visit:

www.sourcebooks.com

The Trials of the Honorable F. Darcy

by Sara Angelini

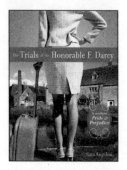

Their attraction is so hot, it should be against the law...

Judge Fitzwilliam Darcy is terribly bored—ready to hang up his black robe and return to the life of a country gentleman—until he meets Elizabeth Bennet, a fresh-faced attorney with a hectic schedule and no time for the sexy but haughty judge. Sparks fly as the two match wits and battle their overwhelming attraction.

Praise for The Trials of the Honorable F. Darcy:

"An excessively diverting entertainment you
won't want to miss."—*Austenprose*

"It is finger-licking, lip smacking, delicious... definitely my favorite modern retelling of *Pride and Prejudice* to date."—*A Bibliophile's Bookshelf*

For a celebration of all things Jane Austen, visit:

www.austenfans.com

Mr. Darcy Goes Overboard

by Belinda Roberts

It is a truth universally acknowledged, that a single man in possession of a yacht must be in want of a female crew...

The balmy seaside resort town of Salcombe boasts the best in bikinis, sandcastle contests, and a fiercely competitive squad of buff local lifeguards as Regatta Week approaches.

And if that weren't enough excitement, Mrs Bennet hears that the splendid villa Netherpollock has been rented by a young man of great fortune. She is determined he'll go out with one of her daughters, until Mr Darcy glides in on his stunning yacht *Pemberley* and she decides he would be the better catch...

Praise for Mr. Darcy Goes Overboard:

"One of the funniest, cutest *Pride and Prejudice* versions I've read."—*Love Romance Passion*

"It's the perfect beach read or a bit of fluffy fun at the end of a stressful day."—*Dairy of an Eccentric*

For a celebration of all things Jane Austen, visit:

www.austenfans.com

The Man Who Loved Pride and Prejudice

by Abigail Reynolds

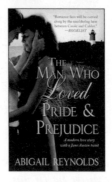

A modern love story with a Jane Austen twist

Marine biologist Cassie Boulton has no patience when a modern-day Mr. Darcy appears in her lab on Cape Cod. Proud, aloof Calder Westing III is the scion of a famous political family, while Cassie's success is hard-won in spite of a shameful family history.

When their budding romance is brutally thwarted, both by his family and by hers, Calder tries to set things right by rewriting the two of them in the roles of Mr. Darcy and Elizabeth Bennet from *Pride & Prejudice*... but will Cassie be willing to supply the happy ending?

Praise for The Man Who Loved Pride and Prejudice:

"This modern romance is by far her finest yet. I read it from cover to cover in one night and I simply could not put it down!"—*Austenprose*

"Reynolds has a great writing style... steamy and surprising."—*The Bibliophilic Book Blog*

For more Abigail Reynolds, visit:

www.sourcebooks.com